THE BENCH

By

N. G. Jones

A CIP catalogue record for this title is available
from the British Library

ISBN: 978-1-907540-15-8

Published April 2010
Printed by Anchorprint Group Limited. Published by N. G. Jones
www.anchorprint.co.uk

To order or make enquiries about this book
email: jonsn@hotmail.co.uk

For Sandi and Ashley

ACKNOWLEDGEMENTS

Thank you to my lovely wife Sandi, without whose support and hard work in editing its content, this book would never have been written.

Thank you to David, for his suggestions and drawings.

Thanks to everyone who has allowed me to bore them with my aspirations of being an author.

As always, all mistakes are my own.

(Love)...... it is an ever-fixed mark that looks
on tempests and is never shaken..
It is the star to every wandering bark.

From Shakespeare's Sonnet CXVI

One

Buster cocked his leg and urinated on the leg of the bench.

"Buster, why is it always that leg of the bench? What's wrong with the others?"

Buster looked up at the man and tipped his head to one side implying it was a stupid question, and the reason was quite obvious.

The man brushed some debris from the bench and took his seat on the left hand side, carefully laying his bag on the ground as he eased himself down.

Buster continued to sniff the other three legs in turn to confirm he had in fact made the correct choice, then sniffed the bag and moved to face the bench. With a Herculean effort he propelled his front paws onto it then gave the man a look that said, "Okay, now."

The man reached down and hooked his arm round the back legs of the dog and in one well-practiced movement scooped him up onto the bench.

Buster shuffled around awkwardly for few seconds then slumped down and curled up with his head on the man's lap. All of which was done with little grace and a loud grunt as he came to rest.

"Those old legs aren't getting any better are they, Buster?"

Buster snorted his agreement and closed his eyes.

The man surveyed the scene before him. It was as beautiful as ever. Off and on he had been coming here all of his life, since he was a small boy he'd taken the hike up the path to this exact spot. In recent months he'd been coming most days, apart from those with the most inclement weather, and he was always accompanied by Buster whose enthusiasm for the walk up the hill was not as great as it had once been.

The man was beginning to struggle with the climb as well, but as long as he was able to he would come to the place that he perceived to be the centre of his world, and when he reached the bench and saw the view he had never once been disappointed.

A rabbit appeared from under a gorse bush and scurried across the camomile grass that formed the path between the yellow-clad plants. Buster raised his head and looked at the bunny with disinterest.

A few years ago the man would not have seen Buster for an hour as he tried to hunt down the elusive meal. He never caught one, but was never bowed by that minor fact. Buster was a hunter, albeit an unlucky one. He didn't need to hunt anymore. The man always brought Buster his sandwiches and they were in the bag that Buster was guarding, just in case any rabbits should try and steal them. Buster knew he was good at guarding, no rabbit had yet succeeded in stealing his sandwiches but he would keep an eye open just in case, even if occasionally they would both be shut.

The man surveyed the distant scene. It was a beautiful, clear spring day, and the sun was bouncing off the white chalk cliffs of

2

the Needles. From the Needles the broad white chalk path of Tennyson's trail stretched along the headland to the east, past Farringford House towards Freshwater Bay and the Downs beyond. Nearer to him, he stared down at the cable car that was taking early season holidaymakers down to the multi-coloured sands of Alum Bay.

All around him was the wonderful smell of spring; new buds were blossoming into life as the gorse bushes revelled in their newfound warmth. On the air he could smell newly-cut grass from the farmers' fields in the valley below, mixed with the sea's own peculiar smell that invaded his nostrils carried from the chalk cliffs that descended hundreds of feet into the sea below. It was the same smell that he had grown up with, a mixture of seaweed and salt.

He looked to his right, down to the benign Solent that lapped gently against the shore on this beautiful spring day. He remembered days it did not look so inviting, dark days that had taken loved ones' lives. Today though, it hosted a flotilla of small boats. Sailing boats borrowing the wind to take them to Lymington and Yarmouth, others bade farewell to the Needles as they set sail to Jersey, Guernsey and France, his beloved France.

Four miles away the ferry appeared, exiting Yarmouth harbour on its short crossing to the mainland, or The North Island as he'd laughingly called it.

He was happy here on Headon Warren, with the rabbits and Buster. This is where he came to reflect on his life. He could have done it anywhere, but in this place remembering had special meaning for him.

"Lunch, Buster?"

Buster was suddenly wide-awake, another job well done. "Ham, I like ham. Please let it be ham." Buster used to like ham and fingers, but for some reason the man didn't, so Buster had rationed himself to ham alone.

Mind you, it wasn't all bad news. In the old days he wasn't allowed on the benches for lunch and had to sit on the wet grass. Now he could have lunch lying down, a fair trade for fingers.

"Hello, Buster." It was that blonde girl with the poodle. 'Why did they always come at lunch time?' Thought Buster. 'Now I've got to get up and sniff him.'

"Hello, Jacques. Isn't it a wonderful day?"

"Yes, it is, Barbara. How is Jess, and yourself of course?" Jacques had always found it amusing that dog owners always addressed to the dog before it's owner.

"We are well, thank you." Barbara delivered it as if she were Jess speaking.

The owners passed a few more pleasantries before Jess and Barbara continued with their walk, then the man eased Buster back onto the bench so he could continue with his fingerless lunch.

Others came and went, including Buster's favourite. A well-upholstered woman who had the good sense to fill her pockets with small dog biscuits for Buster, a habit Buster found attractive in a large woman

Jacques watched the waves venting their wrath against the Needles with an increasing intensity as the westerly wind strengthened. With the strengthening wind came more yachts, drawn out onto the water by the promised excitement of engaging with the elements.

Jacques loved the sea, it had brought him great joy and it had brought him sadness, but it was part of him and had played a role throughout his remarkable life. Even before he was born the sea had played a role in that life.

Buster had decamped for the post-luncheon exploration of his domain, his senses heightened by the ham. It had been a good day so far, ham, followed by a small dog biscuit and now here came Daisy. He liked Daisy, not only did she have the good

4

sense to be a Labrador, but she had a way of sniffing his balls he found quite intoxicating.

While Buster reacquainted himself with Daisy and her charms, the man sat on the bench with that smile on his face again. He was remembering. Buster knew he liked remembering, he would laugh and mutter things to himself that did not involve lunch. Buster liked the man to remember, he was happy when he remembered and Buster loved him being happy. Actually Buster just loved him. He loved the man and he loved ham, oh, and he loved Daisy sniffing his balls.

Also, after the man had remembered, they would usually go back to Buster's sofa which was much more comfortable than the bench. All in all, remembering was good.

This day the remembering was over and the man got up and touched the memorial plaque screwed to the back of the bench and said, "See you tomorrow, old girl." He picked up the bag and called to Buster, "Come on, Buster, back to the sofa."

Buster rather reluctantly left Daisy alone and headed back with the man. It was much easier going down the hill.

* * * * *

Two days later the man once again helped Buster onto the bench, where he performed his small dance before snorting as he laid his head on the man's lap.

He'd already inspected the bench and was pleased to find there had been no other visitors in his absence. The general area also seemed to be in order, so as his eyes closed he knew it was safe to settle down to his main task for the day, guarding the sandwiches.

He'd been guarding particularly well, so wondered why lunch had not been proffered by the man. He opened one eye and was both glad and sad to see he was remembering. Although Buster liked him to remember, sometimes if he did it before lunch, then lunch would be late. Buster loved the man so much he decided to let him remember some more. If it took too long there was always the bark. Something to which he occasionally would have to resort to remind the man that a dog could easily starve to death without a regular intake of sandwiches!

Jacques's remembering had not taken him far. In fact he was on the exact spot they were sitting now. It was the 16th August 1940 and Honeysuckle was tucked under his arm, the top of her head reaching his lower ribs and her mass of dark curls tickling his arm.

Jacques's arm was protecting her from the fight. That is what Jacques did, he protected her and she loved him. She had loved him for so long, she couldn't remember when she had started to love him, it was certainly as long as she could remember! And Jacques loved her, his shadow, the little girl who lived in the fisherman's cottage next door.

It was Jacques's job to protect her. It always had been, but she had sealed that contract in devastating fashion eleven weeks previously. Today it would be much easier for Jacques to protect her.

Honeysuckle had both arms around his waist as the Merlin engine of the Spitfire roared just fifty feet above their heads. Five seconds later the Messerschmitt Bf 109 snarled as it gave chase, it's machine-guns spitting deadly venom at the Spitfire which weaved and kangarooed in an attempt to avoid the bullets.

Even though she was only thirteen-years-old Honeysuckle was not scared. Jacques would look after her.

Jacques watched transfixed by the dogfight that was taking place before his eyes. As he watched, the Spitfire suddenly dived towards the sea and became inverted before turning vertically skywards, the Merlin's propeller eagerly eating slices of air as it pulled it's pilot heavenwards.

Jacques was trying to imagine what the pilot was doing with his control stick and rudders to make it pull out of an inverted dive. Whatever it was, it appeared to have worked. The Messerschmitt had not reacted quickly enough and had been further fooled by the roll off the top of the Spitfire's climb. The Spitfire had now become the predator.

The Messerschmitt turned and sought the protection of the hills and was flying directly towards them. It was below the level of Headon Warren, so they were actually looking down on it with the Spitfire in hot pursuit, it's Brownings venting their wrath on the German plane. Fifty feet below them Jacques could hear the bullets slamming into the cliffs and he could imagine the puff of chalk that each would produce.

The Messerschmitt banked hard right and flew round the side of the hill before levelling it's wings and flying down the valley towards Farringford House, the country retreat that Alfred Lord Tennyson made his home. What would he have made of the drama playing out in the skies above his beloved house?

Jacques raised his hand and cheered as the Spitfire clung to the German's tail. It's pilot squeezed the trigger of the Brownings once again. They purred as they delivered their stream of death.

The tail of the Messerschmitt was reduced to a skeleton as fabric was torn from its bones, then finally it's tail ripped from its body. The canopy opened and the German pilot tried to eject from his flying coffin, but it was too late, he can have been no more than fifty feet off the ground when the guns had struck. The plane hit a copse of trees about a hundred yards from High Down Inn and burst into a ball of flames. The pilot could not have survived.

The Spitfire banked hard left, staying within the valley and flew back towards them at head height and no more than thirty yards away. The noise was deafening as he waggled his wings and waved at the small girl and the boy standing next to her, before opening the throttle of the Merlin and doing a victory roll as it climbed back into the sky to find another kill. There would be many more, on both sides, before The Battle of Britain was over.

Honeysuckle did not like people being killed, but there was a war on and it was necessary. That is what her Mother had told her, and at thirteen years of age she had seen first hand the cold reality of war. This time, as then, Jacques had protected her.

"Come on, trouble, your Mum will be cross with me for not bringing you home as soon as the sirens went off. Don't tell her that you have just stood and watched a dogfight up here. She'll be livid."

"No she won't. She knows I'm with you, and she loves you. Everyone loves you, Jacques." She said it as a matter of fact, and it was true.

He held her bicycle as she nimbly jumped on and they cycled back down the hill, then rode the short distance back to Yarmouth.

Jacques was sixteen, and he was charming. He had the sea in his blood, but what he had just witnessed changed the course of his life. If this war carried on, as soon as he was old enough he would become a pilot.

The man's eyes had been scanning the valley as he relived the dogfight and his fingers had been tickling Buster behind his ear, just as he had tickled little Honeysuckle when she was small. The tickling had woken Buster up and he was hungry, so he was very pleased to see the well-upholstered woman approach. 'Good, a biscuit and lunch at last.'

Two

The heather was in full bloom and particularly fragrant. Jacques decided to go on one of the lesser-used paths on the Warren and see if her tulips had survived the winter. They had, and today they survived Buster's attentions as well.

A cormorant flew overhead, visiting from it's home a short distance away on the Needles and screeched a 'good morning' as it passed, gently soaring on the westerly wind that today whispered over the headland.

Buster sensed that this would be a good day for remembering, but a bad day for lunch. Whenever they visited the tulips the man would enter into a long session of remembering which always meant a late lunch.

Jacques sat on the bench and said, "Good morning, old girl," as Buster completed his inspections.

Within minutes Jacques was in Hanoi in a dimly lit, smoke-filled room with a gin and tonic on the table in front of him.

People surrounded him, all were listening to the dulcet tones of the wonderful voice that filled the bar. The voice was enchanting all who listened to it and he found himself mesmerised by it once again. It was the same voice that had said, "I love you," the previous evening as they had made love in her apartment.

It was November, the year was 1953 and Jacques had now been in Hanoi for three years. They had been good years; the last one in particular had been quite spectacular since he had met Saphine.

After Yvette and what had happened with Honeysuckle, he needed to get away and start anew. Where better than Vietnam? His skills were needed there and it would be an adventure. Added to which, part of him had missed the adrenalin-rush that the Second World War had given him, even though he was glad it was over so his lovely Honeysuckle and others like her could live in peace without fear of occupation, or worse. But the end of the War had brought complications with his relationships, relationships that had been perfect for short periods, but had spiralled out of control. Yvette had been one of those relationships, but that was over and he had moved on.

He was in a new relationship now, with Saphine. She owned the voice that was singing and she was the most exotic woman he had ever met. She was half-French and half-Vietnamese, and the two had combined to form a most exquisite-looking woman.

He looked at the stage where she shimmered through the smoke-hazed room. Her waist-length black hair was curled up on the top of her head, leaving enough for a ponytail to hang seductively over her bare shoulder. Her almond-shaped blue eyes sat perfectly within her otherwise western features, which made up her strikingly beautiful face. Her skin was the colour of honey, and her lips screamed out to be kissed. His eyes traced the line of her body being caressed by a tight red, off-the-shoulder dress that reached to the floor but allowed one long shapely leg to protrude though the slit that ran almost to her waist.

On stage she looked about ten feet tall, the footlights bathing her perfect body in a soft glow. In her bedroom with no clothes on, she barely reached up to Jacques's chest, not an inch over five-feet-two. But what a five feet two she was! "Small but beautifully formed," Jacques would say to her.

Saphine was not her real name; she had made it up, thinking it pretty and different. It was now quite a famous name in Hanoi and was becoming known throughout Vietnam and as far away as Saigon, after a number of successful performances in towns and cities throughout the country. She had chosen the name when she had sung professionally for the first time on the very stage on which she now stood. With the choice of name had come a new life, far removed from the one she'd lived until that point.

Saphine's life up until that day had not been a happy one, though she never complained and would always have a smile on her beautiful face. It was that indomitable spirit, that smile and her beautiful voice that now made her such a success.

She never knew her Father and in all honesty, neither did her Mother. She did know he was a French soldier though, Maman had known several of them! Maman had been a prostitute working in one of Hanoi's many brothels. She had died when Saphine was just eleven years old. Not knowing what to do with the little girl, the brothel's Madame put her to work as a maid and general dogsbody.

She was a sweet child and everyone loved her, but as she began to grow into a young woman, her flowering exotic beauty was being noticed by the clientele who started pressurising the Madame to make her 'best asset' available to them. To be fair to the Madame she protected Saphine for as long as she could, but by the age of fifteen she was working as one of the whores.

To Saphine it was not that bad, as she had grown up in the brothel and it was the only life she had ever known. The hookers were her family and had helped to raise her. She smiled and she was happy, and her reputation as the most beautiful whore in Hanoi rapidly grew. She attracted wealthy customers, all of whom were more than satisfied with the blue-eyed, Eurasian whore.

One in particular became infatuated with her. A French Colonel, old enough to be her Father paid the Madame handsomely for her and set her up in her own apartment in a respectable part of town.

She had sung in the brothel from the age of ten and loved the stage. On stage she was in another world and she was another person, a million miles away from sordid world of the sex trade. The Colonel fell in love with the young girl as she sang; that he could pay to have the singer's body was an added bonus. It was her voice he loved though, and when he owned the voice's body he set about promoting the voice. He got her a job in the club and she was an instant success. Within weeks she was packing the place out, half of the audience in love with her voice and the other half in love with her face and body. Either way, Saphine was a star, and the Colonel's reward was to sleep and have sex with the star he'd helped create.

By the age of eighteen Saphine was earning a great deal of money from her singing and was being accepted within some of the higher echelons of Hanoi's society. She certainly no longer needed the Colonel's patronage, however he was a decent sort and had been good to her, having treated her with respect and genuine affection. Saphine, for her part was aware of everything that he had done for her and she was genuinely fond of him. Their parting was a natural process. He realised that he had lost her when politicians' wives and society accepted her. She had started as his chattel but he had quite naturally become her father-like companion, simply an appendage to the stunning talent that society wanted to embrace.

Saphine had not left him, it was the Colonel who gave her back her freedom. He had never owned her as such, it was an agreement that both had benefited from and in time he realised she had outgrown whatever he could offer her. So over dinner one night he gave her a gold pendant of an angel with wings and said, "It is you, Saphine. You are free to soar with the birds and sing like an angel. You do not belong to me; I must share you with the world. Go, my angel and live the life you deserve."

Saphine had cried. Not about losing the Colonel, for she had not, in fact they were still great friends. She cried because life had been so good to her.

Saphine smiled at Jacques and gave him a little wave with her fingers as she arranged the microphone for her next song. She looked over at the handsome man who had become her lover. He was tall and tanned, his wavy black hair flopping over one eye, the eye she knew to be the kindest emerald-green eye she'd ever seen. He sat perfectly relaxed at the table, his athletic frame at ease with the world around him. Saphine smiled at him, she liked to smile anyway, but she couldn't actually look at Jacques without smiling.

Jacques was the first man she had ever enjoyed sex with. Saphine had grown up with sex being a commodity, a commodity she could supply in abundance, but it was not a thing she enjoyed, sex was a job. That was until she met Jacques.

Jacques was tender, loving and very sexy. From the very first time he made love to her it was different. She had always 'put on a good show' and her clients had never been disappointed, but with Jacques she suddenly wasn't acting. It had confused her at first, but after several occasions she realised what all the fuss was about and how wonderful making love could be. If they had been at home she would have walked over to Jacques right now, pulled her dress up, straddled his powerful thighs and kissed him passionately on his lips.

Jacques was smiling back at her, having very similar thoughts about the sex kitten on the stage. She had been good for him, she had helped put things back into proportion, or at least been the final building block to do so. His smile broadened as he looked at Saphine, yes, she was good for him. To have found her in Vietnam was a huge and unexpected bonus to the job he'd come to do.

After the War, when France had been liberated, they had tried to re-establish their colonies in the Far East, but the world had changed and they had found themselves in a bloody war with the Vietminh, who had decided after years of Colonial rule, and a more recent Japanese control, that Vietnam should be run by it's own people. The Vietminh did not use conventional warfare to fight their cause, they used guerrilla tactics and the French Army's conventional armaments and warfare were not working. So they decided to draw on the experience of some of their less conventionally trained Resistance fighters from the Second World War for advice and guidance. Jacques had been one of the most effective agents during the last two years of the War and was being used as a consultant to the army. He did not have a rank or a title. He wasn't even French. He was effectively a mercenary who had access to the highest level of the French Command. He trained operatives, devised and conducted insurgent attacks whilst structuring the best defences against such attacks from the Vietminh, who were vastly superior in their capability to deliver effective strikes.

It had proved something of a thankless task as the French High Command seemed deeply entrenched in the tradition of conventional warfare whose seeds were planted centuries before, along with it's dated ethics and morals. The Vietminh had their own ethics, 'the ethics of a just war,' where the end justified the means and which did not respect the ideals of a French military regime that still lived with Napoleonic values.

The net result was that the French were losing and they seemed reluctant to take the advice of the one group of French fighters who'd had any success since the First World War, the Resistance. It was almost as if they were jealous of their success

14

during the War, an often ramshackle band of men and women who had not had the benefit of training in the honourable tradition of the mainstream French military. Jacques even suspected some of the idiots would not take his advice simply because he was British, even though his Father was wonderfully, absurdly and proudly French. Something the whole of West Wight had delighted in since his unexpected arrival amongst them.

Jacques could see Saphine waving to someone behind him, then he heard the words, "Hello, Jack, my English saboteur," said with an attempt at an English accent that didn't really work.

He turned round to see Sophie approaching his table carrying a bottle of white wine and two glasses. Sophie waved at Saphine who held up five fingers and mouthed the words 'five minutes' to her friend.

Jacques stood up and kissed Sophie on each cheek, beaming at his good friend. "Hi, Sophie, how are you?"

"Very well, Jack!" She loved to call him by the English form of his name. She would tease him saying, "You're too handsome, and so you deserve an ugly name." But she liked Jacques far more than she admitted to anyone.

Sophie put down the bottle and poured two glasses of wine. "Where's mine?" Jacques asked, whilst making a pretend grab for the wine Sophie had poured for Saphine.

"Hands off! The waitress is bringing you your English gin and tonic, old boy!" Sophie giggled to herself. "Tell me again why Jacques the Frenchman lives on the Isle of Wight. It's so romantic." She made him tell her the story regularly and genuinely loved the tale, though Jacques would only give her the shortened version these days. "Do I have to?"

"Yes, you must or I'll never call you Jacques again."

He sighed. "Okay then. My Father was a French fisherman and he was trying to fix a problem he'd been having with the old engine in his boat. He was giving it a test-run when it failed just a few hundred yards offshore. He signalled for help but no one saw him and the silly sod had gone to sea without any of his safety equipment, which included his lifeboat, which was still hauled up on the beach. Anyway, a southerly breeze soon blew him offshore towards 'les Rosbifs.' Eighteen hours later he was shipwrecked off the South coast of England on the Isle of Wight near Freshwater Bay. There the local fisherman managed to salvage what was left of his boat and get him to the local hospital. In hospital his Gallic charm won the heart of a pretty nurse, and his willing smile, her body. Smitten by the Siren of West Wight he remained to suffer a life of appalling food, worse weather and frightful sexual hang-ups." Sophie was giggling now. She loved the English and their self-deprecating humour. "Her brothers fixed his boat, and he taught them all how to cook properly. Mother was obviously given lessons in the art of l'amour, and hey presto, moi!" Jacques smiled at Sophie. "Is that enough?"

"Yes, thank you, cheri. Your Father was a wise man to stay sur L'isle Blanc. His bloodline is a good one." Sophie was smiling at Jacques, part of her wishing she had been washed up on the shores of his island too.

Sophie and Jacques's relationship went far back, it went all the way back to their Resistance days and they had history, a lot of history. Jacques admired Sophie. She was one of the bravest people he had ever met and she was clever, she was scarily clever.

"What have you got for me, Jack?" Sophie asked, conspiratorially.

"A couple more failed ops that I could tell you about, but they aren't even news anymore!"

"What about the other thing?"

"Yes, maybe you can do it. I've asked a few questions and the feeling is there may be some footage in it that would suit the military. I'll get back to you with dates and plans."

"Great, thanks, Jacques." Sophie was excited, and kissed him on the cheek.

"What happened to Jack? Does this mean you love me again?"

"Of course I love you. I have always loved you, you know that." Sophie leant across and pecked him on the cheek once again, this time adding a mocking display of affection.

Sophie was a journalist working for Paris Match, and was covering the First Indochina War here in Hanoi, but Sophie was far more than just a writer. Sophie had been with the Resistance; she had been captured and shot by the Gestapo then tortured and interrogated before being left to rot for six months in a concentration camp. Where she would probably have died had the War not ended. Sophie and Jacques had a very special relationship born out of being comrades-in-arms, and each owed the other their lives.

Jacques did not know what had become of Sophie after the War and had often thought about her, hoping she had survived but believing she was probably dead. He was more than a little surprised when eighteen months previously someone had tapped him on the shoulder, and on turning round that same person had kissed him full on the lips. He was still in shock when the blonde girl withdrew and he could finally see his attacker. Jacques had shrieked with delight when he discovered his new admirer to be Sophie, an older Sophie than the pretty girl he remembered from France, but one who had matured into an extremely attractive woman. They had been the best of friends ever since.

Jacques studied the woman opposite him. Why would someone as beautiful as Sophie want to go with him behind enemy lines just to get a story? He knew the answer of course, it was the drug. They had all lived on adrenalin for years and many had become hooked. Suddenly the supply had ended, that ending brought it's own high for a while as the novelty of peace brought a different excitement. For him that had partly worn off and for others a depression had followed as they realised their hopes and dreams may not be fulfilled.

He had chosen to become a mercenary, not only because he was running away from the past, but it gave him that shot of adrenalin as well. Sophie had chosen to continue her fight through journalism, and in choosing to report from the front line in a war zone she could get that rush again too. Now she was asking him to take her back into the middle of the battle once again, and he understood why.

Saphine walked over to them, acknowledging the applause as she left the stage. Sophie stood up and embraced her. They were good friends, and they had recognised in each other the same spirit that had fought against adversity. Neither had been bowed by that adversity or even bore it any bitterness, it was simply what had happened in their lives.

Jacques watched them together. Saphine, the survivor and Sophie, one of the toughest fighters he had ever seen. Together they formed a picture of such exquisite beauty that no one could have imagined the strength they both possessed. If he could have added Honeysuckle to the picture in front of him there would be a group of women who could have conquered the world!

Buster was hungry, but the man was deep in thought. A bark was required to get his attention, and lunch.

It worked; the man stroked Buster's ears and said, "What a pair of stunning girls they were, old man. One blonde and the other brunette, quite perfect together."

He started to undo the bag with lunch inside, much to Buster's delight.

Three

Buster walked past the ancient burial ground, or barrow, on the top of the Warren. He sensed that buried deep below him were bones thousands of years old, and a few years ago he would have tried to liberate one of them, but today he could see Daisy down the path about fifty yards in front of him. Tail raised high, and wagging in perfect time to his run he flew down the hill to see his friend, wishing he was just a couple of years younger.

The man smiled at the rejuvenated dog. "What we'll do to impress a girl!" He muttered to himself as Buster ran like a two-year-old to see Daisy.

Eventually both man and dog sat on the bench and got themselves comfortable, one for remembering and one for guarding.

Buster decided that if necessary he would try yesterday's trick again if lunch appeared to be delayed. A loud bark, it had worked, the man had even laughed.

"Now where was I, Buster, before you interrupted? Ah yes,

Honeysuckle."

Jacques was back in The Isle of Wight standing on the paddle steamer about to sail for Lymington and he was looking down at his parents. Standing next to them was Honeysuckle and her Mother, Audrey. His eyes scanned each of them in turn, his Mother, Elizabeth, looked sad and his Father's face was cross. Honeysuckle's Mother looked affectionate, but on Honeysuckle's face was a look of pure dejection. A look he would never forget.

"I'll be fine," he called down to them all.

"I know, but be careful as well," his Mother called back. His Dad just looked at him with a thunderous face. Honeysuckle's bottom lip quivered as she fought back her emotions.

Jacques had joined the Royal Air Force and was leaving to go to flying school. He was both excited and apprehensive at the same time. His Father was just livid. He was not livid that he should want to join up, or even that his choice was the Air Force rather than the Navy. He was angry because his son need not yet have joined. He was underage and had lied to the recruiting officers. He could understand his son's eagerness to get involved after everything he had seen, but he was too young. If he were to lose Jacques before he was really old enough to be in the forces, he would surely have his heart broken. He loved his son more than life itself, he was a fine and brave boy and had already played his part in this dreadful war. He wanted more time with his boy before they took him.

Jacques mouthed the words, "I'm sorry," to him and gave his Father his most disarming smile. It worked; Big Jacques's face broke into a smile. He loved his half-English boy. He had made sure he spoke French fluently though, and taught him how to prepare food properly, something his lovely wife, Elizabeth still had to perfect! But it did not matter. With his son he would prepare for her the finest fish and lobster they caught each day from his fine French boat. The previous evening Big Jacques had prepared a Lobster Thermidor for them all that was delicious, or would have been, had they been French lobsters! It was possibly the last meal he would ever have with his boy, so he had prepared it lovingly.

Jacques watched Honeysuckle's lip quiver, so crossed his eyes and stuck his tongue out at her. It had the desired effect; she couldn't fight back the smile. He always made her smile.

From the day she'd learnt to walk Honeysuckle was by Jacques's side. From the second her eyes opened each morning her first thought was of Jacques, and she was often already in his Mum's kitchen when he came downstairs for breakfast. She didn't have any siblings and her Father had died at sea when she was just a one-year-old and she had no memory of him. He had been a fisherman like Big Jacques. Her Mother ran the village store in the High Street next to the tearooms but most importantly they lived next door to Jacques. So from the age of two, Honeysuckle lived in both houses. At first her Mother had tried to discourage her and apologised to Big Jacques and Elizabeth, but they would have none of her apologies. Elizabeth and Audrey were the best of friends and they all decided that as Honeysuckle grew up some male influence in the little one's life would be a good thing. So Big Jacques became a surrogate father and Little Jacques, a brother.

Strangely, Little Jacques did not mind the arrangement. Honeysuckle had always been there, part of him. She was fun and liked what he liked. She could climb trees better than any boy her own age, she could row quicker than any other kid in Yarmouth and she laughed at all his jokes.

By the time she was five years old Big Jacques, with his son's help, had taught her fluent French and on a nice day she would go out on the fishing boat with them both.

By six, Honeysuckle was one of the gang. There was only one gang in Yarmouth, it was a small place, but she was their resident tomboy. Within the gang there was a second gang, a

21

gang of two who spoke French to each other. When that gang wished they could cut out the rest of the world, at least the world in Yarmouth. In their world everyone spoke French, sometimes to the amusement of others and sometimes to their annoyance. However Big Jacques liked it, soon the Isle of Wight would be French!

Honeysuckle loved it when they talked in French, their own language in their own world where she was alone with Jacques.

When Jacques told her he had joined The Air Force she was angry, just like his Father had been. She had never really been cross with him before, not about anything as serious as this. He would be leaving her and she could not remember a time when he was not by her side. The last time he had left she had followed but this time she could not. It had scared her and she had panicked. In French, he'd explained why he had to go and of course she had understood, but it did not make it any easier.

When he left before and she had followed, it had caused one hell of a stir and she still didn't know if people were angry with her or admired her. She suspected a mixture of both. When Big Jacques had gone to see his family in France, they had always taken her with them on the fishing boat. So why would they not take her this time? All they were going to do was go to France and pick up some soldiers!

When she hid under the tarpaulin in the stowage beneath the cockpit on the fishing boat she had no idea of the scale of the operation she was about to become involved in, or the stir she would cause.

A couple of days earlier, The British Ministry of Shipping had contacted all small boat builders and operators with a view to gathering an armada of small ships to rescue the stranded armies of Britain and France from the beaches of Dunkirk before Hitler dealt them one last final blow. They needed ships with shallow drafts to gain access to the beaches and to ferry the troops to the larger ships that lay offshore. Big Jacques could not volunteer quickly enough and finally gave into the pleadings of his son to join him. Their boat was one of 700 that gathered in Dover and Ramsgate to make the crossing which were guided by bigger ships of the British Navy.

It had been a long journey to Dover and then a wait before the final Channel crossing. They never knew how Honeysuckle remained undetected for so long, but they were thirty-five minutes into the Channel crossing when Jacques went down into the stowage to fetch something. When he heard the sneeze he nearly jumped out of his skin, but he knew instantly who it would be. There beneath the tarpaulin was Honeysuckle with an impish smile on her face, eating a sandwich she had brought with her.

"What the hell? How did you..."

"I had to come, Jacques. I promise I won't get in the way and I will be useful, I know I will."

To Jacques it didn't seem so bad. She was always with him, so why not now? To his Father, it was as if the world had caved in. He was furious and was all for turning back. Honeysuckle begged for forgiveness and made him the same promises. After some time, aided by her only ally she managed to persuade Big Jacques that she may actually be of some use in looking after the men they would pick up. They continued their journey, but Big Jacques wished they had not. Honeysuckle should never have seen the things she did see at such a young age.

They could hear the shelling before they could see the carnage that littered the beaches of Dunkirk. A smoke haze filled the air and with it came the smell of battle. Their job was to take the boat into the shallows and pick up thirty men at a time and ferry them to the waiting Destroyers. The first group they picked up were all French and Honeysuckle, true to her word, proved extremely useful getting them seated and giving them instructions in French. Many were seriously injured, but she never flinched once at their wounds and tended to them as best she could. The little angel who had come to save them bewitched the soldiers, many of who were in shock.

After several shipments of the human debris, Big Jacques could not be cross with his surrogate daughter any longer. She was a tower of strength to all around her and word spread about the 'la petite ange' who spoke French who had come from England to save them.

Throughout the operation an air battle raged above their heads between the Luftwaffe and the Royal Air Force, which Jacques watched fascinated by the dots painting pictures in the sky. Occasionally a plane would burst into flames or crash into the sea nearby. Bombs would explode in the water, but for the most part the soldiers were evacuated without further losses. Each soldier that climbed into their boat beamed when they saw little Honeysuckle with her mop of dark curls and her welcoming, "Bonjour!"

Big Jacques was hugely impressed by Honeysuckle but his son was not surprised, he already knew how impressive she was.

Finally they were given orders to take twenty soldiers back across the Channel to Dover. These boys were British, and led by Honeysuckle and Jacques they sang all the way home, whilst Big Jacques grinned.

In Ramsgate Honeysuckle was put ashore into the waiting arms of her distressed Mother, whom the Navy had managed to contact and inform of the whereabouts of her errant daughter.

As Big Jacques helped her onto the quay he said, "Your daughter has done very well. She is a heroine." He had a proud smile on his face, the smile of her surrogate Father.

Not knowing what to say or do, Audrey just hugged her daughter and cried.

Father and son refuelled the boat and set off in convoy back to Dunkirk to bring the next wave home. They returned twenty-four hours later in a Force 5 gale that had half the soldiers being sick, the whole experience having now become quite unpleasant without Honeysuckle at their side.

Jacques looked down from the paddle steamer at the now smiling Honeysuckle, that wonderful smile on her face, and he was not completely sure of his emotions as he studied her. She was no longer a child, and it had been a child he'd had a lifelong relationship with up until now. The three years difference in their age had always made her his little friend, but she was changing. Ever since Dunkirk her personality had become more mature, and in the last month or two he'd noticed some other subtle changes too, as the small girl was becoming a young woman. Next time he saw her the small girl would be gone, and part of him was sad at it's passing. He had enjoyed the child Honeysuckle and found himself wondering what the woman would be like.

Her hormones had confused Honeysuckle. She knew what was happening to her, she was becoming a woman and with that she found herself having feelings she'd never experienced before. Jacques was suddenly handsome, not just fun to be with. She had fantasised about kissing him, along with other boys of her own age from school, but the fantasy always returned to Jacques. She wondered if it was wrong that she should have such feelings for him. She was fourteen and would be fifteen soon, and Jacques was like her big brother, that is the relationship they'd always had. Unlike her friends though, who all seemed to hate their big brothers and argued with them all the time, Honeysuckle and Jacques were always the best of friends, so was he really like her brother? She was confused. Eighteen months ago it had been simple. When he went to Dunkirk it was her job to go with him and despite what people had told her since, both Jacques and she knew it was the right thing to do. Even Big Jacques had seen it. But now it was different, she didn't like her small breasts and the feelings that came with them. They had changed her relationship with him, and she wanted her big brother back.

As the paddle steamer made the short crossing of the Solent to Lymington, Jacques found himself thinking of Honeysuckle all the time. He was smiling at the little girl who waited at her front door for him to come home from school, the smile he knew so well lighting up her face when he appeared. He loved Honeysuckle's smile, it was mesmerising and seemed to have a life of its own. When she smiled at you it was impossible not to smile back at her and in recent weeks it had become even more beautiful. She had always been a pretty little thing, but when she smiled she was captivating, and as she was turning into a woman that smile was becoming so disarming Jacques had found himself staring at the smile whenever it appeared.

Honeysuckle sat on the pier with her legs dangling over the side of the wooden structure. Her Mum sat at her side and they watched the ferry get smaller as its huge paddles slowly ate up the short distance to Lymington.

Honeysuckle's eyes never left the boat and it was just a speck in the distance when she said, "Will I ever see him again, Mummy?"

"Yes, darling, you will. He will be back soon, don't worry."

Honeysuckle was quiet for a while then said, "You know I love him, don't you?" She was detached, part of her had left on the boat with him and that part was also becoming just a speck in the distance.

Her Mother looked at her. Virtually the first words Honeysuckle had ever said were, "I love, Jacques." She had said it many times since, but this was the first time she had ever heard the young woman say them, and she recognised the difference.

"I know, darling." She hugged Honeysuckle and prayed that the War, or Jacques, would never break her beautiful daughter's heart.

On the boat Jacques was about to eat the ham sandwich his Mother had given him and he was suddenly back in the present.

26

An expectant Buster was nudging the bag by the man's side with his nose, the smell of ham emanating from it had become too much for him to bear.

Four

Buster had watched the man making the sandwiches and there was something new in them. It wasn't a smell he recognised but he was prepared to believe it would taste good. The man had never actually given him anything that didn't taste good! So he set off up the hill with the added excitement of a mystery sandwich to look forward to. His guarding would have to be especially effective today with such a prize at stake!

The man didn't seem as excited about the mystery sandwich as Buster, as he was soon remembering and hadn't made any extra provision to protect Buster's lunch.

Jacques was sitting at the controls of a Lysander Mk III, its wheels no more than five feet above the hedge that marked the edge of the farmer's field, the half-moon giving just about enough light to illuminate the unforgiving hedgerow.

He had made one sweep of the field and was pleased to see the four flares being lit as he came round to make the landing.

He never really knew what would await him as the wheels touched down in the field. They usually selected something quite reasonable, but not always. The previous week he'd put her down in a ploughed field. Thank God the Lysander was a tough little bird, but it wasn't invincible. His friend, Daniel had left one minus its undercarriage in what was more akin to a quarry than a field. Jacques had flown out to France three days later to get him, Daniel having now taught the local Resistance about the importance of flat fields with an approach that would be possible to fly in the dark.

That was the problem; most of the drops and retrievals were done at night with only the moon offering any assistance to land. It was always a trade off, moonlight or the protection of a black sky. In daylight it was too dangerous. The Lysander was slow and ponderous and was perfect fodder for the Luftwaffe's fighters. Any daylight drop required protection from the RAF's own fighters, so they were most effective under cover of the night sky. It was dangerous though, hedges and trees accounting for more losses than the German guns.

This was Jacque's twenty-second sortie, he had been lucky. It was easier when someone just parachuted in, but his squadron specialised in a more personal door-to-door service. Tonight he was going to pick up Yvette.

He met Yvette five weeks previously when he had taken her to Normandy. She was a member of The French Resistance and liaised for clandestine operations with the Special Operations Executive. She had climbed aboard the Lysander dressed as a man with her hair tucked under her beret. She did not say anything to Jacques who was under the impression that she was a he! His other sorties had all been carrying men and they were usually quite chatty. They were twenty minutes into the flight before she finally asked in a thick French accent, "How much longer?"

The accent didn't surprise him, others had been French, but

he was surprised to hear the first female he'd flown and he replied in French, "Forty minutes, Mademoiselle, assuming we find them on the ground okay. It's a dark night and the clouds are getting lower."

It was her turn to be surprised. "You are a Frenchman in The Royal Air Force?" His French was too perfect for him to be English.

Over the thunderous noise from the Lysander's radial engine Jacques explained his unusual upbringing to the shadowy figure sitting behind him. Eventually he had to concentrate on finding the drop zone with his compass and map, he was becoming good at finding fields on moonless nights. From the ground when the sky above was at it's darkest all you could hear was the engine as the matt black aeroplane ghosted through the skies. He knew he was close and his eyes scanned the area for the telltale sign of a flashlight. There it was, he made one low flypast to gauge the field and it's surroundings. As the paraffin flares burst into life in the field below him, he made a steep banked turn and rolled out onto his final high-angled approach path, which brought him safely over the treetops, than he expertly put her down between the flares.

Figures ran out to meet them as Yvette jumped from the plane. She turned to look at the English Frenchman and saw his face as one of the flashlights caught it. He smiled at her.

"Merci, Monsieur," she said and found herself smiling back at him, she couldn't help herself.

"Am I glad to see you!" A very English voice said from behind her.

"Jump in. I'll get you back in time for a fry up," Jacques called to the man who'd been shot down a week earlier and who was becoming frustrated that his repatriation was taking so long due to a spell of inclement weather.

"Finally, a clear night, I thought we'd never get one," the pilot said as he nimbly scaled the ladder by the door to climb in.

He looked back at the strange looking chap who'd just leapt from the plane and saw him smiling at the chauffeur who was about to take him back to Blighty!

Yvette was now busying herself with her fellow freedom fighters who were embracing her affectionately.

"Hey, what's your name?" Jacques called to her.

"Yvette." She took one last look at him.

"Be careful, Yvette. I'll see you soon."

The door closed before she could reply. She was still smiling as her comrades pulled her away to the cover of the woods and their waiting vehicle.

In the intervening five weeks Jacques had thought a lot about Yvette. He wasn't sure as it had been so dark, but he thought she must have been pretty. The boys at the base had confirmed she was, they also told him she was one of the bravest Resistance fighters they knew. He'd been fascinated by the stories about her and was thrilled when the Boss had told him he was to pick her up again that night. He wanted to know more about Yvette.

They used a different field this time and Yvette was soon clambering aboard the Lysander. Still dressed as a man, her face blackened this time.

"Hello, Yvette. Your carriage awaits," Jacques beamed at her.

It had been a rough five weeks and she had lost two close friends, but seeing his face somehow uplifted her and all the pressures she'd been feeling seemed to dissipate. How could seeing a virtual stranger make that happen?

Jacques was still smiling as she strapped herself in. He did not know it, but the next week was going to change the course of Jacques's war.

After his training he had been posted to 161 Squadron (Special Duties). When he'd joined up he anticipated having dogfights over the Isle of Wight in his Spitfire, with Honeysuckle waving at him from Headon Warren. Two things had stopped that from happening. Firstly, his instructors noticed that he seemed to posses an innate natural sense of direction. They teased him that it was because of his life at sea and he'd become known as 'Fish Head!' Secondly, it was soon apparent that he spoke perfect French. Just what was needed to fly the 'Frogs in and out of France!' It was a perfectly natural process to send him to 161 Squadron.

They had given him further training in flying at night with very little guidance, and even given him a quick survival course on how to avoid detection in the 'unlikely event' that he should be shot down.

Jacques had enjoyed it all and was rapidly becoming one of the Squadron's best pilots. He seemed able to find places others could not in the most marginal of weather conditions. He said it was because France was in his blood, and he was becoming the pilot of choice for the more dangerous incursions.

That night he landed back at R.A.F. Tangmere, near Chichester, to refuel before taking Yvette back to R.A.F. Tempsford in Bedfordshire for her debriefing. Tempsford was the most secret Air Force base in Britain, from which the Special Operations Executive conducted their war.

The Special Operations Executive, S.O.E., was set up by Winston Churchill to fight the war behind enemy lines using espionage and sabotage as weapons, and it was the core of the Resistance movement located in Britain. It was known as 'Churchill's Secret Army' or 'The Ministry of Ungentlemanly Warfare,' and supplied arms and personnel to facilitate all manner of destruction on the enemy. In Churchill's own words, "It was designed to set Europe ablaze."

As the Lysander was being refuelled Jacques suggested they get a cup of tea in the Mess. To be honest, he could not wait any longer to see the face of the shadow that had been sitting behind him. He had been thinking about her for the last five weeks, fascinated by what kind of woman would be a Resistance fighter.

He offered his hand along with his ready smile as she stepped from the ladder. Yvette thought it ironic that she had spent five weeks in mud and ditches blowing up bridges and attacking supply routes, shooting Germans and being shot at, then an Englishman should be offering her a hand to take one last ten-inch step onto a perfectly dry piece of tarmac! But he smiled at her and called her Mademoiselle. There it was, that smile, the one she couldn't resist. So she took his hand and allowed him to help her down. It was also the first time they had really been able to take a proper look at each other.

Yvette was smaller than he remembered, perhaps five-feet-three or four, and she could easily have been five-feet wide, her jacket was so large. Baggy trousers were tucked into socks and huge boots, and perched on her head was the same beret she'd worn when he'd flown her to Normandy.

She could have been ten feet-wide for all Jacques cared, because beneath the beret was the prettiest face imaginable. With streaks of black camouflage on her cheeks, she looked like a pussycat with whiskers stretching from her petite nose.

As she took his hand and allowed herself to be escorted from the Lysander, Yvette could also see his face properly for the first time. He was young, she thought perhaps twenty, but he was handsome with spectacular eyes that were both kind and strong. Now standing on the ground she had to raise her head to look up at him. He was tall, over six-feet and athletic-looking, his broad shoulders supporting the flying jacket perfectly, it's fur collar caressed his jaw with it's five o'clock shadow. Yes this Englishman was French, but he had the manners of an English country gentleman, a very sexy one at that.

"Tea, Mademoiselle?"

He had a naturalness to him that fascinated her, and she realised she was still holding his hand and he had made no attempt to let go. She looked at their hands still clasped together but she didn't speak.

"You'd better hang on, the path to the Mess is very uneven," Jacques said quite seriously.

Yvette looked at the fifty yards of pathway that led to the building she had visited before, it was perfectly flat and recently laid. "Thank you, it looks a bit tricky." She continued to hold his hand as he escorted her to the Mess.

Jacques was astounded at his own behaviour. He had never behaved like this with anyone. Actually he'd never really had a girlfriend. There had been a girl in Yarmouth who was nice and had fancied him, but nothing had really happened other than a few kisses and a clumsy grope on the beach by the pier. Honeysuckle had always seemed to be around, which he didn't mind because he preferred her company anyway. But now here he was, quite naturally flirting with a beautiful ten-feet-wide woman who must have been older than his inexperienced eighteen years.

'Oh well here goes, there is a war on, the rules have changed. The worst she can do is tell me to push off,' he thought.

He looked down at her as they walked, and she was looking at him with a slightly puzzled look on her face, then suddenly there was her pretty smile again and she gave him the faintest of nods.

Yvette was only twenty-two years old herself but she had seen more of the horrors of life than anyone she knew, and she'd lived in a brutal world since the War began. She was brave and she was fearless, she had killed many men and crippled others and she could live with it. She'd had sex on a number of occasions and some of those partners were now dead. They had been good men, she had not loved them but she missed them. She had no time for relationships, they would just make her more vulnerable and she had a job to do. When she had defeated the Nazis, she had to find her family.

She gave him a broader smile and squeezed his hand. This Jacques was nice. She needed nice for a while, some strong arms to hold her and she did not have time for courtship, if he proved to be all right over a cup of tea she would sleep with him.

When she squeezed his hand Jacques was suddenly scared, but excitement rushed through his body too. He now knew he would probably lose his virginity to a French girl, and it felt like the perfectly natural thing to do. He squeezed her hand back in acknowledgement of their unspoken agreement.

Tea went well. They made each other laugh and by the time the engineer came to tell them he'd refuelled the Lysander, Yvette was excited at the prospect of sleeping with Jacques.

Back at Tempsford, Yvette stayed in one of the rooms over the Red Lion Inn where she was to rest before getting her brief for the next assignment and return to Normandy. Jacques was given two days off before his next sortie, so the very next night he met her in the pub for dinner.

Jacques was sitting by the bar when she walked into the room. The ten-feet-wide man/girl had transformed into a real girl with curves in all the right places. The pussycat face had on real make-up and bright red lipstick adorned very kissable lips. Her black hair, which he'd never actually seen, formed a bob round her beautiful face. Her hips swayed on perfect legs accentuated by high heels as she walked towards him in a figure hugging green dress.

Jacques stood up as she approached and she raised herself on her toes to kiss him on the cheek. "Bonsoir, Jacques."

Jacques's heart was racing, and he felt terrified. He'd never really been scared before, not at Dunkirk or on any of his missions, but this slip of a girl scared the living daylights out of him. He took a deep breath. "You look beautiful, Yvette." He raised her hand above her head and twirled her round once. "Quite beautiful."

"Merci, Monsieur, and you are very handsome." Her eyes

never left his. Although they had spent only a short time in each other's company, Yvette liked being with him more than any man she'd met. She was pretty sure he was younger than her, but he was self-assured and his eyes somehow gave him a gravitas that made him seem older, they were wise eyes and very sexy.

They had a drink at the bar then went into the small restaurant for dinner. The choice was not great, however the food was fresh and it didn't seem to matter, they were perfectly at ease in each other's company.

Yvette had stayed there before and the landlord loved her. Somehow he'd managed to acquire a bottle of Burgundy, which he presented with great aplomb to the childish delight of Yvette and the amusement of Jacques.

It had been the perfect evening and now they were looking at each other over the remnants of the Burgundy. There had been no talk of the War or their pasts, they were both living in the present. That was all that mattered, especially to Yvette.

"Jacques, will you think I am terrible if I ask you to sleep with me? You are so kind and I need someone strong to hold me." There was a look of shame on her face, almost pleading for forgiveness. "We don't have to have sex, but I need you. I am saying it badly, I'm sorry, I hope you understand?" She was confused at what she was asking of him and looked for his reaction. She hoped she had not shocked him and he had managed to grasp what she was awkwardly trying to say.

"Of course, Yvette. I can sense your pain." His eyes were compassion and strength, and they understood perfectly. She hadn't told him her story, but he could see there was so much she wanted to tell, and he could see the tear in her eye.

"Thank you, Jacques." She was not surprised by his insight. She stood up and led him by the hand from the restaurant and up the old oak staircase to her room.

She kissed him gently on his lips and slowly undressed him, then stood back and peeled the green dress from her own body.

Jacques thought his heart would stop as she stood in front of him and allowed his hands to explore her curves. He thought he would explode when she gently stroked his penis and pushed him back onto the bed.

She knelt astride him and kissed him again and looked into his eyes. As his eyes met hers, he said the most remarkable thing to her.

"Not now, Yvette. I will hold you and share some of your pain. Maybe tomorrow when you are ready."

Yvette couldn't hold her tears back any longer. He was perfect and she needed to cry, she hadn't cried for over a year and this sweet man knew she needed to, even though his body told her he wanted something else.

Jacques cradled her in his arms and she allowed the tears to come, her head resting against his muscled chest. She was safe and even though she cried she was happy.

Jacques was desperate to make love to her, but he could sense it was the wrong time.

"I'm sorry, cheri, I will make it up to you and I'll explain later," she managed to say through her tears.

Jacques could feel her breasts against him and tried not to think about them. His hand rested on her buttock and he could feel the soft hair of her groin against his thigh. His hormones wanted something different, but he knew that she needed comforting, probably more than he needed sex, so he just held her and stroked her hair, occasionally kissing the top of her head.

After what seemed like an hour her sobs subsided. The woman he had been told was the bravest in the Resistance had cried herself to sleep. Jacques enjoyed the feel of her body against his for probably another hour before he too was overtaken by sleep.

He awoke to the most wonderful thing he had ever experienced. Yvette was kissing his penis, then slowly she moved her body over his and eased herself down onto the erection he was convinced would explode before he entered her. He managed to control himself just long enough as her tongue found his and her groin devoured him. How he managed it, he did not know, but she had an orgasm just before his own climax and she collapsed in his arms.

When she'd woken up and found his arms still enfolding her she had never desired anyone so much. He had given her something no one else ever had. He had given her back her humanity and allowed her to grieve.

"Wow, Yvette, I love it when you cry!"

She giggled and her hand sought him out again. "You do don't you?"

This time Jacques was more in control and discovered the joys of sex. In fact he enjoyed sex several more times before Yvette finally allowed him to take a rest.

"Well I must say, not only are you the nicest man I've ever slept with you are the by far the sexiest and best lover a girl could ask for. Where do you get that stamina from, and who taught you?"

"No one. First time, I'm afraid. You just deflowered me. Five times!"

"Oh my God!" Yvette was suddenly on her knees looking down at him with the wickedest of grins on her face. "Really?"

"Yes, really!" Jacques was smiling too, in fact he thought he'd be smiling for the rest of his life.

"Oh my God! How old are you, Jacques?" Yvette suddenly looked concerned.

Lie or not to lie? "Eighteen, nearly nineteen!" He had a look on his face that was asking if it was old enough.

Yvette's mouth was agog as she processed the information. Slowly the wicked grin reappeared. "So let's put all that youth to good use then!"

When they had finished she took his head in her hands and

kissed him. "I will not tell my friends you are only eighteen. It will be my secret, my beautiful English Frenchman!"

"How old are you, Yvette?"

"It's none of your business. Come on, lunch, let's have a picnic."

An hour later they were sitting by a stream in the English countryside, armed with a loaf of bread, some cheese and another bottle of the elusive Burgundy.

"We could easily be in France," Yvette said as she broke off another piece of bread and fed it to him. "It is lovely here, I am so happy."

Jacques was as happy as too. He was lying on his back with his head in her lap, looking up at the girl he'd spent all morning making love with. The sun was warm on his face and the water seemed to play music as it gently meandered through the rocks of the stream.

It was a perfect moment and they were quiet for a while, each wrapped in their own thoughts.

Suddenly Yvette said, "There is something I want to tell you. The reason I was crying and why I just needed you to be there for me." Yvette hesitated.

"Please go on, Yvette, I would like to know." He raised his arm and stroked her cheek.

Yvette looked distant, then said, "My name isn't Yvette. It is Sarah and I am Jewish. Yvette is my codename in the Resistance."

Yvette or Sarah, it didn't matter to Jacques, but he sensed there was more, so he did not speak and allowed her to continue.

"Maman and Papa, along with my sisters, were taken by the Gestapo. I hid in my friend's house and they did not find me. My family was initially taken to Drancy Internment Camp in Paris, but then I don't know where the Germans took them. I know they will be in one of their bloody concentration camps somewhere. People say they are terrible places and many are dying in them. I feel guilty that I could not save them, I should be with them, Jacques." She had said it. Guilty, she had told a boy she hardly knew that she felt guilty. Others in the Resistance knew her story but none knew about the guilt she felt for not helping them and not being with them.

Jacques sat up and held her shoulders. "You should not feel guilt. Your family will be thrilled you are not with them and since they were taken you have fought for them, for France. We will win this war and we will find them. I will help you."

Yvette looked at him. She could see in his eyes that he meant what he had just said and she knew he would help her. She loved being with him, being an ordinary girl with a dress on, just wanting her boy to kiss her. She suddenly felt like a child and he was her protector, and she was not the girl who had probably killed over a hundred German soldiers. It would be so easy to fall in love with him and just let him protect her, but she was not that person anymore. The child had left her the day they took her family.

"I will join the Special Operations Executive and fight with you. When we've defeated the bastards, then we will find your family."

There, he'd said it again. "You mean it don't you? You would do that, yet you have only really known me a day."

"Yes, Yvette, sorry, Sarah." He was still holding her shoulders, his eyes looking intensely into hers. "Anyone can fly the aeroplanes in and out. I know the drill there already and I speak French better than most Frenchmen. They'll jump at having me, hell it's already been mentioned to me by my bosses."

Yvette was experiencing a maelstrom of emotions. Her whole being cried out for her to take him with her, her protector, someone who knows and understands. "It is dangerous, Jacques. They don't take us prisoner, they torture and shoot us if we are caught."

"Then let's not get caught!" He assuredly squeezed her

shoulders.

"Will we be lovers?" It was suddenly important to her.

"Yes we will be lovers, and we will fight our common enemy together."

"What if we fall out, Jacques? You have not seen the woman who kills. You may not like her." There was doubt in her voice, she did not like herself at times and was sure he would see how callous she could be.

"Look at me, Yvette. If that happens then we will continue our fight apart. France is a big place. Together we can be a force, and we will keep each other alive."

Tears filled her eyes. Perhaps this war could be bearable with him by her side.

Two days later Jacques was a member of the S.O.E. and an important part of Yvette's life. She preferred the name Yvette to Sarah.

Jacques passed Buster his mystery sandwich. It was worth the wait. Buster had no idea what it was, but it tasted like chicken, so he would add mystery sandwich to his long list of likes.

Five

After lunch the man didn't get up to go home, but he nestled back into the bench for more remembering.

Buster generally preferred to go home to his sofa after lunch, but it was a warm summer day and he was enjoying the sun on his black fur, so he quite happily settled in for the duration.

Jacques had got into the habit of remembering Honeysuckle between each of his other recollections, and after remembering the day he lost his virginity to Yvette he felt a little guilty about Honeysuckle. It was a wonderfully sunny day, so he decided to stay a while longer on the Warren and think of her.

He looked out to the Solent and in the distance the ferry was approaching Yarmouth harbour, sailing boats miraculously avoiding its path with a nonchalance that always amused him. The water was much busier than when he was a boy, but despite everything he still loved the sea and he'd bought his own small sailing boat and had sailed it for a number of years after he had returned to the Isle of Wight in retirement. His thoughts went back to his dear Father and wished that he could have sailed it with him before he had passed away, the French flag would of course have been flying proudly from the stern of the yacht.

The ferry was almost in the harbour now and he was back on the Isle of Wight with Honeysuckle, well not quite.

He was on the paddle steamer approaching Yarmouth all those years ago and standing at the end of the pier was Honeysuckle, waving at the approaching boat.

He was glad to be going home for a short break before becoming operational with the S.E.O. Other than for a couple of days about nine months ago, he had not seen his parents and he had not seen Honeysuckle at all. She had been visiting her aunt with her Mother on the mainland and was distraught when she returned to find she had missed Jacques. She had sat with Jacques's Mother for hours in their kitchen and pumped her for every word he had said and for information on all he was doing.

She wrote to him regularly and he wrote back whenever he could. The letters were always written in French, hers were diaries of what she had been doing, but she never told him how much she missed him. He did not need a soppy girl wasting his time with that stuff when he had a war to fight.

His letters to her were still the letters of a big brother, they did not mention his friend who had died whilst training or the crash landing he'd had to make in the Lysander when it's engine had failed crossing the coast after retrieving an airman from France. They'd been lucky, he had just enough altitude to be able to glide the beast to terra firma, thus avoiding a dip in the cold sea, something they all dreaded as survival time was limited to just a few minutes. That was the problem with single engine aeroplanes, when the engine stopped working they either became boats or stationary vehicles! Anyway, this time he was a hero and saved the valuable aircraft. The engineers drove down

43

to a field some fifty yards from the coast in Sussex and changed the magnetos. So Jacques got to do a rare daylight take-off and returned to Tempsford.

His letters did not mention anything that could scare his little Honeysuckle, and they had not mentioned Yvette or the fact that he was no longer a pilot, but a spy and a saboteur. In a modern world he could even have been described as a terrorist. No, his letters were about her world and the world of his own childhood.

Jacques knew the speck on the pier would be Honeysuckle, and he found himself wondering what the small girl he'd not seen for eighteen months would look like. The speck got larger and made a little leap for joy when it saw Jacques wave back at her. Slowly the speck became a person, a person Jacques could barely recognise.

She was a mere fifty yards away now and Honeysuckle was a young woman. Her Mother had allowed her to wear make-up, and she had grown at least six inches in the past eighteen months. Her hair had also grown and was a mass of dark waves and curls that hung over her shoulders and framed that smile, a smile that lit up the whole world around it.

Jacques would have been speechless had she been standing in front of him and he was glad he had a few minutes to prepare himself before greeting her.

As he stepped from the boarding ramp she flew into his arms. He was wrong, she'd grown more than six inches, and there were the heels as well. She seemed at least ten inches taller than when he'd last seen her, and she had acquired a figure, one hell of a figure.

His face was buried in her curls as she hugged him to her. Eventually she pulled away and held his hands. "I've missed you, Jacques."

Jacques was still mesmerised by the woman she had become. He stood shaking his head, but saying nothing.

44

Honeysuckle was delighted at the effect she was having on him. It is exactly what she had wanted and she gave him her smile once again, her generous mouth and eyes bewitching him. He just stared at her, still speechless.

"Say something then," she said, tossing her head to one side.

"I can't. I don't believe what I see before me. You are stunning. My little Honeysuckle has turned into a beautiful swan."

"Are you saying I was an ugly duckling?" Her smile had turned into an attractive pout.

"No, you weren't ugly. You just weren't, this!" His hand gestured towards her as if he were presenting a princess.

The pout went and the smile returned. He couldn't take his eyes of it. His only defence against it was to pull her to him and bury his head in her curls again as he hugged her once more.

Honeysuckle was in heaven as she felt him close to her.

"Where are my parents?" Jacques said after a while.

"They are making tea and I am to take you straight there."

Jacques's parents were now perfectly aware of how Honeysuckle felt about their son. Elizabeth had seen it first and had asked Honeysuckle's Mother, if what she thought she saw in Honeysuckle was true. "Oh yes, it's true, she is besotted by him. It was seamless, the nature of the infatuation just changed from that of a small girl to that of a young woman!"

"Oh dear, Audrey. I know he loves her, but I don't know if he loves her like that. She has always been like his little sister." Elizabeth had looked concerned.

"I know, but Honeysuckle knows that too. All we can do is leave them to their own devices and wait to see what develops."

Big Jacques didn't get it at first, he had noticed his surrogate daughter grow into a woman, but his wife and her best friend still had to explain to him in words of one syllable that Honeysuckle had also changed inside which had altered the situation with his son. Still confused, he eventually grasped the nettle and simply said, "Why would she not love him? He is French!"

The three of them had deliberately allowed Honeysuckle to meet him alone. They knew that what he saw would astonish him, and if their darling Honeysuckle were to have him, he must see her as a woman, albeit a young woman.

Over tea they studied Jacques's reaction to her. It was perfectly obvious that he saw her as a woman, but was she still his little sister?

During the few days he spent at home they were as inseparable as ever. It was the school holidays and Honeysuckle usually helped her Mother in the shop, but she had refused her daughter's help and insisted she spend the time with Jacques.

They had tea in the tearooms, and sat on the pier. They walked to Freshwater, and cycled to Headon Warren. One day they took a picnic and walked some of Tennyson's Trail to Brighstone before getting the bus back along the stunning coast road, which the army had built, and they watched the waves crashing against the rocks beneath the chalk cliffs.

Another day they took a picnic to the beach and sat in the late summer sun until the sun set in the west beyond the Needles.

During these perfect days they talked. No longer the talk of children, but the talk of adults. Jacques told her all the things he had not said in his letters. He told her about the night in Normandy when he had been picking up a Resistance member and they were attacked. He told her about the bullets that hit his plane as he took off. He told her about friends who'd died at the hands of the Luftwaffe, and the bravery of the Resistance and the S.E.O. But he did not tell her about Yvette, or the fact that he was now a part of the S.E.O. and he was not sure of the reason why.

He did know that he still enjoyed her company more than any person he had ever known. She was the most natural and delightful person to be with and when she smiled he wanted to kiss her, because her smile had a life of it's own that almost hypnotised him.

Why could he not tell her about Yvette? He wanted to share it all with her and he felt guilty that he was deceiving her in some way, but something was stopping him.

Honeysuckle was in paradise every second that she spent with him. She was sixteen and she knew she was in love.

She had been a little apprehensive about his coming home. In the previous eighteen months her mind had built him up out of all proportion, and she was aware of it. What if they had lost the special relationship they had? What if the war had changed him? What if he didn't like the woman she was turning into? Or was she still just being a silly little girl with childish fantasies?

The time they had spent together told her that what they had was special, and the way he looked at her told her that he saw the woman she had become. And his eyes told her that he liked that woman.

They had spent their first days together as adults and there was hope, but he had not made any sort of advances to her, but that didn't matter because she was only sixteen and that would come later. She would make sure it did, but if he would just kiss her once she would know how he really felt.

They spent their last day together on the beach and it was wonderful. Their conversation never ceased even when they swam in the surf, as whenever their heads appeared above the waves again they would resume talking. They would run back along the beach to their towels and dry off before eating yet another of the morsels their parents had prepared for them.

In the late afternoon Honeysuckle said, "Come on, let's go back to Yarmouth and row up the Yar to the tidal mill like we used to when we were little. The tide will be in and we can have our last swim by the little beach there, it's lovely.

"It sounds good to me," Jacques replied, already gathering

up their towels.

Back in Yarmouth they grabbed the tender to Big Jacques's boat and Honeysuckle rowed him up the river to the mill, as she had done a hundred times before. He just lay back and encouraged his slave to row faster. At the age of ten she would just giggle all the way there, that giggle had now become the most wonderful husky laugh as he told her, "Put your back into it, wench."

They were escorted by a myriad of birdlife as she pulled harder on the oars. Terns skittered to their right in the reeds and gulls followed them up the estuary. A heron stood motionless in the salt flats waiting to see what the tide would bring for his supper. Shortly the sun would disappear behind the headland, which looked down on Yarmouth with its Norman Church spire nestling perfectly in the middle of the town, whilst the old castle guarded the harbour entrance, woefully inadequate for any modern day battles.

Honeysuckle loved Yarmouth, it was where she had grown up with Jacques, and here by the mill was her favourite place. She associated it with Jacques, her slave to his master, here they had always been alone together. She had not visited the mill or their little beach for eighteen months, she hadn't wanted to, it would not have been the same without him.

They beached the tender and stepped ashore, surrounded by perfect tranquillity. The only noise was the mill wheel turning gently on the tide some four hundred yards away.

A little egret landed gracefully on the far side of the estuary opposite them as Honeysuckle peeled off her summer dress to reveal her unnervingly curvaceous body, which was covered only by her swimming costume.

All day it had bothered Jacques that he should find himself looking at her, trying not to imagine her as he'd seen Yvette.

She grabbed his hand and led him to the water, then she dived gracefully into the deep clear pool, her long legs giving a dolphin kick as she disappeared from view.

Jacques shook his head in disbelief as he had done all day whenever she was not looking, and he followed her into the private pool that no one else seemed to know about. Beneath the water he watched her swim with a beauty and grace that a dolphin would be proud of. Her glorious hair streamed out behind her as she glided through the water, then she did two things that Jacques would never forget.

There, five feet under the water she actually smiled at him, like a mermaid who lived in the sea perfectly at home in its depths. There in the water the smile was even more remarkable and even more beautiful. Then she took his hand, and still under the water they both swam the short distance to their little sandy beach.

At the beach she allowed him to stand up then circled him under the water before rising up in front of him like a siren, her body brushing against him. With her soaking wet hair framing her now unsmiling face, she assuredly took his head in her hands and kissed him. She waited for his lips to part so she could explore his tongue. They did.

Jacques had been mesmerised by the whole thing from the moment her ankles had flicked her beneath the surface. When her body touched his he had wanted to hold her, but his hands had not moved. When her lips had touched his he had no option other than to open his mouth and let her kiss him, he could not have stopped himself in a million years, he knew he was in the presence of someone quite extraordinary.

The kiss was over, and there was the smile again. Not embarrassed or demure, but her radiant unselfconscious smile. "There, it is done, Jacques. It had to be done."

Jacques just stood there in complete shock, but knowing it had been the most remarkable moment of his life. More remarkable than the day he'd spent with Yvette all those months ago and those days he'd spent with her since. He did not know what to say, he just stood there with his mouth open.

Honeysuckle laughed at him, it was a nervous laugh, should she have done it? What was his reaction going to be? She already knew what one of his reactions had been, she could feel it against her stomach and butterflies had swarmed inside her when she felt him.

She waited with an anxious look on her face, like a small child waiting to be chastised, then he laughed.

"Well, little Honeysuckle, so you've grown up!"

"I'm sorry, Jacques, I've fantasised for so long about kissing you. I couldn't stand it any longer and you are leaving tomorrow, I…"

"It's okay, Honeysuckle. I liked it, but you are only sixteen and…."

"I know, but I had to see if our relationship could ever be anything more. Not now, but when I am older and the War is over." She looked anxious, wanting some sort of affirmation.

It was an unasked question and Jacques was totally confused. He loved Honeysuckle, he had always loved Honeysuckle, but could he be falling in love with her? He knew one thing, he didn't feel the same way about Yvette, but how the hell did he feel about Honeysuckle? Yvette was a woman, an incredible woman, and Honeysuckle was? What was Honeysuckle?

"Honeysuckle," he wasn't sure what he was going to say to her as she stared expectantly at him. "Honeysuckle what we have is remarkable and quite frankly I'm confused about what just happened. You know I've always loved you, but it was always as a brother, and now," he hesitated, she looked forlorn at what he was about to say. "I don't know, that may have changed. You are only just sixteen and still have a lot of growing up to do."

All Honeysuckle heard was, it may have changed. "I love you Jacques, and when I'm older and the War is over it may be possible?" There was a look of hope on her lovely face, and desperation in her eyes.

The War had a long way to run yet. A thousand things could happen, he needed time to think about what had just taken place and he needed time to think about Yvette. Who knows what could transpire over the coming years? He had to leave Honeysuckle with hope though, but hope tempered with reality and part of him wanted to share in that hope.

"It is possible, Honeysuckle, but I must tell you some things that may scare you and you must be realistic about the future and what it may bring."

It is possible Honeysuckle, again that was all she heard, but she would let him talk. Her silly Jacques thought he was wiser because he was older, he had no idea of what the future held. But Honeysuckle knew without any doubt in her heart.

"I have joined the Special Operations Executive and will be working in France, liaising with the various French Resistance groups and preparing for the invasion that will eventually come. When we liberate France the war will be close to an end. It is very dangerous work and many of us are getting killed. I haven't even told my parents yet, but I will tonight before I leave tomorrow." He waited while it sank in. "If you love me, Honeysuckle, either as a sister or as the woman who just kissed me, you must prepare yourself for the possibility that I may not return." He did not mention Yvette, there was no need, not yet.

Honeysuckle then did the third thing that he would never forget for the rest of his life. She touched his face and said without any doubt in her voice, "You will be fine, my darling. We will be together." Then she reached up and kissed him on the lips, gently and assuredly, his equal in years and his elder in wisdom.

From that moment on she would never just be his 'little sister' again.

That night he told his parents about his new role in the War. His Mother was scared as was his Father, but his son, their wonderful son, would be fighting for France.

That evening all three of their parents watched fascinated by the way the pair now interacted. There had been a change, firstly they were not talking to each other incessantly in French and when they looked at each other the childish smiles had gone, but something else passed between them.

Even Big Jacques noticed the change in them and took his son to one side and clumsily tried to say, "I hope nothing err.. She is only sixteen you know..." Torn between love for his son and that for his surrogate daughter.

Jacques laughed. "Don't worry, Papa. All we did was talk. We are a long way from that." It was only a small lie.

Audrey stood with her arm in Elizabeth's as the children said goodbye to each other on the quayside. The look on Honeysuckle's face brought a lump to their throats as she wrapped her arms around Jacques then leaned up to allow him to kiss her. It was not a passionate kiss, but neither was it the kiss of an older brother.

As the ferry sailed out into the Solent, Jacques's heart was heavy. There was so much he'd left unsaid to her, he believed it was to protect her but he knew in part it was to protect him. He thought of Yvette and felt guilty. Was he guilty of betraying them both?

It was quite late when Buster and the man left the bench. The man talked to the bench for quite a while before they finally set off down the hill. He spoke to it every night and touched the plaque before they left. Buster did not know what he said, but the man was laughing as he talked and he seemed particularly happy.

Anyway, the net result was that Buster missed Countdown on the television, he liked Countdown. Dinner always came after Countdown and he'd been confused when his bowl was offered before it came on. 'The man must have forgotten!'

52

Six

The man hadn't forgotten the sandwiches today though, and they smelt like ham. Yes, his favourite. So he flew up the hill to sniff and prepare the bench for the man when he and the ham sandwiches finally caught up.

When the man arrived Buster was sitting proudly by their bench with all potential sandwich thieves seen off. Before long they had both assumed their respective positions.

Almost instantly Jacques was on the paddle steamer once again, still wonderfully baffled about what had happened with Honeysuckle. He was reliving her breathtakingly dramatic kiss and the smile she'd given him under the water. All he could imagine was that she'd been a mermaid in another life or another place. He knew he would treasure the moment for the rest of his life, however long that may be.

With that feeling of mortality, his thoughts returned to the R.A.F. training school at Brackley, near the village of Croughton in Northamptonshire. He'd arrived with the other recruits, all of them wet behind the ears, and three of them were dead within a month. He remembered the exhilaration he'd felt the first time he'd pulled back on the stick to get the Tiger Moth airborne, with his instructor sitting behind him seemingly confident with his student's ability to fly the beast. They'd practised steep turns and the relationship of pitch and power; how to climb and descend; the effect of drag and the importance of flap settings for take off and landing. All of this was done in one glorious hour before it was time to bring her in to land. The landing was the only part of the flight he was not in total control of, the instructor had asked Jacques to 'follow him through on the controls,' as he demonstrated the landing technique. After that he did every landing himself as they practiced 'circuits and bumps,' as his instructor described his practice landings. By the end of his first week's flying the instructor stepped out of the aeroplane to 'take a pee,' and asked Jacques to pick him up when he landed next time. Jacques was half way round the circuit before he realised he was alone and he had been sent for his first solo flight. It was the most excited he could remember feeling. That night his first friend died.

R.A.F. Brackley was designated as an Emergency Airfield and was kept permanently lit to accept returning, damaged aircraft that had taken hits on their bombing raids into Europe. That, and it's other role as a training base made it a prime target for night bombing raids by the Luftwaffe.

Freddie died instantly when the bomb hit his billet. The siren had just alerted them to the impending attack but he had no time to get to the bunker. It seemed daft to Jacques that they should light up the approach and runway to lead the enemy straight to the door of one of the Air Force's most important training facilities, but he was told resources were limited and it was strategically placed near a number of bomber stations who needed all the help they could get to retrieve their wounded ships.

Two weeks later another friend, Dickie, was cut down by MG 17 machine-gun fire from an attacking Messerschmitt 109 as he'd tried to run for cover.

It was a strange environment. Jacques swung from elated highs as he flew the marvellous birds that he had become part of, to deep sadness as another colleague died. Young men he'd only known briefly were being killed even before they had been trained for battle. They all knew their chances of surviving the War were slim and even before his elementary training was complete they were resigned to the fact that death was part of their life. But the high he got when he flew the aeroplane excited him. The adrenalin rush as he pulled the aircraft out of a spin, or did a barrel roll made the danger almost worthwhile.

His third friend had died in a Tiger Moth because he did not recover the plane from a spin he'd put her into too close to the ground. They took risks, all of them, their future would rely on them taking risks and gambling that they had enough air between them and the ground to stay alive. One instructor had said, "It's the ground that ultimately will kill you. The bullet, or the fire will injure you, but it is the ground that kills you."

They were prophetic words for Jacques in particular, as he was posted to 161 Squadron. The ground killed everyone they lost, the ground they couldn't see because it was too dark.

At first he was disappointed when he got his posting. He'd wanted Spitfires or Hurricanes, and he was good enough, they'd told him that. They also told him he was too good and his talents were needed for more clandestine activities.

Those activities brought their own adrenalin rush, especially at the beginning as he gambled against the ground as he practised night landings in appalling weather on the darkest of nights. Initially these landings were into fields he knew, later he was sent to find a field in parts of the country he'd never even heard about before. When he was proficient he was given his first sortie to France.

It was weird, he felt as if he was going home. He was English and had lived all his life in England, but his Father had done a good job in convincing him he was French too. That night, as he flew over the French coast, he felt a strange calm inside, a sense of belonging. He'd smiled to himself as he had the sudden thought, 'Thank God Dad was not German!'

Often he would have to turn back when he couldn't locate the flashlights guiding him in. Once he'd got so low in an attempt to see them the branch of a tree clipped his wing. The next night he flew a little higher, you could get too much adrenalin! It had taken five attempts to get that particular saboteur into France. He was English and had been a schoolteacher, teaching French. Now he was a demolition expert and there was a bridge that needed taking out by a certain date, they were even carrying the explosives in the hold to do the job. His name was Peter, but had quickly become Pierre when he realised Jacques spoke French. It was Pierre who first suggested Jacques's excellent French might be of more use on the ground. It had got him thinking, and something inside was pulling him to France. Then he met Yvette.

After that memorable encounter with Yvette he was convinced that he was destined to be in France and to be with her. Sure, he was young and his seduction had been one of the most exciting things that had ever happened to him. She, and her body had completely bowled him over and he couldn't stop thinking about her. Meeting her and losing his virginity, somehow seemed part and parcel of his destiny.

When he'd gone to his Commanding Officer and said he wanted to apply to join the S.O.E. the Boss had said, "Not surprised, you're more Frog than Brit. I'll see what I can do, but we'll be sorry to lose you."

Two days later he was on a train to London to be interviewed by the S.O.E. in their headquarters at 64 Baker

Street. Colonel Gubbins and Vera Atkins, the woman who ultimately become his handler and prepared him for active service, interviewed him. The young man who spoke French perfectly impressed them. He had proved his bravery by working with them already and appeared to be friends with one of their best agents. They did not know just how friendly! His soul appeared to be French, and he was motivated. Their only reservation was his age, he'd finally told them the truth, and the fact that he had never actually lived in France, despite appearing to know more about it than England. But he had a proven military background, and he had one other thing. He had charm, and charm could be as effective a weapon as any other, especially when trying to stay alive in an occupied country whilst undertaking clandestine operations.

He spent two more nights of bliss with Yvette before taking the train to Guildford where he was picked up and driven to Wanborough Manor for his initial training. He was taught how to use guns, surprisingly the only guns he'd fired up until now were on an aeroplane, and explosives. His knowledge of explosives would become integral to his work along with other methods of sabotage. He did a course on wireless telegraphy, and how to live secretly in occupied territories. They taught him how to kill with his bare hands and how to take another's life without them uttering a sound. He was taught how to be an assassin and he was taught how to save a life. At the end of this training he was sent to Scotland where the Commandos toughened him up on courses in the Highlands to a level of fitness he'd never thought possible. At the end of it all he was a killing machine that could have a real input into the outcome of the War.

It was this killing machine that had gone to visit Honeysuckle, but all she had seen was her Jacques. He had told her something of his training, but had avoided the more radical aspects of it. Yes, he was a different man when he'd gone to see her, but when he left again, he was once again her Jacques. And

Jacques was still confused.

He was about to enter a world he had tried to imagine, and live in a country he'd always loved yet rarely visited. The reality was not what he had expected, but the life he led there did not disappoint him.

Vera Atkins had been working on his cover, he was to become Philippe Villon, a wine distributor. It would allow him to travel freely in both the free and occupied France. She spent a day teaching and testing him on his family history, then a day teaching him about wine. Initially he would join up with his friend Yvette, who would introduce him to the real art of sabotage. In time he was probably going to be given the task of leading another team from within her group, which was growing fast as more joined them, and together they would undertake whatever was needed. Later they would start to organise the various groups of the Resistance into a more co-ordinated fighting force to prepare for the eventual invasion by allied troops. He was not given a time scale, nor told when he would be brought back to England for debriefing or further instructions, but he was told he would certainly be coming back before the 'final push.'

On April 3rd 1943 he reported to Tempsford where his old friend Daniel from 161 Squadron, flew him to a field somewhere in Normandy.

As he jumped from the plane he yelled, "Thanks for the ride, see you soon." Then started running towards the flashlight in the woods.

Yvette had come to meet him personally and his heart leapt when he saw the cat's whiskers smudged on her face. It had been nearly three months since he'd last seen her in England and he had never stopped thinking about the nights they'd spent together.

There were two other men with her who she quickly introduced, then smiled at him but made no attempt to kiss him. Three months earlier she couldn't keep her hands or her lips off him, but this was business and they had to leave before the Germans arrived to investigate where the shadowy English plane had landed.

Within a minute they were in the back of a van driving like maniacs without any lights on, trying to put as much distance as possible between themselves and the drop off point.

It was probably thirty minutes before the van came to a halt outside a farmhouse and all four went inside. Yvette's colleagues were called Alain and Pierre. They were older than her, yet deferred to the young woman. A third man appeared and introduced himself as Albert, he was younger, about the same age as Yvette, and he was English.

"Albert is our radio operator, Philippe, trained by the S.E.O. He has been with us for six months," said Yvette.

It sounded strange when she called him by his new name. "Good, radio telegraphy is not my strongest point. If I had to do it the Germans would be here before I had the first word transmitted." He continued to talk in French and smiled at Albert, who returned it with interest. The other two were less trusting of the new Englishman they had just been sent. Jacques knew he would have to prove himself to get their trust.

Albert spoke first. "I have prepared a daube while you were out. Rabbit, a fresh rabbit that I shot this afternoon."

Pierre replied, "Bon, daube is the only food you can cook!" Then slapped his young English radio operator on the back.

"It smells good, Albert. Come, we'll clean up before we eat, then I'll explain our next job to Philippe," she paused, "mes amis, Philippe's Papa is French and he has already worked with us. He is a good man." Then she turned and left the room, climbing the wooden staircase to the creaky floorboards above.

"French eh? You may be alright," Alain said with a smile. Pierre's moustache just twitched.

"Come on, Philippe, I'll show you to your room and how we escape from this shit-hole if we need to," Albert said, grabbing Philippe's bag. "This is heavy, what the hell do you have in it?"

"Presents for you all, or perhaps they're presents for the Germans!" He smiled and followed Albert.

"In here, you're in with me. There is the bathroom. Yvette lives in luxury on her own and the other two are in here. I'll let you have a wash then I'll give you the rest of the tour." He turned and clumped down the stairs again.

Yvette appeared from the bathroom drying her face with a towel. She saw him and pulled him into her room and kissed him passionately. "I've missed you, cheri." She kissed him again then said, "They don't know about us, we must keep it like that for now. They are superstitious about relationships within the group. They think it is bad luck so I must appear aloof around you whenever we are with them. I'm sorry, cheri, I will make it up to you." She gave him her wicked smile and her hand caressed his already hard penis, then she was gone.

Jacques, or rather Philippe washed and returned to the kitchen again.

"So what is the set-up here?" He asked.

"Alain and Pierre are brothers, real brothers, and this is their farm. I am their little sister and Albert, a cousin. We work the farm, badly, and the house is used to harbour prisoners-of-war who have escaped, along with the less lucky airmen who through the network find their way here. The farm also acts as one of our arms caches. There are a number in the area, so our resources are spread out and growing, they are supplied by the S.E.O. who also finance us. We are about a hundred at the moment, but people are joining all the time and we operate throughout most of Normandy. It is our playground!" Yvette was smiling. "We go further afield as well, when London wants a special job done, or we see a target ripe for picking!"

Alain took up the explanation. "The various groups have been too autocratic in the past and resources have been wasted.

60

We are beginning to work more closely with groups like the maquis next door in Brittany, but that brings it's own dangers. Small is safe, family is better." He looked at his brother. "If too many know your business, torture can loosen their tongues, so we are careful when we meet new people. To the Gestapo we are just bad farmers, which is actually what we were before the war!" He laughed at his own joke, an infectious laugh that Philippe grew to love.

"But I am a wine distributor. So where do I fit in, surely not here?" Philippe asked.

It was Yvette's turn to explain. "For a few weeks you'll stay here, but there is a priest's hole you may have to get used to hiding in when people come. I still have to set up your cover with hotels and bars. It should be easy, we have people there already and they will have more contacts. We even have some samples of the wine you're going to sell and distribute, we will sample a bottle in a minute! Tomorrow we will visit your employer and he will circulate your name to his customers, so within a few weeks the name Philippe Villon will be known, and then you will move here from Toulouse and we will put a face to that name. And you will get to drive your own van." She smiled at him. "It's being prepared as we speak, an Aladdin's cave of arms and explosives beneath the crates of wine!"

"Don't worry, you won't be idle, Philippe." It was Alain again. "There is work to be done tomorrow night. And we're expecting a couple of 'unlucky' pilots later in the week, and if you are bored you can be a bad farmer with me!" He laughed again. Philippe already liked him, Pierre's moustache just twitched.

After their daube, which really was extremely tasty, Albert showed him round the farm and it's outbuildings. In one of the barns an underground room that they accessed through a trapdoor covered with hay, housed a plethora of arms, ammunitions, explosives and everything needed to detonate.

them.

"This lot has been supplied by the S.O.E."

Another barn played host to what looked like a junkyard of scrapped vehicles. "There are eight vehicles in here and two of us can reassemble any one of them in an hour. I can paint one in two hours and change registration plates in two minutes. The Germans think they are just junk that a lazy farmer cannot be bothered to get rid of. That lorry will carry thirty men." He pointed at a chassis half-covered in straw with one wheel removed. Its flatbed and canopy were chucked haphazardly in the corner of the barn. "Remove the chicken's eggs and change two spark plugs, put the bonnet back and it's the fastest lorry in Normandy!" He smiled proudly at his prized vehicle. "The only problem is getting petrol, so we steal it from the Germans."

Other barns were actually used by the farm. Two cows mooed hello, and chickens clucked around his ankles as the two men walked back to the farmhouse.

"Any visitors, French or German, you sit in here until we tell you to come out." Albert pushed the top left hand corner of a wooden panel he had counterbalanced. It clicked and the panel swung open to reveal a space about twice the size of a coffin with a mattress on the floor and a book lying in the middle. "You may get bored," he said pointing to the book. "We've left it here with a torch for our guests. I don't know what it is, I'm not much of a reader myself," Albert added rather dismissively.

They joined the others in the kitchen who were already poring over a hand drawn map. "Philippe, your first job." Yvette pulled him closer to the map. A railway formed its centrepiece, arrows and crosses obviously signified other things and he waited for Yvette to explain.

"As you know, one of our main jobs is to disrupt the German supply lines and their communications network. We have learnt from our people in the railways that the Germans are bringing a freight train to Caen. It will be carrying arms and a number of soldiers to replenish their dwindling garrison, courtesy of our attentions and those of the maquis! When we have finished with the train their problem will have become even more intense. As the Allies prepare to invade, the Germans will try to move as many soldiers as possible to the coastal regions to defend against allied landings. In time we will become very active, disrupting and yapping at their heels, but for now it is attacks like this that will be most effective. We need to lay the explosives tonight under the cover of darkness. The train will be well guarded with the usual machine guns that give 360-degree cover. We don't know yet if there will be sufficient troops to warrant the usual anti-aircraft carriages. If they are there, so much the better; our people in the railways will be able to let us know which carriage carries the soldiers, they are the main targets. If we can detonate the explosives as their carriage passes, then that will cause maximum damage. Guns are useless if there is no one to fire them!"

"Do you want me to set the charges?" Pierre asked.

"Yes, but take Philippe with you and show him the tricks of the trade the S.E.O. didn't teach him. You are our top man, so who better to learn from?" Yvette knew how to get the best out of her people. Pierre did not know whether to make his moustache twitch or smile, so he did both.

"I think this will be the most effective place to attack the train." She pressed her finger onto the map. "The train will have slowed for the station at Lisieux, where we will have the signalman arbitrarily put a speed limit on it after it passes through. There is cover in the woods about fifty yards from the track and good access back to the road for the getaway."

"How many men?" Alain asked.

"Just our little band for this one, boys!" She looked round the men and saw their smiles. She knew they loved to keep it within their own group. Although she was young she was totally accepted as the leader, each one of them owed their life to her in some way or another and they had all played their part in looking after her. Yes, this was what they liked, small and devastating. All for one and one for all!

"Philippe, are you okay going with Pierre tonight?" Yvette watched his reaction.

"Of course. I want to learn from the best," he said with a genuine respect in his voice.

Yvette smiled to herself. Her boy was good, good at a lot of things! She looked for Pierre's moustache to twitch, it didn't, just a smile. This was going to work. It had taken a month before Pierre had accepted Albert, but hopefully after the next two nights they'd all think of Philippe as one of them.

That night Pierre and Philippe set off in the most ancient Citroen Philippe had ever seen. They were heavily armed and carrying enough explosives to derail a dozen trains.

"It's simple, Philippe, if we are caught with this lot all we can do is shoot our way out," Pierre said as they loaded the last box of explosives.

"Just say the word, head saboteur, and I'll start shooting." Philippe gave him a disarming smile, which was greeted by a wide grin.

It was about an hour's drive to the site of the proposed attack. At one point Pierre stopped the car by a gate and opened it, then drove across a number of fields before emerging back onto a tarmac road.

"What was all that about?" Philippe asked.

"Avoiding a German checkpoint. You'd think the idiots would move it occasionally. Still, Albert has raised and toughened the suspension on this old girl. She loves the fields." He laughed. "Now, when we get there we must be careful, they patrol the railway. We must work fast and then cover up our wires."

They were able to park by the forest as Yvette had indicated. One hour later the charges were set and the wires to the detonator were laid along a ditch that led to the woods and then covered with leaves and undergrowth.

"Good, the real fun will be tomorrow," Pierre said as he fired the old banger back into life. It's engine purred like a brand new vehicle.

Back at the farm they grabbed a few hours sleep before the sun came up. Later in the morning they made their final preparations for the attack. At two o'clock in the afternoon a boy arrived on his bicycle with information for Yvette. The train was estimated at 23:00 hours and it would have three anti-aircraft carriages with the ensuing weaponry and skilled artillery forces. The attack would have to be clean and lethal, but more importantly their retreat would have to be rapid.

Before they left Yvette appeared in the kitchen, her face camouflaged with dark streaks. This time she had deliberately accentuated the cat's whiskers for Jacques's benefit, who had told her how sexy they had looked.

Jacques was finding it difficult not to take her in his arms. Since their first date he had never been in her presence without being able to kiss her, and now as she smiled at him through her whiskers he was in agony. His nineteen-year-old hormones were getting the better of him.

"She is very pretty, our Yvette, non?" Pierre had caught him almost salivating at the pussycat.

"Yes, she is very pretty," Philippe replied, his face turning red at having been caught in his fantasies.

"Don't let her pretty face fool you, Philippe, she is deadly." Pierre was quite serious. Later that night Philippe would learn just how deadly.

They took two vehicles that Albert and Alain had been working on all day, purely so they had a spare in case of a fault or attack. Pierre and Alain left first and the other three followed about half an hour later. They took separate routes and arrived at 21:00 hours. Yvette and Alain stealthily swept the woods and surrounding area for anything or anybody who may interfere with their night's work. All seemed well, Yvette had chosen the spot carefully as it was well away from any other habitation.

"You will like this, Philippe. We are going to use a Waffen S.S. blasting machine, the M40. We stole it a year ago. It has it's own generator that sends 300 volts to detonate the explosives. It's bloody marvellous, the Germans really do make the best kit, you know!" He laughed and his moustache wagged like a dog's tail. He connected the wires to the detonator. "I love it when they are killed by their own equipment."

It was 22:00 hours and the expected advance train carrying floodlights and about twenty men came down the track. The lights swept the landscape for any sign of possible terrorist attack, occasionally troops would jump from the carriage and investigate anything they thought might be suspicious.

The powerful lights lit up the woods around them as if it were daylight, but caught no trace of the five people buried under leaves, or the ends of the rifle barrels that protruded about an inch from their cover as their eyes stared unblinking though the sights.

The train moved on without any soldiers disembarking and searching the surrounding woods. Yvette had chosen the location well as the woods were considered far enough away, but there still might be foot patrols, especially as the road was nearby. However the vehicles were well hidden under the nets with a tapestry of woodland life woven into them.

It was a waiting game now. 22:45 hours, and Yvette could hear a vehicle approaching along the road about two hundred yards away.

"Shit, I thought they might search this area as it's so close to the road," Yvette whispered. "Philippe come with me, but quietly."

The armoured car pulled into the side of the road about a hundred yards from their own vehicles. It was an Sd.kfz 232. 'Six wheels and four crew, perfect,' thought Yvette. It stopped exactly where she thought it would. "We'll take the driver and the machine gun operator first. Look, the fool is standing up with his head out. We must make sure they don't get a chance to transmit their position. Then we take the other two who will be searching the woods, give them one minute so they are out of sight. I'll kill the gunner, okay? Silence, no guns, understood?" Philippe nodded.

Exactly as Yvette predicted, two S.S. soldiers got out of the armoured car and stepped into the woods with flash lights and their guns at the ready.

Yvette and Philippe were perfectly positioned to strike. She had studied one hundred yards of road when they'd arrived and picked hiding places for twenty possible scenarios. She had driven up and down the road at least ten times, imagining where anyone could pull in and what vehicles they would probably use. There would be no traffic along this road until daybreak, yet it seemed to be human nature to park the vehicle on the verge, or if a definite parking place presented itself, 90% of the time a driver would take it. That is exactly what had happened.

Philippe and Yvette were no more than five yards away when the two soldiers crossed the road to the woods they were about to search.

Exactly one minute later Yvette leapt like a panther onto the armoured car, and before the gunner realised what was happening a six-inch hunting knife had severed his jugular artery. Yvette's hand over his mouth prevented any sound from coming from the dying man. His body slumped back into the vehicle, then she dropped a tear gas canister into the tank and closed the metal turret lid trapping the driver.

Jumping from the armoured car and using all her body weight she ripped the aerial from its side, thus preventing any transmissions being made. The driver struggled to get his head into the fresh air and as he pushed the turret open again Philippe snapped his neck.

The total noise level was not enough to alert the other two soldiers to what had happened. Gesturing silence to Philippe they followed them into the woods. Four minutes later Yvette had slit the throats of the two clumsy soldiers as they trudged noisily through the undergrowth. They never heard the panther's approach.

As the last man died, the moonlight caught Yvette's beautiful catlike face and Philippe saw a look in her eyes he had never seen before. She was covered in blood and there was a mixture of bloodlust and hatred on her face. She saw him watching her as she wiped the knife on her sleeve.

Jacques was not sure what had just passed between them. She did not avert her eyes or look away, she just stared back at him without saying a word, a blank malevolence in her eyes. She defiantly fixed his stare for another second then gestured that they should rejoin the others.

Jacques looked at the bodies on the ground and he remembered the man he had just killed. It was his first ever kill, he did not have time to think about what he had done or time to judge Yvette for her part in it, because there was still work to be done.

In the distance they could hear the train approaching as they reached the others. "Albert, wait with the vehicles. Take off the nets when you hear the explosion and start the engines. We'll leave in the same ones we came in. Do you remember the routes we've chosen, and did you open the gates as we discussed when we planned the routes last week?"

"Yes, we did the gates on the way over. It's been dry and any fields we have to cross should be okay," Pierre replied.

"Good, we'll see you two back at the farmhouse and we'll all help Albert dismantle the vehicles," Yvette said.

The train slowly approached the charges they had laid. One, two, three carriages in and Pierre pushed the plunger that would signal the end of life for over seventy young German soldiers.

It was spectacular. The explosion lit up the night sky and highlighted the carriage flying high into the air with flailing bodies falling like water in a fountain to the ground below. The rest of the train was ripped from the track as the explosives and the screams of ravaged bodies shattered quiet night air.

Alain pulled Philippe's arm as he knelt mesmerised by the pyrotechnic display. Pierre had already cut the wires to the M40 and had it tucked under his arm as he started to run. Another hand grabbed Philippe's arm and pulled him to his feet, it was Yvette. He looked into her eyes, they had changed. Once again there was the vulnerability he'd seen the night she'd cried whilst laying in his arms, the woman he knew had returned. They ran as fast as they could to the vehicles, which had their engines running, and were ready to go.

They knew they would have a good start on any pursuers and they knew the countryside like the back of their hands. Though it did not stop a frantic drive from the scene of their crime.

They arrived back at the farmhouse within fifteen minutes of each other. Yvette, Philippe and Albert were last to get there because they stopped for five minutes whilst Albert radioed that the outcome of their mission was positive. He always did this away from the farmhouse so the source of his signal could not lead the Germans to their refuge. When they arrived, one vehicle was already partly dismantled. The second was quickly put to bed in various parts of the barn and all the weapons returned to the subterranean bunker before they retired to the kitchen to debrief the mission and drink a toast to a liberated France.

"You are strangely quiet, Yvette, are you alright?" Asked Alain.

"I'm fine, just a bit tired. I'll go and leave you boys to it," she replied. She looked at Philippe as she said it. He had seen her, he had seen the woman she could be, the woman she did not want to be. Would he judge her? Would he hate what he had seen? He was the best thing that had happened to her since this living hell had begun.

She looked for a sign in his eyes. Something that said he understood. Was it there or did she revolt him? His kind eyes smiled at her. She wanted to run over to him and hold him, try to explain why she was the way she was and try to make him love her again. His eyes did not say that he was disgusted, they reached out to her and she wanted to be in his strong arms again.

Meeting Jacques had changed her. She had never felt any disgust or remorse for her actions; all her victims deserved their fate. But now Jacques was here it was different, she had been shocked at her own reaction to what she had just done and what she'd become. She had killed countless Germans, many with her own bare hands just as she had done this evening, but she had never questioned herself or thought about trying to justify it. When he'd watched her killing them the look on his face had cut her to the quick. It wasn't disgust, it was shock. He had seen the monster that lived inside of her, the monster she had always denied.

So now, if she could not be with Jacques she needed to be alone so she could search deep into her own soul to see if the young, happy-go-lucky child that Sarah had once been still existed. When she had been with Jacques in England she had been that person again and it had felt wonderful. But did that Sarah only exist there or could that innocent child be reborn again in her beautiful France?

Jacques watched the enigma leave the room and his heart went out to her. He had seen the hatred in her eyes as she'd killed the German soldiers and wondered what terrible demons had inflicted such pain on the soul of the beautiful woman he'd given himself to.

They both lay in their separate beds, each wrapped in thoughts of the other. Sleep was slow to come before the short night's rest was over and the five terrorists became bad farmers once again.

Buster hadn't seen the man smile much in the past hour or two and he was glad when he was back in the present, offering him a piece of pork pie and saying, "Yvette, what a woman."

As far as Buster was concerned pork pie was almost as good as ham, and now the man was smiling a lot and tickling him behind the ears, so all was well again. Buster preferred it when the man's remembering brought smiles and laughs.

Seven

It was raining quite heavily with strong winds blowing up the side of the hill and round the glass conservatory of Headon Cottage.

Headon Cottage is where Buster and the man lived; it was situated half way down the hill on the Totland side of Headon Warren. Today the remembering would be done in the conservatory, sitting on the wicker sofa. It wasn't Buster's favourite sofa but the man liked it and the view was wonderful.

The man placed his cup of tea on the table by the chair and stroked Buster. "No walks today, old boy, it's horrid out there. Tea and cake inside our dry little nest."

Buster's ears pricked up at the mention of cake, he was particularly partial to a slice of cake, especially after a ham sandwich!

The man settled into the inviting cushions of the sofa, making sure his tea was within reach after Buster had taken his place next to him with his head on his lap.

It would be a Honeysuckle day. Every other day was a day

for remembering Honeysuckle, but this was one day he would not be proud of.

After Honeysuckle had kissed him in their private pool by the mill, he had never stopped thinking about her and his reaction to her kiss. Over the next six months his relationship with Yvette had become both intense and immensely physical, yet his private thoughts would often turn to Honeysuckle and whenever he thought of her there would be a smile on his face. He couldn't think of her without seeing her own incredible smile, or the aquatic smile she gave him from beneath the water, not to mention her siren kiss that had aroused him so much in their pool, and it warmed his innermost being. It was the constant that helped him through times that were brutal and cruel. Her smile helped him deal with the killing and havoc he wreaked on his enemy, it helped him deal with the death he handed to countless men who he knew in his heart were probably good people who had just become caught up in the same war as him. Her smile was the light at the end of the tunnel. Her innocence, the reason he did what he did. Honeysuckle and her smile were constantly with him, as was her kiss.

So was Yvette. Where Honeysuckle was innocence and virtue, Yvette was experience and wantonness, but she was also vulnerable and complicated. If Jacques was being honest, it was Yvette's physicality that had mesmerised him. He was young and she had taken his virginity and he loved every second of their carnal relationship, but there was more. He cared for Yvette, and believed he could be in love with the defenceless girl that lurked within the ruthless woman she had become.

Lusting after Yvette whilst thinking about Honeysuckle all the time left Jacques with an uneasy feeling. He wanted to be infatuated with Yvette, to worship more than her body but he couldn't get Honeysuckle out of his mind and he didn't want to, she was a huge part of his life and always had been. He was totally confused about his feelings for Honeysuckle. Until his last visit she had been his little sister, but now what was she?

He decided he would write Honeysuckle a letter and give it to one of his old colleagues when they made a pick up one night. How naïve could he have been? He allowed his adolescent feelings of guilt and his honourable desire to be truthful with Honeysuckle to cloud his judgement. He wished he'd never written that letter, and as the Lysander got airborne he knew he'd made a mistake.

He'd been in France for seven months when he wrote it and had become a battle-hardened veteran, already having seen a number of colleagues die or disappear at the hands of the Gestapo. He could cope with the killing, he did not enjoy it but it was necessary. Each life he took, or saw taken, gave him a primeval desire to procreate. He was unaware that it was a perfectly natural reaction to death. In Yvette he had a willing partner who was driven by the same longing, but whose demons sought more from their sex. For her, being with her perfect Jacques was a cleansing process, his purity and goodness in some way easing the culpability for her deeds and the shame she felt for the enjoyment she experienced when killing the people who had taken her family.

They needed each other for similar yet different reasons. Their relationship was no longer a secret from the rest of the group, it couldn't be, but on operations it never got in the way of their work. Jacques had an apartment in Caen close to the depot from which he distributed his wines. He had a permit for a van and all the correct papers to allow him to carry on his business, so he was able to travel freely. The first time he'd been stopped he was nervous, but his perfect French with a slight Normandy accent made the process a simple one and subsequent checks had proven less uneasy. Yvette would regularly stay with him at the apartment and the fact that she was his girlfriend added to their cover. This was France and there was a war on, that they were not married did not appear to be a problem. They would walk hand in hand for all to see, and smile at both the police and the Germans with equal warmth. All became accustomed to the love-struck young couple taking coffee in the cafés near the barracks, train stations and communication centres of Caen, or Pernod in a bar near the docks of Le Havre. There was nothing suspicious about the couple holding hands and staring doe-eyed at each other. If anyone had noticed, often a couple of days after one of their romantic interludes an arms dump or radio mast close to the point of their assignations would be blown up, but nobody did.

They were good, one of the best teams in France. When London gave them a specific job they never failed to deliver. In between assignments they devised their own targets and ways to disrupt the German war effort.

More recently they'd been instructed to co-ordinate the various Resistance groups to prepare for the allied invasion of France. No date was given and it was still some way off, but it was felt that to maximise the effectiveness of the Resistance a closer working relationship had to be formed. They had travelled extensively meeting other leaders, and a network of communications was established between them all.

One visit had taken them to Paris for a romantic weekend, to make contact with the recently formed Prosper network. They met with Yvonne Rudelatt and Andre Borrel, both of whom Yvette had met before within the S.O.E. They had been parachuted in to set up the new network around Paris in preparation for the invasion.

They also met Sophie for the first time, the girl Jacques would subsequently meet again in Vietnam several years later. They both instantly liked Sophie, she was amusing and initially Jacques thought, possibly just a tiny bit mad, but her colleagues said she was brave beyond belief. Sophie and Yvette became instant friends and she had joined them for a simple meal in a small Rive Gauche restaurant on their last night in Paris.

Jacques watched fascinated at Yvette talking with Sophie. Sophie brought a side out of her he had never really seen before; a young woman who was interested in fashion and make-up; who liked to dance and loved the ballet; a woman who loved to cook and exchange recipes; a woman who wanted a normal life.

He sat quietly and listened to them. Here was the wonderful, vulnerable girl that lived beneath the facade of the warrior. He hoped he would see more of that girl. Yes, Sophie was good for Yvette and most probably, Yvette was good for Sophie. Together they could be girls again, girls like Honeysuckle whose life had not been scarred by the War.

During the course of the evening they only talked once about the Resistance and it was Sophie who brought up the subject. "I'm a little scared about our new network, Prosper, I don't even like the name."

"Why?" Asked Jacques.

"Because it is so new. There are people involved we have never met before. Too many new faces whose backgrounds we do not know about. What we are going to do is hugely important, prepare Paris for the invasion, but it is all being put together too quickly. It cannot be secure. We are going to fly in over sixty agents over the coming months and vast amounts of arms and explosives. As you know, our groups have been small, tight knit, almost family. I am nervous, it doesn't feel right."

"Then be careful and do not trust anyone, Sophie," Yvette said, the cool Resistance fighter once again. "If you need us, we will be there for you."

"Thank you, thank you both." They had known each other just thirty-six hours but there was total trust between them.

That night in their small hotel, Yvette said, "I like Sophie immensely, we must look after her, Jacques."

They made love and eventually fell asleep in each other's

arms. It was probably the most intense lovemaking they had ever had. Relaxed, on their romantic weekend, Yvette could be herself, and when she thought he was asleep she whispered in his ear, "I love you, Jacques. Don't be cross with me, but I think I am going to have your baby."

Jacques was not asleep and when he heard her words he froze, a maelstrom of emotions flooded through him. He knew he was not supposed to have heard and he laid perfectly still, his mind racing, trying to work out the connotations of what Yvette had just whispered to him. Then his thoughts turned to Honeysuckle, and just as every other time he thought of her he was confused. Why did he have such a feeling of loss?

The next day, when he was back in his apartment in Le Havre he wrote the letter to her, but not before he'd had a long conversation with Yvette.

When they awoke in the early hours and had made love once again, he said, "I heard you, cherie. I heard what you said about the baby and it is fine, but are you sure?"

Yvette was crying. "Yes, pretty sure, I am six weeks late. You are not angry?"

"How could I be angry with you? How do you feel about it?"

"I'm not sure." She managed a smile. "It's not great timing is it?"

"No, but if it is meant to be, so be it. That is if you want to have a baby?"

"I do, Jacques." Then she added something that demonstrated all her torment and angst. "Do you think it will make me human again?" There was a look of need on her face, seeking validation from him.

Once again Jacques's heart went out to her and he saw the girl he could love. "Don't be silly, you are human. One very beautiful and loving human." He kissed her gently on the tip of her nose.

Yvette tilted her head back and her tongue sought his, she needed more proof that she could love. Jacques, feeling her need, obliged.

* * * * *

Honeysuckle ripped the envelope apart, anxious to get at its contents. She recognised his writing and couldn't wait to get to read his words. Since she had kissed him in the pool barely a minute had passed without him being in her thoughts. She had already planned the rest of their life together.

It would start in France, where she would join him in the Resistance. She had even written to the S.O.E. offering her services as a fluent French speaker, just as soon as she was old enough. Vera Atkins had had replied, saying they would be interested when that time came, but hoped the War would be over long before then. They would get married in St. Agnes's Church, the prettiest Church on the island with it's thatched roof, nestling in the grounds of Farringford House just a short distance from Yarmouth; they would have five children, all with French names; the first would be conceived on their private beach by the pool upstream from the mill where she had kissed him, and they would make their home in one of the cottages that lay sheltered below Headon Warren, her favourite spot on the island. In this paradise they would live a perfect life farming, or fishing, or maybe both. She knew some of these dreams were just the child in her, but the woman in her also knew that she wanted to give herself, her heart and her body to the man she loved.

As she read his letter her mood swung from excitement to despair.

My dearest Honeysuckle,

I'm sorry it has taken so long to write to you, but I am sure you appreciate how busy we are. I would like to tell you about our work here but it would be dangerous, so I hope you understand.

I often think of you all, and I trust you are keeping everyone in order back home, especially Big Jacques!

Jacques got to this point in the letter and did not know what to write next. He knew his next words would break Honeysuckle's heart, and that was the last thing in the world he wanted to do.

I have thought about our last meeting many times, and the kiss we had at our pool. It is because of that kiss that I feel I have to tell you something. Please forgive me Honeysuckle, but I have met a girl here in France.

When I see you next I will tell you all about her and our relationship. It is complicated and I hope you will understand.

I do not know what to say to you in a letter, my sweet Honeysuckle. Please try to forgive me, and let me explain face to face. I hope to be back in Blighty for a few days shortly.

I intended to write you a much longer letter, but now it seems inappropriate. I thought you should know about her, it is only fair. I also appreciate that writing these words may appear cowardly and cruel, and they may be, but it is not what I intended.

You must know that I will always love you, but as things now stand it must be as your big brother.

At this point, for the first time and after months of agonising over Honeysuckle, he finally realised that these last words were fundamentally untrue. He stared at what he had written. He did not want to be her big brother, and without a shadow of doubt in his heart he knew that he wanted the woman Honeysuckle had become.

A tear rolled down his cheek. There was no choice, he knew that his duty was to look after Yvette and their child, and the feeling of loss he felt was excruciating.

Then he imagined Honeysuckle opening the letter and the look on her face as her beautiful smile turned to bewilderment, and then to anguish. The thought of it brought more tears. But he could not let her carry on believing that they had a future together as a couple. That would be crueller.

Perhaps when she learnt of the baby she might understand, but he could not tell her about that in this letter. He needed to tell her in person.

Please forgive me, my dearest. You are still young and I know you will find someone you love far more than me.

You have been, and always will be my best friend. The friend I will always love.

Jacques x x x

Honeysuckle stared down at the letter, she thought that her whole world had ended. At first she could not cry, she was in denial. Then for the first time in her whole life she was angry with him. She screamed abuse at the letter and the man who had written it. Then they came, tears that hardly stopped for a week.

Her Mother heard Honeysuckle's shriek upstairs in her room. She flew up the stairs to see what brought on such an outburst from her daughter to find her curled up in a foetal position, sobbing and making agonised noises as if she were a kitten that had been run over.

She sat and put her arms around her daughter. "What is wrong, darling?"

Honeysuckle did not respond, she could not speak. Then her Mother saw the letter on the bed by her side. She picked it up and read it.

Her heart went out to her beautiful daughter and her mind

went back to the day Jacques had left to join the Air Force, when she had sat with Honeysuckle at the end of the pier. She remembered praying that Jacques or the War would not break her daughter's heart. Both had conspired to do so.

She curled up with Honeysuckle and stroked her hair. "My poor, darling. It will be fine, just wait and see."

It was not fine. How could it ever be fine? Finally Honeysuckle found the words she could not say before. "I hate him, Mummy. I hate him!"

Buster knew it had not been good remembering. He didn't like the man to be sad, he much preferred it when he smiled. Having said that, Buster did a bit of his own remembering back to when he was a puppy and he first saw a person smile. He had been scared, thinking he was about to be bitten by their bared teeth. He soon learned that they showed their teeth when they were happy and not angry, and after happy teeth there was usually a treat!

Eight

The storms of the previous day had cleared the air and it was a perfect summer day. Jacques sat with Buster's head on his lap, looking out past the Needles towards Swanage and the headland of Studland Bay, where the rocks of Old Harry stood proudly like sharks' teeth from the sea, mirroring the other jaw that was home to the Needles on the Isle of Wight.

Jacques was glad to be back on his bench, especially on such a beautiful day. He decided it was too perfect for the dark thoughts of yesterday, so he would to go back to Hanoi and more hedonistic times. There would be plenty of time to revisit the War and the myriad of problems it threw at him.

Buster had been pleased to see the smile on the man's face again and almost ran up the hill to claim the bench for 'remembering and sandwiches.'

All four legs of the bench had been fine, and he was sitting bolt upright on the seat when the man arrived, proud that he was able to get up without the man's help. Somehow it was easier in summer.

"Well done, Buster. Life in the old dog yet." Jacques produced a dog biscuit by way of a reward for the sprightly dog.

Buster had known that it was coming, as he'd seen the man put the treat in his pocket back at the cottage and knew exactly what he was doing when he rushed up the hill and appeared to be clever. Being clever always got a treat.

"Yes, Hanoi today, Buster. Hanoi was a good place for a young unattached man." Buster watched him smile.

Jacques was back in the club with Saphine sitting on his lap, her legs crossed towards him showing a heart-stopping expanse of shapely leg to the rest of the club's clientele. Each one of which she made eye contact with as she sang her song.

Sophie sat opposite them, smiling and amused at the look of lust that Jacques could not hide. As Saphine gracefully rose from his lap, somehow brushing the entire length of her leg across his groin, Sophie laughed. "I think you need to cover that up!" She pointedly looked with more than a disinterested glance at his erection, which was pressing against his light flannel pants.

Not trying to hide it, Jacques looked down. "She does that, you know. Something about her."

"Umhh, I've noticed." Her eyes widened.

They flirted, especially here in Hanoi. They'd always flirted slightly and Yvette had found it amusing. Sophie was quite simply a flirt.

In the wake of the War, Europe had become puritanical once again, returning to the moral values they all believed they'd been fighting for. Hanoi never had those values, love and sex were readily available without judgement or censure. To Sophie and Jacques it was a comfortable place to be, somewhere they could continue the flirtations they had started years before.

After the lawless years of the Resistance, the confines of the new moralistic, straight-laced Europe had proven inhibiting.

They were both on the run from that, along with other things from their past.

Sophie lent forward and touched his penis. "Mmm, nice!"

Jacques made no comment and did not move, he allowed her hand to rest there as he looked down at it before they both burst out laughing.

They had never had sex or anything more than a kiss on the cheek. But in their minds they had, and it was a game they loved to play. Saphine knew, and Yvette had never taken offence. Saphine loved Sophie, she was round-eyed, blonde and beautiful and she admired her intelligence. Once she had suggested to Jacques that Sophie joined them in bed. She did not have western hang-ups about sex, after all she had been a prostitute! However Jacques, although giving it a fleeting thought, was far too ingrained by Victorian values to really entertain the idea. As Sophie touched him, he found himself thinking about it again before an image of Honeysuckle wiped the idea from his mind.

Sophie laughed again. "You're having a Honeysuckle moment, aren't you?" She knew him well, and had become his confidante during the past year. She knew all about Honeysuckle and how a different look appeared in his eyes whenever he thought of her, often followed by a guilty expression that would appear from nowhere, as it did now.

"Shut up, or I'll take you up on your offer one day, and you won't like that!" He looked at her hand, which had deliberately started to stroke him at the mention of Honeysuckle, as her eyes mockingly became moon-struck.

"You're right, I'd hate it!" She pinched his erection and took her hand away. Her eyes betrayed the lie.

"Ouch, that hurt!" He yelped.

"It was supposed to, but it has taken care of your erection!" She was staring at his groin.

"Poor Jack!" She fluttered her eyelashes at him. "Would you like me to rub it better?"

"Get off me. You bloody French are all sex mad!"

She gave him a look that made the innocent young Jacques want to run a mile, but the older Jacques, the French Jacques, the Jacques who had known Yvette and Saphine allowed his eyes to smoulder back at her.

"Oh my, Jack, those eyes. One day I will have you!" She was perfectly serious.

Jacques knew that one day she would, and he would not be complaining.

Saphine finished her set of songs and came to join them. "I've been watching you, you've been flirting with my girl." Saphine kissed Sophie on both cheeks and threw a less than threatening look at Jacques, before resuming her position on his lap. "Come on, let's eat. I'm starving."

As quickly as she had sat down, she stood up and taking both their hands she led them from the club.

They went to their favourite street restaurant which did some of the best food in Hanoi, where they were greeted by Fatty who had kept their usual table free for them, it was the only one beneath a fan. Whenever Fatty knew Saphine was coming to eat, people would sit at that table under pain of death!

Saphine kissed Fatty, who blushed then bustled with excitement. "What I get you?" Remembering the other two, he then shook hands with Jacques and accepted a kiss from Sophie, without blushing.

"The usual please, Fatty." Saphine gave him a smile that caused the beetroot pallor to return to the amiable restaurateur, who cannot have weighed an ounce over six stones.

They sat at their table and soaked up the continuous bustle of street life that enveloped them. It was late, but life in Hanoi made no allowance for the late hour. Street vendors still sold their wares to shoppers who had only recently finished their day's work. The road was full of tuk-tuks and bicycles, all fighting for space with mopeds and scooters. No obvious traffic pattern was apparent and Jacques, as always, marvelled at how they managed to avoid each other. Brightly painted lorries were the kings of the road which appeared to take no notice of their fellow road users.

Jacques loved the scene. The vitality of life in Hanoi always excited him, along with the aromas that invaded his nostrils from all directions. Most were the pleasant smells of food being cooked, but not all. At times the drains would impose themselves on the more delicate fragrances of satay or sweet corn. This particular spot was his favourite as a perfume shop was situated directly opposite whose fragrances overpowered the more offensive offerings from the street.

Fatty appeared with a tray which held three Bia Hoi and passed them to his guests. Jacques held the cold bottle of beer to his forehead and brushed it against his cheeks before pouring some into a glass and downing its contents in one go. The girls sipped the cool nectar a little more demurely.

Fatty was the proud owner of one of the few refrigerators in Hanoi. It usually did not hold beer, but when Saphine was coming he would always find room for half a dozen.

Sophie spoke first. She asked the question she'd been dying to ask since she'd met up with Jacques in the club. "Am I on? Will they let me come, Jacques?"

Jacques knew she'd been dying to ask, and deliberately had not told her. She teased him all the time, now it was his turn. "Maybe."

"You horrid man, tell me." She slapped his arm.

"Okay, they will let you come, but you have to do three practice parachute jumps before we go."

"That's ridiculous! I did dozens of them during the War." She looked angry.

"I know, but this is the French Army, not the Resistance. They think you are just a 'stupid girl' with crazy ideas above your station." He smirked at his friend who slapped him again.

"Seriously though, thank you, Jacques. I know it must have been difficult persuading the idiots."

"Mon plaisir, Mademoiselle. I've set up the practice jumps for Thursday. I think we'll be going in sometime next week. I should know by Thursday."

"You two are mad. It's just one big game to you. Adrenalin freaks, I read about it in the newspaper. You are both adrenalin freaks," said Saphine.

Sophie and Jacques looked at each other. It was a good description and they were not going to deny it and had even discussed between themselves why they did what they did, and came to a similar conclusion. They both shrugged their shoulders in the ultimate Gallic gesture and smiled at Saphine.

"You will be careful, won't you? I love you both." Saphine was serious, she did love them both in different ways, but was quite sure she could love Sophie in a very similar way to Jacques!

Food was arriving at the table with an increasing pace. Chicken and cashew nuts, spicy beef with ginger, noodles, fried rice, chilli prawns and pad chow were all devoured by the hungry group who did not have one spare ounce of body fat between them.

As they tucked into the feast that Fatty was supplying, Sophie asked, "Do you still think the French Generals are making a huge mistake, Jacques?"

Jacques took a swig of his beer then answered, "More than a mistake, they are committing suicide!" He paused, then continued, "The idiots still think they can fight the Vietminh in their own country using conventional warfare, despite everything we've told them. Surely we showed them how effective guerrilla tactics could be during the War back in France, but it was in our own country then and we knew it like the back of our hands. We knew what could be achieved by terrorism and the Germans were our targets, but here, we are the targets. We cannot win this war, we should walk away. They think by taking Dien Bien

Phu airfield and creating an air-supplied base there, they can cut the Vietminh supply lines from Laos, and that will draw the enemy into a conventional battle that would cripple them. Sure we can easily take Dien Bien Phu, but can we keep it? I doubt it. Firstly, the Vietminh snipers will pick off patrols at ease. French tanks and artillery are useless against the 'shadows', which inhabit the jungles. The Germans were virtually unable to touch us, their only weapon was to strike back maliciously at the innocent, and with each strike they lost another battle to win the mind and hearts of the people whose country they occupied. That is what will happen here. Will they listen to me? Oh no, not these arrogant twits. Secondly, I have witnessed the remarkable ability the Vietminh have for moving their own equipment around their country. Should they wish to, they could take us on at our own game, their logistics can cope with any large-scale arms movements. In recent months the hardware they have access to seems to be growing, supplied by China, who I believe is also supplying the expertise in how to use it."

"You make it sound hopeless. I like hopeless causes!" There was a sparkle in Sophie's eyes.

"It probably is. So when we get there and have set up the base, when I'm up country outwitting the Vietminh, I will be forming my own personal withdrawal plan. If you are silly enough to still be there when it all goes wrong, you will be very welcome to join me."

"Thank you. How wonderfully gallant and English of you, Jack," Sophie said in her best English.

"Are you sure you really want to do this, just to get a first-hand story about the shortcomings of the French military?" Jacques was serious now. "It really could be carnage."

"I will love the excitement, and anyway, the first phase should be okay, you said so."

"Yes, I think it will, but we could become sitting ducks. The only way in and out will be by air. If the Vietminh have anti-aircraft guns, we will be in the trouble. And guess what? The imbeciles don't think that they do. Only think! Fucking idiots, the lot of them!"

"Now, now, Jack! If it's the disaster you think it will be, I will report it as such. The Generals will not be getting a free endorsement of their policies. If they are shown to be 'fucking idiots,' I will destroy them in the press. At the very least, I will report the futile waste of lives defending a far-flung colony against the people whose home it really is. And I will mention the irony that Resistance fighters are now the occupying force."

"Yes, it is ironic, isn't it? Why am I here?" Jacques was almost talking to himself.

Sophie took his hand. "Because you are a thoroughly decent man, Jacques, an honourable Englishman, who still harbours ideals and morals that are more relevant to Victorian Britain. If you had been completely French, you would have fled to join the French Foreign Legion. Unfortunately, mon brave, you have some things in common with the fucking idiots!"

Jacques laughed. As always, Sophie's insight impressed him. "I can't wait to read the articles when they are published."

"They will be incisive. War is futile, and I will dedicate the rest of my life to spreading that word." Her eyes blazed at him and a wicked smile appeared on her lips. "Unfortunately, it turns me on!"

"You are incorrigible, Sophie," said Jacques, smiling at the very sexy woman in front of him.

Saphine had been listening to their conversation and watched them flirting. She didn't mind, it was natural, she flirted with Sophie as well. "When you two finally consummate this relationship, can I be there?" She said and she was perfectly serious.

Sophie exploded with laughter. Jacques blushed. Saphine just looked puzzled at both of their reactions. "Is it so terrible?" She asked.

"Non, cherie, it would be lovely. But poor Jack is English and his sensibilities would never allow it." He blushed some more. Saphine shrugged and tucked into another prawn.

That night when he made love to Saphine, his English sensibilities were put aside briefly as he imagined the girls together before he managed to put such thoughts out of his head and resumed a more conventional seduction.

On Thursday morning he collected Sophie from her hotel and drove her to the airfield were she was to do her three parachute jumps. She looked a million dollars wearing slacks and a tailored blouse, which hugged her chest. Bright red lipstick accentuated her generous lips and mascara set off her blue eyes, with her long blonde hair framing her pretty face.

"Bloody hell, Sophie. You're not going to the club!" Jacques said, smiling at her. "You're going to a military base."

"The boys deserve a bit of glamour in their lives. Don't worry, after they've dressed me in some dreadful army outfit I won't look so glam."

Needless to say she was well received by the 6e Bataillon de Parachutistes Coloniaux. They were almost fighting over who should teach her. Sophie never let on that she had already done over ten combat jumps and completed a weeklong course with the S.O.E. By lunchtime she was their heroine, and by the end of the day she was legend!

Jacques watched it all, and completed the three jumps with her. At the end of the day, the sergeant who had finally won the battle to train her, pinned her wings to her chest with a mixture of pride and lust.

Afterwards they all retired to the bar where Sophie completed her charm offensive on the Regiment. In the bar she told them about her past and the Resistance, her interrogation and her internment in the concentration camp. The piece de resistance that won their hearts was when she eased her blouse from her shoulder along with one lace bra strap to reveal the bullet wound inflicted by the Gestapo. The twenty guys that huddled around her were genuinely proud to have such a woman to go into battle with.

As they drove back to Hanoi Jacques said, "That was impressive. A whole battalion, all lusting after you at once."

"It was fun, wasn't it?" She had an impish smile on her face.

Jacques glanced over to her and wondered about the woman who had left a French battalion infatuated with her. She was an enigma, every man she met loved her instantly, and she was quirky and fun. Yet she did not have a boyfriend and never spoke about any other man she may have had in her life. She had been his confidante ever since she had arrived in Hanoi, but she would never talk about her own relationships.

Jacques decided it was time to find out. "You know all about my love life, but you have never talked about yours." Once again he was inviting her to open up about her personal life, as he had done many times before.

"I won't have one until you sleep with me." As always, she evaded the question.

Jacques slowed down and pulled over to the side of the road. He turned the ignition off and turned towards her.

"Tell me now, or you don't come to Dien Bien Phu with me, and I certainly won't sleep with you."

"Oh Jack, you spoilsport. Just sex then, no sleeping?"

"Neither, now spill the beans."

Sophie was suddenly serious. She looked at Jacques, sizing him up, deciding if she would finally confide in him. She liked and respected Jacques more than any man she had ever known, and if she was being honest with herself she loved him from afar. She knew if things had been different and his life less complicated they may well have been a couple. But there were other reasons why she had not seriously tried to consummate that love. There was Saphine who she loved, and despite their teasing of Jacques she was actually old-fashioned enough to know that she would hate sharing him, and he was Saphine's boyfriend. But there was another reason, another man to whom she had given her heart years before.

She stared at Jacques. It was only fair that he should know, after all he was her best friend and the more she thought about it the more she realised she wanted to tell him. "Okay, Jacques. There was a man, a brave man with a good heart. We met in the early days of the Resistance and I fell madly in love with him, but the Germans killed him. My own incarceration and torture were as nothing compared to the loss I felt when he died. A little like Yvette, I waged my own vendetta against them for a while. But unlike Yvette, I learned that people are people. Some are good and some are bad, and not all Germans are bad. My personal war ended a long time ago, now I fight against all wars. Hardly anyone ever knew quite what he meant to me, and we did not even know each other that long."

"What was his name?"

"Didier, his name was Didier, and he was a lot like you, Jacques." She touched his cheek. "Don't worry, I am not trying to make you a substitute. You know I love you and I know you love me too, but it is an inopportune love and it is also the love that two comrades-in-arms hold for each other. Your heart lies with someone else, cheri, and I want you to fulfil that love. It is what you deserve." It was the most serious she had ever been with him, even when they had been under fire during the War.

Jacques liked the serious Sophie. He almost felt as if he were in the presence of a different person. He had heard a rumour that she had lost a lover during the War, but there had not been time to dwell on personal loss during the conflict. Like Yvette, no mention had ever been made in public of their loss, but better than most Jacques knew what she must have been through. He suddenly found himself reliving emotions he had felt for Yvette.

"How do you feel about it now? You never talk about your

loss."

Sophie looked at the man who had devoted himself to her old friend Yvette. The man who selflessly tried to ease the hurting of the girl racked with the pain of her own demons. She had watched from afar as his strength and compassion had given Yvette life. At times she was ashamed that she'd wished it were her that was receiving that attention. Though at the time it had encouraged her. Here was a man, a decent man, she knew she could love like Didier. That same man with those kind eyes was offering to share her pain now, as he had shared Yvette's.

At that moment she desperately wanted him. She wanted to love him and be loved by him, but she knew it would never happen.

"I came to terms with it a long time ago, Jacques." She managed to say instead of taking his face in her hands and kissing him.

"Will you marry, Sophie?" He asked.

"Yes, if I meet the right man. I've only ever met two that I would put in that category. One is dead." The look in her eyes told him who the other man was. Then she giggled as the old Sophie returned. "There is always Saphine of course, she would have me. I love her too, but I'm not sure about the lesbian part. We just flirt and tease, but occasionally I genuinely find myself wanting her physically. Is that terrible?"

"You're asking me? Christ, I can't look at her without wanting to screw her!" They both laughed.

Sophie needed to change the subject and it was her turn to probe. "What will happen with you and Saphine? You know she is nuts about you, don't you? She told me you are the only man she has ever enjoyed sex with."

"I'm nuts about her too, but it is mainly physical. Saphine is strong and she is a survivor. The people of Vietnam love her and she loves them. I can't see her coming to live with me in a Breton cottage, or a two-up-two-down on the Isle of Wight!"

"Actually I can't see you doing that either." She smiled at him.

"Maybe not, but Saphine and I will part naturally. Probably when the French have been thrown out of Vietnam. It will be a mutual parting and without malice. I will never forget her, or what she has done for me. Until that moment we will enjoy each other."

"So screwing me once would not be out of the question then?" Sophie slid across the bench seat in the car and pushed herself against his arm. The serious time was definitely over, but they were both glad they'd had the conversation.

"No, not out of the question. In fact, as we are baring our souls, I can categorically say that I would like that very much."

Sophie clapped her hands together with glee. "Good, I will leave you in no doubt when the moment comes." Then more seriously she asked, "Will we still be friends afterwards?"

"Of course, Sophie. We will be friends and I will always love you, and we will always have the memory of each other locked in coital bliss."

"Don't, I'm not sure I can wait!" She laughed, then leant over and kissed him. Not the kiss of a friend, but the kiss of a lover. "Mmm, perfect. I knew it would be. Take me home then go and seduce our Saphine."

Buster had one eye open watching the man. This remembering had been nothing but smiles and at regular intervals, laughs as well.

The rotund lady approached with her pockets bulging with dog biscuits. 'What a fine summer day this had been,' thought Buster.

Nine

The next day was just as beautiful and by mid-morning Jacques along with Buster were once again sitting on the bench.

For Jacques it was to be another Honeysuckle day. There was no such thing as a bad Honeysuckle day, whenever he thought of her his heart leapt, but sometimes there were recollections he wished he did not have. However, these recollections were part of their lives and if he was going to review his life they all had a place and were paramount to how it developed.

Before he took his mind back to the War, he gave Buster a chew that was almost the size of his own leg. Buster needed spoiling, he was no longer a young whippersnapper who needed to stay trim so he could hunt and romance any lady dog who passed by, he had done all that and needed some comforts in his life.

Jacques was once again on the ferry. Yarmouth was still in

the distance and he strained to see if Honeysuckle was waiting on the pier. She was not.

Both he and Yvette had flown back to England to get a briefing about the build up to the Normandy landings They spent three days at Wanborough and 64 Baker Street learning the codes that would be transmitted by the BBC, which would trigger their pre-planned operations to destroy German communications and supply lines. Each had been strategically selected and would be targeted in a sequence that would cause the maximum amount of mayhem.

After the briefings they had been given forty-eight hours leave. Jacques telephoned his parents to say he would be home for a day and a night, and asked them to tell Honeysuckle. His Mother had been quite offhand with him on the telephone. He knew the reason why.

Yvette had wanted to come with him so she could meet his family, and had been upset when he started to make up reasons why she should not. "Let me tell them about the baby on my own. It will give them time to get used to the idea. Next time you will come with me, I promise. I'm sorry, cherie, it will be better this way."

Yvette begrudgingly agreed and stayed with a number of their comrades from the Resistance. Sophie was included in the group, so they decided to pamper themselves for an evening at a nearby hotel.

Jacques left the girls and with a heavy heart set off to the Isle of Wight to see the real reason he had not wanted Yvette to accompany him.

As he stood on the deck of the ferry, he wasn't sure what to expect when he got home or what he would say to Honeysuckle when he saw her. He strained once again to see if she was waiting. One hand waved from the pier as he got closer. It was a hand he was very pleased to see and the owner of the hand was smiling affectionately at him, but it was his Mother. By her side, Big Jacques stood expressionless as he stared at his son. "Oh dear," Jacques muttered to himself. "This is not going to be easy."

As he stepped from the boat, his Mother embraced him. "It's so good to see you again, Jacques. You must tell us all about what you've been up to." There was no censure in her voice.

"Maman, Papa, I have missed you." He was looking at his Father as he said it.

Big Jacques's eyes chastised his son, but he couldn't maintain the cool reception, it was not the French way. He grabbed his boy and wrapped his arms around him in a bear hug that squeezed the breath from Jacques. "Mon fils, comment as-tu?" He said, crushing him some more.

"I'm fine, Papa, but thirsty. I need some English tea."

"Bien, and then a bottle of red wine I have been saving." He slapped his brave son on the back. As violent a manoeuvre as Jacques had encountered since leaving for France.

Over tea he painted a picture of his work in France, using only broad strokes without any detail. His Mother was alarmed at the dangerous nature of the Resistance, but would have been far more alarmed if had told her the full story. His Father listened intently to all he said, his pride growing with each story told.

One glass into the red wine, Jacques asked almost defensively, "How is Honeysuckle?"

There was a short silence as his Father looked at his Mother, who then said, "She is well, but very unhappy." She paused. "You have broken her heart, Jacques."

It was like an arrow through his own heart. "I know, Maman. I am so sorry. I've been dreading this, but I must tell you why I wrote to her." His parents waited expectantly.

"The girl I mentioned in the letter, she is pregnant." He waited for their reaction. They just stared at him. "Her name is Yvette and she is French, she is beautiful and brave and fights for the Resistance because her entire family were taken by the Gestapo and sent to one of their concentration camps." He added this in an attempt to justify his actions.

His Mother raised her hands over her mouth as if in prayer, as her eyes grew large with shock. Big Jacques's moustache twitched just like Pierre's.

"Mon Dieu, Jacques, you don't do things by halves."

"Non, Papa."

Still looking shocked, his Mother said, "Do you love her, Jacques?" As she waited for his answer, her shock turned to compassion for the girl and her son.

Jacques wanted to be truthful with his parents, but there was an involuntary hesitation before he answered, "Yes, Maman, I do love a lot about her. She is the bravest person I have ever met and she is very beautiful, but she is vulnerable and what happened to her family has affected her deeply. You will like her, I promise you." He did not know what to say next.

"Does she want the baby?" His Mother asked, not judging.

"Yes, she does. It is as if she needs a baby to replace the family she is convinced are dead, but she was shocked when she found out she was pregnant and we have discussed abortion. Especially given all that is happening in our world." He was trying to defend her now. "It was an option, but we decided together that we want to have the baby. She will end her active involvement in the War a few months before the baby is born."

Big Jacques had said nothing, but was processing all he had heard. "French and beautiful, you say? And a good lover?"

"Yes, Papa."

"Bon, it is the French way. She will be welcome in our family." He hugged his son once again, whilst Jacques watched his Mother, waiting for her approval.

She suspected it was a disaster in the making, but one she had no control over. He would need their support over the coming months and years and he was a fine human being who

98

probably did not deserve to have to make such choices at such a young age. But these were strange times and he had become a man too quickly, she would give him all the support he needed. "Yes, she will, Jacques. I can't wait to meet her." Then as an afterthought she added. "I will write a letter to Yvette and you can take it to her. I'm sure she is lovely."

"Thank you, Maman. She would like that." He smiled at his Mother. He knew she was trying to help and appreciated it. "Honeysuckle, Maman. Does she hate me?"

"No, Jacques. She will always love you, but your letter turned her from being the happiest girl I'd ever seen to the saddest one. None of us could understand why you wrote it, but now we do. You must go to her and explain. I don't know if it will help her or make matters worse. If it were just a girl she may have thought she could get you back, but a baby is another thing. Be kind to her, her childish dreams of you easily transcended to womanhood, and those dreams are currently shattered. She is a year older than when you last saw her, but she has grown up, in part thanks to your letter."

"Will she be at home?" Asked Jacques.

"No, she is working in the Officers Mess over at the George Hotel. The military has requisitioned it. If you ask me, they have turned it into a recreation facility! But they say they are doing 'important war work' there. They love Honeysuckle though, she works in the bar and restaurant. It has been good for her. All the male attention has helped her deal with your letter, and there has been a great deal of attention!" His Mother raised her eyebrows.

"Do you think she would mind if I go over and see her?"

Big Jacques looked at him. "Of course she will mind. You broke her heart." He did not mean it to sound as harsh as it did, and when he saw the look on his son's face he added, "But she is a woman, she will want you to see how attractive she is to other men."

"Jacques, don't be so unkind, Honeysuckle is not like that."
His Mother suddenly smiled. "Well, maybe she is a little, all girls
are. Be prepared, Jacques, a year ago she was pretty, now she is
quite beautiful." She was not teasing him, she said it quite
seriously.

Jacques walked the two hundred yards to the George
Hotel, which was situated next to the pier, with its gardens
running down to the water's edge. At the door a Sergeant
stopped him and said, "Civilians are not allowed inside without
written permission."

Jacques had forgotten he was no longer in uniform and
realised he must have cut a rather bizarre figure in his casual
French clothes, with his hair flopping over his eyes several inches
too long for the Services.

"I'm sorry, I should have thought." He padded each of his
pockets in turn to find the identification papers he always carried
when he was in Britain. Eventually he produced the much-
needed ID, just as the Sergeant's face was beginning to scowl at
the sloppy youth who stood before him.

The look on the Sergeant's face changed as he read his
papers. Flight Lieutenant, Royal Air Force, seconded to the
Special Operations Executive. He had heard a great deal about
the S.O.E. and their bravery, but he had never met any of them
before. He saluted the officer. "Sir, thank you, Sir. Please come
in."

Jacques had forgotten all about saluting and without
thinking slapped the Sergeant on the back and said, "Thanks."
Before walking past him.

The Sergeant watched a little dumbfounded at the enigma
that had just walked in. Shaking his head he muttered to himself,
"Bloody hell, what chance have we got of winning this war?"

Jacques knew his way around the George, so walked
straight to the bar where he assumed they would have set up the
Mess.

It was only six o'clock in the evening but it was already busy, in fact busier than he had ever seen it before. His appearance did not go unnoticed as several of the officers looked disapprovingly at the stranger who had walked into their bar. He scanned the room for Honeysuckle, he should have known where she would be. A large group of men were huddled around the bar and a gap suddenly appeared, there behind them stood Honeysuckle.

She had not seen him and she was smiling at the men who were quite obviously smitten by her. She threw back her head and laughed at something that had been said to her then smiled at her admirers whose eyes never left her face.

'Quite beautiful,' his Mother had said. An understatement, a year had seen Honeysuckle blossom into the loveliest girl imaginable, and her smile had become even more entrancing. He stood by the door about thirty feet away from where she captivated her audience. His heart was pounding and all he wanted was to walk over and take her in his arms.

Suddenly she noticed him and the smile faded from her face. She did not scowl or even look angry, but for the first time in her life the smile left her face when she looked at Jacques.

The poignancy of moment was not lost on him. From the very first day that she smiled, whenever she saw him her face exploded into the most joyous of grins. When the smile left her face Jacques's heart sank, as he realised how uplifted he had always felt when he saw her smile, no matter what age she had been.

The others in the group had noticed the interchange between the two of them, and the looks they were giving Jacques became even less friendly when they saw the effect he'd had on their Honeysuckle.

Honeysuckle just stood and looked at him. He had no idea what she was thinking. But all he could think of was that his actions and his letter had stolen her smile.

A member of the group walked over to him and said, "Can I help you?" His tone suggesting the only help he wanted to offer was to eject the longhaired stranger from the premises.

Jacques gave him a disarming smile, but his eyes never left Honeysuckle. "Hello, my name is Jacques. I'm an old friend of Honeysuckle and I'd like to talk to her."

"Should you be in here?" The man was now giving Jacques a disdainful look. "This is a military establishment."

Still staring at Honeysuckle, he handed his papers to his protagonist who eagerly took them, anxious to find the evidence that would allow him to evict the stranger.

"It's okay, Simon, I will talk to him." Simon perused the papers, visibly annoyed at their content.

"Flight Lieutenant, eh?" Then he noticed the secondment to the S.O.E. "I suppose your appearance is down to working with the Frogs!"

For the first time Jacques actually looked at the man. Smiling he said, "Probably, old boy."

Simon was confused. Everything about the way he had been addressed was correct, yet he knew he had just been assessed and charmingly dismissed by a senior officer who was probably capable of killing him with a single move. Then he watched as the girl he thought he had fallen in love with walked over to them.

Jacques was also watching her. Her curves had developed even more since he'd last seen her, accentuated by a tight skirt and tailored blouse. The girl had gone and Honeysuckle was now a confident and desirable woman. Her hair was longer too, the mop of curls tied up loosely away from her beautiful face. As she approached, Jacques wondered what on earth he would say to her.

Honeysuckle spoke first. "Hello, Jacques. This is my boyfriend, Simon." She flashed Simon the smile that had always been reserved for Jacques.

For the first time in his life Jacques was jealous. It had

always been his smile, and he had lost it to another man. He remembered writing the letter and the feeling of loss he felt as he sealed the envelope, and how writing the letter had finally made him realise his true feelings for her. Now he felt that loss again, but it was magnified tenfold as she stood before him.

He turned to Simon. He didn't like Simon. "Hello, Simon, very pleased to meet you." He offered his hand. Simon accepted it and they shook hands, neither really wanting to.

"Simon is a Spitfire pilot. You may remember him, Jacques. He lives at Farringford House, near Freshwater." All of this was designed to turn the knife in Jacques's heart.

She knew that ever since the day they'd watched the dogfight on Headon Warren Jacques had wanted to be a Spitfire pilot, and Farringford was one of the most beautiful homes in West Wight. As Jacques looked at Simon, he remembered the boy he'd met a couple of times during the school holidays. He recollected a stuck-up little toad who went to a boarding school on the mainland and came back in the holidays to sneer at the poor island folk. It wasn't true of course, Simon had actually been okay and friendly enough, but right now he didn't like Simon!

"Jacques was, is, my next door neighbour, Simon. I told you about him, he is part of the S.E.O." She had missed out the part that she was besotted by Jacques, and always had been.

"What you do must be very dangerous, Jacques." Simon was making an effort and trying to restart their meeting after it's prickly beginning.

"What we all do is dangerous." Jacques would have to meet him half way. After all, the fact that Simon was her boyfriend was his own fault. When he told Honeysuckle the full story about Yvette and the baby, he would drive her deeper into Simon's arms. No, he didn't like him, but he would try for Honeysuckle.

"How long are you here, Jacques?" Asked Honeysuckle.

"Just one more day, then we are being dropped back into

Normandy."

"We'll talk in the morning then, Jacques, just come round. Simon is taking me out this evening." Jacques had just been dismissed without even the slightest of smiles.

She turned and went back to her duties at the bar. "Nice to meet you, Jacques. Sorry I was a bit pushy."

For the first time Jacques looked properly at Simon. He had grown into a handsome man and he flew Spitfires. If Honeysuckle liked him, he was probably all right. Jacques forced a genuine smile and said, "You're a lucky man, Simon. My little next door neighbour has grown into a stunning woman." He shook his hand again and left the bar.

That night he never stopped thinking about Honeysuckle and what he had lost. With it came guilt that he should desire her so much when he had such a striking girlfriend who was soon to be the Mother of his child.

The next morning after a feast of bacon and eggs that his Mother had been saving for his arrival, he went and knocked on Honeysuckle's front door. Audrey answered. "Come in, Jacques."

As always she hugged him, but her eyes did not portray the disappointment in him that he had expected. Had his Mother already told her best friend about his predicament? "You look well, Jacques. The long hair suits you. Honeysuckle will be right down. Would you like a cup of tea? Maybe some eggs?"

"That is very kind, but Mum has already stuffed me full of at least a month's rations!"

They made small talk for a while until Honeysuckle appeared wearing slacks and a body-hugging blue sweater, her hair now cascading around her face. Once again his heart leapt and he felt guilty for desiring her so much. Then she smiled, the smile she'd always saved for him.

"You look great, Honeysuckle." He stared at the vision in front of him, then not knowing what to say next he added, lying,

"I liked Simon."

"Good, so do I. Shall we go for a walk and you can tell me all about your girlfriend?" It was said very pleasantly, but very pointedly.

They walked along the short High Street, past the Church and towards the mill. "So what is she like and what is her name?" Honeysuckle was determined to behave in an adult fashion.

"Yvette, she is French."

"Come on, more than that."

"She is in the Resistance with me." Jacques genuinely did not know what to tell her, or how to tell her why he had really written the letter to her.

"She must be very brave." Honeysuckle was beginning to feel a little threatened by Yvette. She was bound to be pretty and now she was a romantic figure who fought for her country and not just a homebound young girl like herself. If she were being truthful to herself, she still harboured hopes that Jacques would fall for her when he saw her new curves.

"She is incredibly brave, Honeysuckle." Again he was at a loss as to what to say next.

"Do you love her terribly?" This was the one question Honeysuckle really wanted to ask him. Their entire future, along with all her hopes and dreams depended on his answer.

They had reached their private pool near the mill. Jacques took her hands and sat her on the rocks by the water's edge. She was looking into his eyes almost begging him for the right answer. In her eyes Jacques saw the child again, the child that used to hang on his every word. He saw the young girl who worshipped the very ground he walked on, and he saw the woman that he knew he loved but could not have. He knew what she wanted to hear and he knew what he wanted to say to her, but he could not.

"It is complicated, Honeysuckle. Yes, I love her, or at least part of her."

Honeysuckle watched him, puzzled. What was he saying?

"I have to tell you everything that has happened, Honeysuckle, and why I wrote you that beastly letter."

Still holding his hands she said, "Please go on."

There was no easy way to say it. "Yvette is pregnant." He saw the look in her eyes. "Please don't hate me."

There it was, all hope gone. Jacques would never abandon a girl he had made pregnant, neither would she want him to. She did not mean it to happen but her eyes filled with tears and silently they rolled down her cheeks. Through the tears she knew without a shadow of a doubt that her Jacques really did love her, but he was too decent a man to let another girl down. All she felt was despair for them both.

"I'm so sorry, my darling Honeysuckle. It should have been us. I know I have ruined it."

Through her own tears she could see his. She reached up and brushed them from his cheeks. She had to be strong for them both, but there was one thing she needed. "Tell me you love me, Jacques. Just once. Tell me you love me as a man loves a woman."

"I love you with every ounce of my being and I always will, Honeysuckle." He could hardly get the words out.

"Then I will always have your love, and you will always have mine, my darling."

They did not kiss, but held each other in an embrace that lasted forever, each wrapped in their private thoughts.

It was Honeysuckle who eventually broke away. In a strange way she was happy, it was as if her biggest fear had been lifted from her shoulders, the fear that he did not love her the way she loved him. Even though she knew she could not have him physically she had his love, she had the love of the one person in the world she held above all others. It would have to be enough, it was not what she dreamed of, but he loved her and now he needed her support. She would be strong and she would give him that support because he was hers and she was his, no matter whom they married or whomever else they may fall in love with.

"Come on then, you rogue. What have you been up to?"

Jacques managed to smile and told her about the sexpot Resistance fighter who seduced him.

"That was to be my job! I do not want to hear any details. It would appear your virginity is no longer there for my taking." She was trying to make light of it, but it was one fantasy she would have to forget. Then she added, "And before you ask. Yes, I'm still a virgin. I was saving myself for you, so let your cheating heart bleed!" They both managed a contrived laugh. There was a degree of melancholy in their forced smiles as they each thought of what could never be.

Honeysuckle suddenly felt compassion for him and said, "Seriously, Jacques, will you be happy? And what is Yvette really like?"

They had always been truthful with each other and this was not the time to be anything less. "I think we will be happy, but she is complicated." Honeysuckle was quiet, inviting him to continue. "She is Jewish, and her entire family were taken to a concentration camp, they may well be dead. Actually they probably are dead. It has affected her deeply and she has issues with the Nazis."

"I'm not surprised." Now Honeysuckle's heart went out to the poor woman.

"She is possessed by a hatred and bloodlust that is not natural. Yet at the same time she is a vulnerable and loving woman. I think, no, I know she hates the person she becomes when she kills and hates so intensely. I think our relationship is her antidote to all she loathes about herself, and she believes having our baby will reinstate her feeling of humanity. She may well be right. She is capable of great love, and I believe she really loves me almost as passionately as she hates the Nazis. She is a

107

good person, but scarred."

Honeysuckle heard the words and found herself a little alarmed that his Yvette could hate more than she could love. "I'm sure she loves you passionately, what girl would not?" She stroked his cheek again.

All he was saying helped her made sense of the nightmare she'd found herself in. He was giving his whole life to another woman for all the reasons she loved him. "My darling, you are a good, gentle man. Now I understand. I hope and pray that you will be happy."

He hugged her again desperately trying to make it platonic, but it was not. They were both young and beneath the hug was a real physical need for each other. Honeysuckle closed her eyes and imagined him naked next to her, then tried to put the thought out of her head. How could she be strong for them if she wanted him so badly? Her thoughts turned to his happiness and all that he had told her. She needed to find out more about Yvette, as deep inside she felt unease about Jacques's description of her. She found herself doubting that theirs would be a happy relationship.

Then she felt guilty as she found herself thinking if they were unhappy there was still a chance for her. She must not think like that, all she wanted was for Jacques to be happy.

They spent the rest of the day together. At times behaving like ten-year-olds, and at other times being adults discussing parenthood and life after the War. Honeysuckle admitted to him how she had planned their life together, and how it was to start when she joined the S.O.E. She even showed him the letter from Vera Atkins saying they would consider her. "I don't think I'll be doing that now, someone else got there first!" She'd laughed.

"Now it's your turn. I've told you all about Yvette, what about Simon?" Jacques asked.

"Ah, Simon. He's infatuated with me."

"I bet they all are!" He looked a bit peeved as he said it.

That was good, she thought, 'I like him lusting after me and being jealous, it serves him right for getting someone else pregnant.'

"Actually, Simon is quite sweet and a very good kisser." She would rub it in a little more.

"Is he? That's nice!" They both laughed.

"I've been seeing him for about four months. Actually not long after your beastly letter." Maybe they could still have fun she thought as he winced. "He is stationed at Ibsley in the New Forest with one of the Fighter Squadrons, so he's lucky to be so close to home. It was his first posting and he thinks they are getting ready for the push. After his training he had some leave and he came home to Farringford. I met him on my first day in the Mess. Now whenever he is off duty he comes to see me on his motorbike."

"I don't blame him," Jacques paused, "how do you feel about him?"

"I like him, he's fun and very handsome but if you had not sent me that horrid letter I would never have noticed him. As it is, you did, so I kissed him and it serves you right!" She watched for the pain in his eyes, it was there. "Anyway, we've been on some dates. He's nice and I suppose I will have a relationship with him now I can't have you."

She didn't mean to sound cruel. She had Jacques's love and he had hers, but this ghastly war made life precious and she had to live her own life. The second nicest boy she had ever met was mad about her and the tales he told about his friends being killed broke her heart. Simon deserved to be cared for, to have a girlfriend to cherish. His life would likely be a short one and he deserved some happiness in the merciless world in which he lived. He had made it quite plain that Honeysuckle could fulfil that role. "Do you mind, Jacques?"

"How can I mind after what I have done? All I want is your happiness."

Honeysuckle looked at him and fought back her retort, he

did not need to feel any more guilt. "Thank you," she said.

"Will you marry Yvette?"

"Yes, I suppose so when the War is over. I'm afraid our child will be born out of wedlock, I don't see how we can marry before then."

Honeysuckle couldn't resist it. "Another bastard in your family then!" But she said it with her beautiful smile lighting up her face and her eyes twinkling.

"You, rotter! I suppose I had that coming." But he did not let her get away with it completely and began to tickle her waist as he had done a thousand times before when she was a child.

She shrieked with delight as they engaged in the wrestling match that would always follow his attack as she tickled him back, eventually ending up on the sand, arms and legs wrapped around each other with her curls in his face. At exactly the same time they realised the intimate nature of the skirmish, and Honeysuckle turned her head towards him giving him a look of such carnal intensity he thought he would die if he did not kiss her. He moved his lips towards hers.

"No, don't, Jacques. I could not bear it and I would not let you stop." She put her hand to his lips. "If you kiss me now the rest of my life would be unbearable, and so might yours."

She was quite right, of course. Jacques knew that he would never desire anyone else the way he did Honeysuckle at that moment. Her animal intensity just inches from his face and the look in her eyes that said take me, but you can't have me, would haunt him forever.

They lay locked in their embrace for an age, as if each of them were daring the other to defy the unwritten rules they had made. Each knew that if one made a move the other would not resist. Eventually Jacques took her head in the crook of his arm and pulled it to his shoulder laying his cheek on her soft curls he closed his eyes, not daring to look into hers any longer.

Honeysuckle's heart was beating heavily. 'Yes, he loves me,' she thought. Her eyes closed too, as they clung together for the next half an hour without speaking a single word.

To Jacques, it was the most intense half hour of his life. The most complete he had ever felt. Honeysuckle savoured every second, knowing they would probably be the most important moments she ever spent with him and also realising they would have to sustain her through all the times he would not be with her.

Buster opened his other eye. The man had not moved a muscle for ages. He usually grunted or laughed occasionally, but he had sat completely still, to the point that Buster had become alarmed and decided both eyes were to be used for guarding.

Suddenly the man snapped out of it and said to Buster, "Hungry, old boy? I am, let's tuck in. She always left me feeling hungry for more."

Ten

Buster was hoping the man didn't do the sitting still thing again. The man was not as young as he used to be, and it wouldn't do if he were to keel over on the bench. Buster was not as quick as he had once been and even though it was downhill all the way to get help, he decided if the man did the sitting still thing again he would bark very loudly to snap him out of it. Not only that, but he'd seen some cheese and onion crisps going into the bag, which were his favourite crisps and he was already salivating thinking about them, so the man would need reminding about lunch sooner rather than later.

It was another fabulous summer day, which had enticed more than the usual trickle of ramblers from their beds. On a day like this the man would find it difficult to remember whilst having to wish 'good morning' to the stream of walkers who were passing by the bench as they walked the Coastal Path to the Needles.

Buster didn't like ramblers. They had clumpy boots and

sticks, and he could not understand why so few of them had dogs and more importantly, dog treats. He had given up barking at them though, the man didn't seem to like it, and just occasionally one of them knew how to tickle him properly behind the ears. A good tickler had actually just given him an apple core, so perhaps today's ramblers would be a better bunch. He would keep both eyes open though, just in case an army of them arrived with sticks. He would have to bark at an army.

As they settled into their positions for remembering, Jacques said, "This could be an Yvette day." Buster was pretty sure Yvette was not lunch, so paid little attention.

Jacques was sitting squeezed up against Yvette in a Lysander, which in itself was not unpleasant, but he couldn't stop thinking about Honeysuckle. His old pal Daniel was flying them back to Normandy after their briefing for the invasion of Europe, and for old times sake he'd allowed Jacques to fly a couple of circuits before they had set off, which Jacques had enjoyed more than he thought he would.

As he helped Yvette into her parachute harness in the ridiculously small space, he asked, "Can you manage this, Mum?"

She loved it when he called her Mum. She was five months pregnant and could feel the baby kicking as she struggled into the harness. "Just about, but this will be the last time." She giggled as he caressed her now voluptuous breasts.

Their brief was to co-ordinate the sabotage operations and preparations for the Allied landings in Normandy. Yvette was going to be involved for just two more months then would rest at the farmhouse and await the arrival of their baby. As they waited for the drop point to arrive they had been discussing babies' names.

"I'd like an English name," said Yvette. "It's time you had an English name in your family."

Jacques was instantly with Honeysuckle once again, remembering a conversation they had once had about calling all their children by French names.

"Honeysuckle, if it's a girl."

He was instantly brought back to the present by the sound of her name. "Your neighbour, when you were little. The little girl you told me about. That's such a sweet name. What do you think?" Asked Yvette.

"Yes it's lovely, but I've lived with it all my life. I'd prefer something different." He couldn't bear to be reminded of her every day. "Perdita is nice, it could be shortened to Perdy," he added, trying to sow another seed in Yvette's mind.

"I like that. Yes, Perdy. And for a boy, I like Derek or Simon." Jacques looked at her. Bloody hell, was he to be punished forever? "They're okay, but there are nicer names I'm sure."

"Okay, we'll talk about boys' names later. I think we must be nearly there."

Daniel located the flares and positioned the Lysander about one mile upwind of them. "Good luck!" he yelled as they jumped from the door into the rushing wind that raced over the wing's aerofoil. They went into a free fall, and perfectly positioned themselves to land in the field where the brothers, Alain and Pierre had lit the flares. Jacques made sure he landed first and released his harness before running anxiously to where Yvette was about to land. He need not have worried, she landed perfectly like a feather fluttering down to earth. He gathered her parachute whilst the boys retrieved his, and within minutes they were in the van on the way back to the farm.

"Good to have you back. When is it to be? When do we drive these Nazi scum from our land?" Pierre asked.

"About six months time, Pierre. We have much to do and our role will be vital." Jacques replied, although to them he was still Philippe.

"I can still be of use right up to having the baby." Yvette was keen to stay involved.

"No, not a day past seven months, Maman!" It was Jacques again. She liked it when he was forceful. The brothers smiled. Yvette's baby, although being something of a shock had brought happiness to them all. Philippe was a good Frenchman and a good fighter and they approved of her choice. They even knew he was really called Jacques, they had heard Yvette call him by that name often enough and teased them whenever the mythical Philippe was mentioned.

Back at the farm, Albert presented them with one of his famous daubes and some freshly baked bread. Yvette devoured copious quantities of the stew for both herself and Perdy, which she had already decided her baby would be called, should it be a girl.

Replete from the daube, Yvette gave an outline of their assignment and the people they needed to contact in the run up to the invasion. The next day Philippe and Yvette would drive back to Caen, where he would resume his life as a wine distributor after returning from taking his girlfriend to visit his family in Toulouse. Their next stop would once again be Paris, where a great deal of work needed to be done with Sophie and the newly-formed Prosper network, in preparation for the advance on Paris.

Back in their love-nest in Caen, they spent the night in each other's arms. Yvette was as happy as she had been since the day the War had started, despite her demons she had a future with a wonderful man and their beautiful baby. Jacques thought of Honeysuckle but he was also swept away with the loving woman he held in his arms and rejoiced in her newfound contentment. Perhaps it could work.

The next day they left to meet Sophie in Versailles, along with others from her group, which had steadily been growing over the previous months. Francis Suttill was now in charge of the Prosper network and they were to meet with a man called Henri. He had been a pilot in the French Air Force and was going to work with Jacques to locate suitable landing fields for all the arms and explosives, which were to be flown in. There would be up to one hundred missions and the logistics of finding suitable arms dumps would be a problem.

Sophie opened the door and hugged Yvette. "Look at you, you look gorgeous, positively glowing." She turned to Jacques. "And you are very handsome too, Daddy!" Then she dismissed him as being superfluous to the rest of the conversation by putting her arm around Yvette and walking her to the small kitchen for baby talk, leaving Jacques with a sweet smile.

She did come back with a bottle of beer for him before returning to the kitchen for more baby talk. He sipped the beer listening to the girls giggling, when there was a loud knock on the door. Sophie was instantly in the room with him, her pistol in her hand. She put a finger to her lips as Jacques eased his weapon from his jacket.

There was another knock. "Sophie, c'est Henri."

She lowered the gun and looked through the peephole and unlatched the door. "What are you doing here? Our meeting isn't until seven." She frostily asked the tall blond-haired man who walked through the door.

"I wanted to meet your friends. I hear one is a pilot." He smiled at Jacques and offered his hand. "Henri, we will be working together. It is a pleasure to meet you."

"Hello, Henri." Jacques considered the man who shook his hand. He had sharp features with intelligent eyes that looked coolly at him above thin lips that worked overtime in an attempt to offer a warm smile. Behind him Sophie still looked disapprovingly at the intruder.

Yvette appeared at the door to be introduced to the new arrival. She had remained in the kitchen, her weapon cocked to create the element of surprise should their visitor have been wearing an S.S. uniform or a leather coat.

"Mademoiselle Yvette, I presume." Henri stepped confidently towards her and offered his hand once again. Yvette took it and said hello, but did not return his ingratiating smile.

Whilst he drank the beer Sophie offered him, he chatted to the three of them oozing a superficial charm. Jacques enjoyed his company and his conversation, especially about flying. Yvette listened and observed him without saying much but responding amicably to his questioning about her obvious bump. Sophie said nothing but her eyes never left Henri, and her expression never softened.

After he left and Jacques had said how pleasant Henri seemed, Sophie said, "Do not trust that man, Jacques. There is something wrong about him. He is too pleasant, and never says anything erroneous. Keep a very close eye on him when you work together.

"Why?" Jacques looked surprised.

"I understand, Jacques." It was Yvette.

"Call it a woman's intuition. He asks too many questions and is too eager to be everyone's friend. He wants to know everyone's business." Sophie was being wonderfully irrational.

It was enough for Yvette who had decided she loved Sophie the first time they met. "He's slippery. Sophie is right, be careful."

Jacques knew better than to argue with the pair of them, so promised he would treat Henri with a degree of respectful guardedness.

That evening they met him again, this time he came with Francis Suttill along with three other men. Despite only having one brief meeting Henri greeted them all as long-lost friends, whilst Francis, though polite was more circumspect and far more to Sophie's taste.

Yvette quickly took to Francis. On two occasions they had just missed meeting each other, once at Baker Street in London, then later at Wanborough the S.O.E. training establishment. He had attended another invasion briefing a week earlier and had been spoken of with high regard. She was told he was an impressive figure with an incisive mind and excellent leadership qualities with inspiring motivational skills. She had looked forward to meeting him.

Francis was a tall, lean man with a wonderful bird-like hooked nose beneath kind eyes which when he smiled were framed by an explosion of laughter lines. Listening to him, Yvette remembered the description she had been given of him at Wanborough. Yes, this was a man she could work with, and their co-operation would be key in a successful campaign.

Next to him, Henri sat with his weak smile permanently painted on his face. Sophie's eyes still never left him. Their meeting lasted several hours as the logistics were worked out and the targets assigned to the various factions within the Resistance. The next month would see Henri and Jacques pick the sites for the shipments. The following month they would retrieve those consignments of weaponry and explosives, and during the months leading up to the invasion they would be used on various targets. London would control the whole operation using the coded messages they had been given, which the BBC would transmit. All this would lead up to a glorious crescendo of destruction that would herald the allied invasion and its liberation of France.

However once this was accomplished their work would not be over. They would then wreak havoc on the retreating forces of Nazi Germany as the Allies continued their push to rid France of the vermin, which had infested their country. And in Paris, they would arm the civilian population to drive the Nazis from their beloved capital before the Allies marched triumphantly down the Champs Elysee.

Once the meeting that helped determine the liberation of France was over, Yvette and Sophie seamlessly slipped back into talk of babies as if Jacques were not there. He sipped another beer whilst wondering about Henri and the seed the girls had planted in his head about his trustworthiness. He listened to them giggling in the kitchen, two young women who had remained alive for five years because of their instincts. He would watch Henri closely.

Jacques spent the next week with Henri assessing drop zones and landing sites along with their environs for safety and ease of recovery. It proved far more difficult than Jacques had expected. It was not easy to find a field flat enough for landing a reasonable sized aircraft for the supplies to be offloaded, or more often where they could be parachuted in and collected with ease and with a minimum of risk to the Resistance.

A week later he returned to Normandy where he went through the same process with Albert and Pierre. This reconnaissance, along with others like it allowed more than 10,000 tons of arms and stores to be delivered, enough to arm over 200,000 Resistance fighters along with the 2000 extra personnel that were flown in from Britain.

Amongst the 2000 were a large number of female agents, as they possessed the advantage of being able to move freely around the country without attracting attention, unlike male equivalents of a similar age who would normally have been conscripted into forced labour, or rotting in prisoner-of-war camps.

Over the coming months Jacques formed the reception committee for a number of these girls, some only a few months older than Honeysuckle and with each girl that arrived he half-expected to see her face.

While Jacques was preparing and co-ordinating the drops, Yvette and Sophie were organising the campaign of sabotage with the various maquis. Telecommunications and railways were hit, bridges demolished and roads paralysed. Sophie refused to allow Yvette to actually take part in any of the operations, but the now-heavily pregnant Yvette was busy planning, assigning and organising the resources for each of the raids.

Henri had regularly met with Jacques, who had taken heed of the girls' advice. By the end of that first week he was in firm agreement with them, Henri was slippery! At each meeting he found himself fending off questions about personnel and arms caches in Normandy. At one point Jacques got angry when he asked about proposed operations. "Henri, you know that our survival depends on subterfuge, so stop asking me these fucking questions." Henri just gave him his most ingratiating smile and apologised.

Some of his questioning about Sophie and Yvette had so riled them all that they had Albert, the radio operator, call London to voice their concerns about the reliability of the ex-French Air Force pilot they had sent to co-ordinate the supply lines.

Unfortunately their suspicions were dismissed.

Albert walked into the kitchen of the farmhouse where the others were gathered. His face was anxious. He had been making one of his routine calls to Sophie's radio operator in Paris and received some worrying news. "Francis Suttill has been taken."

"Merde," yelled Pierre, his moustache twitching furiously.

Francis probably knew more about the campaign being run in France than anyone, except for maybe Yvette. He certainly had all the details of the Prosper network's operation.

Alain turned to Yvette. "You must leave. It must be that prick, Henri. You are not safe. If they have taken Suttill it is just a matter of time before they come for you, Yvette."

Yvette was thinking. "No, what does Henri know of our operation and where we live. I have never told him anything, what about you Philippe?"

"Nothing, I told him to fuck off and stop asking questions," Philippe replied.

"So we should be safe here. We have kept everything to

ourselves. Outside of our group, Sophie is the only one who knows about the farm and she is completely reliable."

"We're safe for now," Alain interjected.

The reference brought a concerned look to Yvette's face, but she continued. "We have an arsenal of weapons and explosives here, it would be impossible to move them all at short notice, and where to? Hiding this stuff is difficult. Moving it to one of the other sites would draw attention to them and we may lose two caches. I say we take a chance on this one."

Albert said, "I'll have one of the cars permanently ready, in case you need to make a rapid exit, Yvette."

"No, I will stay and fight with you," she said.

Jacques, the brothers and Albert just looked at her and then Pierre said, "No, you will take our baby and start a New France."

She turned to each of them in turn and saw the resolve and love in their eyes. She put it down to hormones, but the tears welled up inside her. "I love you all." It would have been useless to argue. She pulled herself together then asked Albert, "Has anyone else been arrested yet?"

"Yes, Andree and Gilbert."

"The two men we met with Francis." Yvette was almost talking to herself. "Sophie, how is Sophie?"

"Fine, her radio operator said that they have left her apartment and moved out to the country."

"Good. If the whole Prosper network falls apart the plans are in tatters, but it sounds as if she may still be able to run it. When it is safe to use the radio again tell her to come here, Albert. We need to rethink some of those plans." He nodded and gave her a reassuring smile.

"It is only a matter of time before they start picking up more of the Prosper people." Pierre was about to say what they all knew. "Francis will break, or one of the others."

In reality it was not that bad. Whoever had talked did not

give them much intelligence and as a result the majority of personnel within Prosper were left alone. A number of arms dumps were raided, but several others remained untouched. Each one taken was unguarded so no Resistance fighters were killed. Whoever had talked had protected their people well. Close to Paris two arms drops had S.S. reception committees, here a number of the Resistance were killed and others captured and interrogated, but nobody was sure if the Germans had just been lucky or they had been tipped off.

Sophie avoided the attentions of the Gestapo and was able to re-organise the compromised Prosper network. This time Henri was sidelined, as she could not be sure if he had actually given Francis to the Gestapo. She was not going to take any chances, so Henri was kept firmly in her sights and fed misinformation in an attempt to trap him. She never knew if he was aware of this, but he never gave any of this misinformation to the Gestapo, so all she had were her suspicions.

Sophie visited them at the farmhouse and final plans were made. Jacques worked closely with Sophie to facilitate the final consignments, during which time they built a great trust and mutual respect.

Yvette's group in Normandy appeared to have been left alone, and their build-up to the invasion was all going according to plan. The baby was due in four weeks time, and Yvette was no longer arguing about going out on missions when the Sd.kfz 232 tank drove through the gates of the farm.

Jacques was with Sophie briefing a group for the retrieval of an arms drop. Pierre, Alain and Albert were preparing the distribution of arms from other caches with their comrades in Le Havre. Yvette thought it just a routine visit by the S.S. They happened fairly regularly and the fools had never suspected anything out of the ordinary about the farm, she assumed today was no different so she made no attempt to get to the vehicle in the barn.

The officer knocked respectfully on the door and gave her a friendly smile when she unlatched the bolts and opened it. "Bonjour, Mademoiselle," he said, as he eased the pistol from behind his back and gently held it to her forehead.

'You bloody fool,' she thought. She was happy, revelling in the idea of motherhood and she had let her guard down. For the fist time in five years she had finally let her guard down. "Merde!"

The black Mercedes crunched on the gravel as it drove across the farmyard. Two leather-clad Gestapo agents stepped menacingly from the rear and walked towards her as three S.S. troopers held their rifles at shoulder height pointed directly at her head.

The senior Gestapo officer leered at her through horn-rimmed spectacles, a smirk appearing at the side of his mean lips. One year ago she would have broken his neck before the first bullet cut her down, and she would have died quite happily knowing there was one less Nazi walking the earth. Now, there was Perdy, and Perdy must have her chance in life. So she stood perfectly still and stared into the tiny slits that passed for eyes in small man in front of her. He was the most contemptuous looking man she had ever seen, standing not one inch over five-feet-three.

She stared at him and wondered at the arrogance of the self-styled master race who had seen fit to take her proud and handsome Father along with the rest of her family to their probable deaths.

"Madamemoiselle Yvette. You have much to tell us, come and join me in my car." He raised his arm, gesturing her to join him.

She couldn't help herself, the hatred welled up inside her and she spat at the little reptile. His snide grin just grew wider as the rear of the hand he'd raised to show her to the car slapped her violently across the face, his chunky ring breaking the skin on her cheek. "This will be fun, Yvette, or whatever your real name is."

The smile suddenly left his face and he grabbed a handful of her hair and dragged her to the Mercedes, where the driver roughly tied her hands behind her back and manhandled her into the rear of the car before the two Gestapo slid in, one either side of her.

She flinched as the weasel-eyed midget placed his hand on her heavily pregnant stomach and said, "A French bastard, eh?" His hand moved to her breast and he squeezed the generous globe. "The little bastard will not starve if he is lucky enough to even be born."

Yvette had been about to spit at him again but suddenly realised the nature of the threat, so closed her eyes and allowed him to grope her.

Sophie's radio operator got a call from Albert. "They have Yvette, Sophie," he yelled as he ran into the room where she was discussing that night's retrieval with Jacques.

"What?" Sophie was on her feet, grabbing her coat before he could tell her the rest. "The Gestapo have taken her. Two hours ago. She is still in the prison in Lisieux. They will be interrogating her."

Jacques was already half way out of the door on his way to the van with Sophie in hot pursuit. "If she is there, Jacques, we can still get her."

"I know, but they will soon take her to Gestapo headquarters at Avenue Foch. There she will be tortured and then at best will disappear into one of their concentration camps. At worst they will kill her and our baby." He was calm, this was what he had been trained for. Panicking would not help. If they were to save her they needed to be calm.

Sophie yelled to her radio operator, "Tell Albert to get as many men as possible to the police station. Tell him we will be there in two hours."

Albert, Pierre and Alain had already leapt into action and had thirty well-armed fighters in the back of the lorry on their way to the police station.

Normal procedure would have seen Yvette taken straight to 84, Avenue Foch, but the weasel could not wait to get his hands on Yvette and extract as much intelligence as he could before reporting to his seniors so he could receive their accolades. He also had a fetish about pregnant women, and what he wanted to do to Yvette could not be done at Gestapo headquarters. It was this fetish that was to cost him his life and save Yvette's.

In the prison cell Yvette was tied to a chair and stripped to the waist. He'd dismissed his colleague who had no appetite for what he knew was about to happen. He was waiting in the reception till his superior had finished, hoping he would not take too long.

Her breasts fascinated the weasel, it seemed to Yvette that most of his questions were being addressed to them and not her. She knew her only chance of survival was to keep him there as long as possible. Here, her friends stood a chance of rescuing her. Once she was spirited away she would be dead and so would Perdy.

He asked about her colleagues and her part in the Resistance. Nicely at first, but when she refused to answer he slapped her hard across the face.

"I don't know anything, I'm not in the Resistance." He slapped her again, this time harder. In his eyes she saw something new, a lustful look appeared between the slits and his lips parted, savouring her pain.

"We know you run the Resistance here." He stepped towards her and took her nipple between his fingers, pinching it as hard as he could as he slapped her across the face again. "Who is your radio operator?" Her other breast became the recipient of his lecherous attention.

125

She averted her eyes. If she looked at him her loathing would take control of her and she would snap. She needed time.

Between inflicting pain on her breasts he would stroke her belly. Quite gently at first, then he started to talk to the child inside. "You will like these, French bastard. They are ripe." He leant down and bit hard into her nipple.

Suddenly he was on his knees, his ear against her stomach. Then he started sniffing her belly like a hunting hound. "Do I smell Jew in there?"

Yvette tried to show no reaction, but she must have made the slightest of moves as she tensed.

"Ha! Yes, I smell Jew." He laughed out loud. He pulled the other chair over and sat in front of her, his legs splayed out either side. He removed a packet of cigarettes from his pocket, and then pulled one out and lit it.

Yvette was watching him now. Smugness had been added to lust. She had never wanted to kill anyone as much as she wanted this man to die.

Without warning he took a long draw on the cigarette and stubbed the burning end into her belly. "There, bastard Jew. You must get used to the smell of burning flesh." Which he followed with a chilling laugh. It scared her, it scared her for Perdy's sake.

The cigarette found her breast this time. She noticed his spare hand was stroking himself now as he inflicted pain on her, and saliva was actually dribbling from his mouth.

"So, bastard Jew." He was talking to her stomach again, the cigarette hovering an inch above her belly button. "Shall we drown you in good Aryan sperm?"

He put the cigarette back in his mouth and started to release his belt. 'Oh my God, he is going to rape me,' thought Yvette. 'I am about to give birth and he is going to rape me.' Her brain was racing. There would be a way, a way she could kill him even with her hands bound. He would have to move her if he intended to penetrate her. There would be a moment, he would

126

let his guard down and she would kill him.

His trousers were round his ankles and an angry penis poked at her stomach. "There, bastard Jew. This hose will drown you. What do you think?" He gave that evil laugh again. He turned his attention to Yvette, striking her breast with his open hand then pulling hard on her nipple once again. "Jewish bitch, I will fuck you till I kill your bastard."

He untied her from the chair and pulled her to her feet by her hair and spat in her face as he did so. Moving behind her he lifted her skirt and pulled her pants down then ripped them from her legs. His fingers greedily explored her vagina and she could feel and smell his foul breath on her neck. She closed her eyes and gathered herself. She would not let it happen. She would rather die than let him harm her Perdy. "Wait."

It was the first word she'd spoken since the 'interrogation' had begun. He'd been disappointed, they usually screamed or cried. "So the Jewish bitch talks."

He stepped back and allowed her to turn round and face him. She was smiling and pushed her breasts hard against his chest, then raised her head as if to kiss him.

Fascinated he watched, surprised by her compliance. There was an agonising shooting pain as her knee crushed his testicles. As he doubled up in agony Yvette sunk her teeth into his neck directly into his jugular vein and her jaw locked. Like a rabid dog she shook his neck, her teeth slowly penetrating his skin.

He fought wildly, trying to free himself from the frenzied woman who was intent on literally ripping his throat out. The pain from his groin subsided as the blood began to flow from his neck. He wrestled her to the floor but could not free himself. He knew he was about to die and in a last ditch effort to free himself he punched her hard in her stomach.

The pain was excruciating and as a reflex action Yvette released his neck.

Another blow followed, then another. She fell doubled up

in agony as he hit her child. Now he was on his feet and kicking her. The kicks were striking every part of her body as he continued with his vicious attack. Slowly he realised that the maximum pain and hurt could be extracted by kicking her unborn Jewish bastard child.

He was laughing when the bullet blew the front of his skull apart and covered the inert Yvette in blood and brains, before his dead body slumped and fell on top of her.

Jacques leapt forward and dragged him from Yvette. He lifted her in his arms like a child and carried her sobbing from the cell and up the stairs to the reception area of the police station.

The other Gestapo officer lay dead on the floor along with three soldiers. Two policemen stood, their hands aloft staring into the gun barrels that pinned them to the wall. Outside, over thirty men knelt, their guns raised, guarding the entrance and waiting for the S.S. troops to arrive at the scene of their raid.

Yvette's attacker had been too engrossed in his sick fantasy to hear the gunfire in the street above.

Sophie waited for Jacques to reappear. He had leapt down the steps to the cells and she'd heard the single shot, the shot she prayed had brought an end to the Gestapo swine's life.

She had been covering the steps in case it was the German who appeared. She did not know what to expect when Jacques appeared carrying Yvette in his arms. She was shocked to see her half-naked body covered in blood and the sobbing girl in his arms. She stepped towards them and pulled Yvette's skirt down to cover the trickle of blood that issued from between her legs. She looked at Jacques to see the pained look on his handsome face as he just shook his head.

"Get her to the doctor, Jacques. I know you have a sympathiser who will help. We will make sure you get away safely. Now go!" Sophie almost pushed him towards the van as the first shot ricocheted off the wall next to them.

128

Jacques eased her into the seat, and as he arranged her dress to cover her bare breasts he saw the cigarette burns around her nipples. "It will be fine, darling. I'll take you to Doctor Arnaux. You will be fine."

Yvette did not speak, she just stared into the darkness she saw before her. Already she had stopped sobbing. Her baby was dead. Her hope, her future, her Perdy was dead. She knew it the way she knew that night followed day.

The doctor administered to her wounds and examined her thoroughly, paying particular attention to the baby. Then they took her to the secret room in the attic where many others in the Resistance had recuperated from injury and where several had died. She lay on the bed and curled up into a ball, still not talking or responding to any questions the doctor asked. Jacques too was ignored, as if he was not there or invisible.

"Come, Jacques. Yvette must rest." Dr. Arnaux led him down to his rooms again.

"How is she?" Jacques asked anxiously.

The doctor looked at the young man who he knew to be Yvette's lover and the Father of her child. "She is in deep shock, Jacques. Physically she is not too bad, nothing broken, just the burns and bruising. But..." he hesitated, "the baby, your baby. I think the baby is dead." He let it sink in. "I cannot hear a foetal heartbeat, and Yvette has severe interior bleeding. She has been badly beaten."

Jacques was now in shock himself. His mind raced. How would she deal with this? His brittle hellcat might disintegrate. He was quiet, wrapped in thought.

Then the doctor answered a question Jacques had been finding it hard to ask. In fact he had already jumped to a conclusion about the answer having seen her half-naked and the German with his trousers round his ankles. "I don't think she was raped. There is no bruising there or any sign of sexual activity."

It was a small blessing, but one he found comforting beyond all reason. "Good. She could not have lived with that." How she would live with the rest of it, he did not know.

An hour later Pierre arrived at the doctor's. "How is she?" He asked.

The doctor answered, "Comfortable, she will survive."

Jacques inwardly questioned his prophetic words, but said nothing. Instead he asked Pierre if everyone had survived the fight with the S.S. Pierre's moustache twitched. "Come on, Pierre. How bad?" The moustache warned him that it had not gone well.

Pierre paused. "One dead, Jean. And they have..."

"Come on!"

"They have Sophie."

"Bloody hell, no. Not Sophie as well!" His anguished tone quickly gave way to anger. "The fucking bastards. Is she alive?"

"Yes, she was shot in the shoulder, but it took her down whilst she was covering our escape. We tried to get to her but their fire power was too great." Pierre looked thoroughly downcast.

"I know you did, Pierre. Come on, we'll get her back. Like we did, Yvette."

"No, they took her straight to the Gestapo headquarters. This time Sophie belongs to them."

Jacques was acutely aware of what that meant, almost certain death after agonising torture is what Sophie, Yvette's best friend, had in store. It would be the final straw for Yvette, if there were any straws left to break. Jacques had never felt so helpless in his life.

Pierre saw the look on his face and snapped him out of his despond. "She will not talk, no matter what they do to her. The girls never talk, only the men."

Jacques found himself smiling. How true, every woman he'd met in the Resistance had been brave beyond belief, and had pain

130

thresholds he could not imagine. Still, his heart went out to Sophie and he prayed her end would be quick.

Once again Pierre snapped him back to the present. "Yvette is not safe here. They will be looking for her. After the show of force we put up to get her back, they know she is important."

The doctor interjected, "She can't be moved yet. Probably within the next forty-eight hours her body will abort her dead baby."

Pierre looked at Jacques for conformation of what he'd just heard. Jacques nodded at him. "Merde. The bastards." But he was soon in control again. "After that. She cannot return to the farmhouse, it is compromised. They will start a massive manhunt to find her."

"England, I'll take her back to England. She will be safe there, and it will give her time to heal."

"She won't want to go," Pierre said.

"I don't know. She will not speak. She is in a deep shock," Jacques said.

"It is a good idea. In her present state she is no use to the War effort. In England, her mind can heal as well as her body." It was the doctor. "Though she must remain here for now. What she is about to experience will not be good."

Pierre went to fetch Alain and Albert. The four of them would pay with their lives rather than have them take Yvette again. They waited at the doctor's home for the Gestapo to come and for Yvette's baby to leave.

Thirty-six hours later she went into labour to abort her child. Jacques had expected screams. Yvette gave birth to Perdy, the little girl who never drew breath, in perfect silence without shedding a single tear.

Four grown men shamelessly shed all her tears on her behalf.

Three days later Yvette and Jacques boarded the Lysander

131

for England. Vera Atkins met them; she put her arm around Yvette and smiled at Jacques. "Come, my dear. We have a nice room for you."

Jacques stayed with her for twenty-four hours. She never spoke to him or anyone else. She didn't cry or even look perplexed. She was dead inside.

There was no question of Jacques not returning to Normandy. There was too much to do, the invasion was drawing near and he was desperately needed. But he needed something too. He needed his own healing process to begin. He needed Honeysuckle.

He had twelve hours before Daniel flew him back to France, so he borrowed his motorcycle and drove to the Isle of Wight.

He told Yvette he was going back to France and kissed her on the forehead, then she spoke her first words. "I'm sorry, Jacques," and a tear appeared in her eye.

It was too much for Jacques, who hugged her and cried into her shoulder. Her arms involuntarily wrapped around him as he implored her not to feel guilty, but she didn't say anything more and no more tears appeared.

Jacques tickled Buster behind his ear. "That's about as bad as it gets, Buster."

Buster was glad the man had spoken. There had been no smiles and no one had passed by with treats. His muzzle nudged the plastic bag containing the sandwiches. 'I had better remind him,' he thought.

The man laughed. "Sorry, old man. You must be starving. Ham today, your favourite."

Eleven

Today it was busy on the Warren. 'Probably a ramblers day,' thought Buster. Several new dogs about, he wasn't very happy. He preferred the spring and autumn, just his usual friends to sniff without all the newcomers. The man preferred it too, less interruptions in his remembering, though last time he was so deep in thought no one would have snapped him out of it. Hopefully today would be better and he wouldn't have to wait so long for lunch!

Jacques looked at the rock he used to sit on with Honeysuckle when they were children. It was just feet from the bench he now occupied with Buster. It seemed much bigger all those years ago and the indentation that made a natural seat for them had gathered soil over the years and a sprig of white heather had seeded itself. The rock had stood at the side of the path, but the years had seen the path move and it was now almost completely surrounded by gorse.

They had parked the motorcycle at the bottom of the hill and walked to their rock. He had telephoned the exchange in Yarmouth and Katherine, the lady who worked the exchange, had walked the short distance to Honeysuckle's house to tell her that Jacques would be there in three hours time. Luckily she was at home, as Jacques had already set off for Lymington and the ferry.

She was waiting on the pier, waving to him as the boat approached. For the first time in days Jacques felt his spirits lift.

When he disembarked, they hugged each other and without preamble he said, "Come on, jump on the back, I need to talk to you."

Honeysuckle looked quizzically at him, but realised he was not going to expand as he was already sitting astride the bike offering her his hand.

Luckily she had on a loose-fitting skirt, which she was able to hitch up and she was immediately behind him. Her arms wrapped around his waist and her head rested his back as he started the engine and gunned the throttle. She held on tightly as he sped off a little too fast towards the Warren.

Slightly flustered, Honeysuckle eased herself from the pillion seat calming her mop of curls and said, "What is this all about, Jacques?"

"At the top, on our rock. I'll tell you there." Without saying anything more, he took her hand and led her up the winding path to the place they had spent so much of their childhood together, their place and their rock.

Once they had arrived, and a little out of breath he sat her down. He did not sit himself, but looked down the valley to where the Messerschmitt had crashed and beyond, to Farringford. He was searching for the words, wondering what to say to her. He had left Yvette twelve hours before he needed to because he had an overwhelming need to be with, and talk to Honeysuckle. Now he was there he felt guilty for leaving Yvette and he did not know what to say.

Honeysuckle could see the anguish on his face and the pain in his eyes. She waited for him to begin in his own time.

It seemed an eternity and all she wanted to do was take him in her arms and soothe away his obvious hurt, but she waited.

Eventually he turned back towards her and with tears in his eyes said, "The baby is dead. It was a girl. The Germans murdered her."

The enormity of what he'd said took a while to sink in, then she leapt to her feet and took him in her arms and said, "My poor, Jacques. My poor, poor, Jacques."

It was her turn to become tongue-tied. What could she possibly say? She gave him time to continue.

"The Gestapo took Yvette and assaulted her. Then they beat her badly and kicked her in the stomach until our child was dead." He wanted to release the tears that had formed in his eyes, but like Yvette he found it hard.

Honeysuckle let go of him and held him at arm's length. She saw him fighting back the tears. "You can cry, Jacques. It's alright, you know."

He managed a weak smile. "I have cried, and I will again. But now I am so angry, I find it hard to cry."

"I understand. It must be terrible." She kissed his cheek. "Come, sit with me. You need to talk about it. It will help." As always she knew what to do and how to deal with him.

They sat next to each other on the rock where they'd had so many conversations. Children's conversations, but they were adults now and needed to have an adult talk. She held his hand as they stared out towards the Needles, then squeezed his fingers in encouragement.

Jacques told her the entire story of how Yvette was taken and about the sadistic bastard who assaulted her. He told her about the rescue and how the Gestapo had captured one of his best friends, Sophie. Honeysuckle did not interrupt, but allowed him to relay the awful events in his own time and in his own way. However she noticed he did not speak of the effect it had all had on the woman who was going to be the Mother of his child. The woman, it had been taken for granted, that he would marry when the War was over.

When he finished by telling her that Yvette had apologised to him, she was almost in tears herself and had to wipe away a tear that rolled down her cheek. He did not see it; he was still staring, unseeing at the English Channel towards France.

"How is Yvette, and how do you think she will cope with it all?" She asked.

"That is the problem. She did not speak a single word until she made that apology, and she has not spoken since. She has not shed a single tear, she is bottling it all up inside. She believed that the baby, our baby, had given humanity and self-respect back to her. At the moment she is like a dormant volcano, she has been in denial and she has felt guilt. But when the anger comes, as it will, and the volcano erupts it could be catastrophic." He was still staring ahead.

Her poor Jacques, what a tangled web he found himself in, a domestic nightmare in the middle of a world of intrigue and betrayal. Still a young man, he had witnessed a world and events therein that beggared belief. What could she say, or do that could help him? All Honeysuckle knew was that talking would help. They had always talked when something was wrong, but it was a long way from losing a pet rabbit to losing your baby, and in such circumstances.

"You wanted the baby, didn't you?" She was still holding his hand.

"Yes. Yes, I did." He paused. "At first I didn't. I felt trapped. I felt as if all the choices I should have in life had been taken away from me." He turned to face her. "I thought I had lost you because of the baby. So I blamed the baby. But after I saw you last, I knew I could never lose you. Not the important part of you." He had to continue, to explain. "Yvette changed too. She was always a vibrant and sexual girl, but the prospect of motherhood altered her. She became gentler, content, wholesome if you like. From being trapped, I saw a life and a relationship that could work." With the idea of the baby he became wistful again. "She was called Perdy, you know. I was actually looking forward to the idea of having Perdy."

Honeysuckle saw his eyes moisten once more. With that, she cried herself. She cried for him.

Her crying is what Jacques had needed, now he had to care for her. "Don't cry, Honeysuckle. I can't bear to see you cry. Just talking to you has helped me. I will be fine, and I'm sure Yvette will be too." The last part was a lie, he was sure she would be far from being fine.

"I'm sorry, Jacques. It must be so awful for you. I will always be here for you, you know that?"

"Thank you, dearest Honeysuckle. I know." He took her hand and stood up. "Come on, let's walk down to Alum Bay."

They followed the path that led down towards the multi-coloured cliffs that formed the backdrop to the sands of the bay and past the gun emplacements that defended the Solent.

"What will you do now, Jacques?"

"I will fly back to Normandy tonight. The allied invasion will happen soon and there is still much to do. Now Yvette is gone, I am in charge of the Resistance operations in Normandy, which will cripple the German armed forces. It is important work, and I'm afraid the War will not stop to allow grieving hearts to mend. We are just the latest casualties in a long list of broken hearts."

"What about Yvette?"

"She will recuperate here in England. How long that will take, or what she will do next? I do not know." His heart went out once again to the woman he had left in the hospital. "It will appear callous, but I have to leave her, and I pray she will be alright."

"Would you like me to go and visit her? As your friend, your little sister." Honeysuckle was quite serious. She felt nothing but compassion for the woman she had never met, the woman who had taken her Jacques.

"I don't know. At the moment in her present state of mind, I don't think it would achieve anything. I really don't know."

The path and steps down to the beach were steep and they walked in single file, a comfortable silence between them as they were both wrapped in their own thoughts. At the bottom her hand sought his again and they fell into stride beside each other.

Honeysuckle was ashamed. On the walk down she had allowed herself to imagine that without the baby he may be free of Yvette, and that she may have him back. The whole world thought she was so perfect, so generous of spirit, so caring. Yes, she was ashamed because she knew she was not. How could she have such thoughts when such a terrible thing had happened?

She continued to walk, now in a self-conscious silence by his side, wishing she had not had those thoughts.

Jacques suddenly snapped her out of her self-loathing. "How is Simon?"

"He's fine, just fine." She was smiling to herself, glad that he had changed the subject before she could become selfish again.

Jacques noticed the smile on her face. Despite all that had happened he felt a pang of jealousy that the mention of Simon should make her smile. "What are you smiling about?"

The sun appeared from behind a cloud and illuminated the kaleidoscope of colours that formed the rock face behind them. "Nothing."

"What sort of nothing?" Now he was smiling too. "You're still seeing him, obviously."

"Yes, when he comes home."

"Still a good kisser?" He was teasing her now, like an older

138

brother.

"Yes."

"Come on, tell me. I know there is more to your relationship than just kissing."

"Okay then. He asked me to marry him." She was still smiling as she waited for his reaction.

Jacques stopped walking. "But, but you're only eighteen, and only just that. You can't...."

She was laughing at him now. The look on his face was wonderful. Indignant. Hurt. Jealous. Yes, he was jealous, and she could see that the thought of her marrying someone else would tear him apart. Suddenly she was thinking, 'I can have him again.' Guilt followed.

"What did you say? Did you say, yes?"

Poor Jacques. He was distraught. Every other problem in his life had suddenly disappeared. All he could think about was losing Honeysuckle, and it showed. It was written all over his face for her to see.

Honeysuckle relished his pain for a while before she put him out of his misery. "Don't worry, Jacques. I will not marry him."

"Good. You are too young." He looked stern.

She couldn't hold it in any longer and burst out laughing at him.

"What's so funny now?" He looked cross.

"You, your face, you look like you are sucking a lemon. So cross and disapproving." She screwed her face up into an imitation of his.

It worked, he joined in with her laughter. "Do I look like that? I'm sorry, it's none of my business." His face relaxed.

It was Honeysuckle who looked serious now. "Yes it is. It is your business, Jacques. We are completely part of each other's lives, and I love that you were upset at the thought of me marrying another."

She put her arms around him and hugged him, her head on his chest. She could have kissed him, but the time was not right.

"So what did you tell him?" Jacques was still slightly perplexed.

"Don't be angry with me, but I said I would think about it. I won't marry him, but he was about to go back to his squadron and there is only a fifty percent chance that he will return. Well over half of his friends are already dead or injured. I couldn't send him away without hope, thinking I did not care for him. I do care for him, but I do not love him, Jacques. When the War is over he will see that, and he will realise his infatuation with me was born out of all the imponderables that war has brought."

She was still holding him and did not see him close his eyes in relief when she said she would not marry Simon. He knew only too well the pressures that Simon would be under and Honeysuckle was right. Even the belief that you had a chance of getting a girl like her would get you through the War. It was exactly what was sustaining him, how could he begrudge it to another man.

She remained in his arms, as just a few hundred feet away a Spitfire roared over the Needles heading towards the New Forest. The unmistakable noise of its Merlin engine finally pulled them apart as they watched it fly past towards the sanctuary of home, where perhaps it's pilot would find the embrace of his sweetheart. It could easily have been Simon.

The poignancy of the moment spoke to them both and answered all the questions that did not have to be asked.

After lunch, which included another mystery sandwich, Jacques took Buster down to the beach at Alum Bay. They didn't go there very often, it was a steep walk down and neither was getting any younger.

Buster liked the beach and remembered his own antics with stick and ball. For old times sake he had rushed into the surf before discretion overcame his valour, after a large wave had crashed over his head. Shaking himself down he trotted back to the man's side.

He hadn't seen how brave Buster had been, the man just stared out over the Needles then turned his head slowly towards the New Forest as he traced the imaginary path of the Spitfire.

Twelve

It was quieter today, fewer ramblers and more clouds than yesterday. Buster idly pondered the connection between ramblers and clouds, and if there was a connection between ramblers and sandwiches. But came to no real conclusions.

The man was already on the bench, patting the space by his side. Buster made one last inspection of the area before putting his front paws up and waiting for the man's helping hand. He was stiff after yesterday's adventure on the beach.

"Something different today, my little furry friend. Back to Vietnam, I think."

Jacques sat in the C19-Flying Boxcar with his parachute between his legs. It was November the 20th 1953, and Sophie sat next to him.

"How long is the flight, Jacques?" She asked.

"A couple of hours," replied Jacques.

"Waiting, we used to do a lot of that, didn't we?"

"Yes. It was always the worst time." He remembered the times he'd lain in wait with Yvette for an aeroplane to land or a train, or truck that was to be their target. Sometimes they would wait for half a day or through the night. They would talk to each other to while away the time. He had waited with Sophie on many occasions too. She was great to talk to, always humorous and companionable.

However, there was one conversation he had never had with her. One he wanted to have since he had met up with her again in Hanoi. He had tried but she would always avoid it. Maybe here, going back into battle she would talk about it.

"Sophie, I want to ask you something and this time I want an answer."

"Yes, Sir." She saluted in due deference to his tone.

He laughed, she always made him laugh. "You have never spoken of it, but what happened when the Gestapo captured you? As your friend I would like you to share it with me." He looked seriously at her.

She returned his look. "It's no big deal, Jacques. One of the reasons I've never talked about it to you is because of what happened to Yvette. I did not want to open old wounds and it is in the past."

"No big deal! They shot you, interrogated you and left you to rot in a concentration camp. No big deal!" He loved this woman.

"Okay. You want to hear it, then here it is." She looked again at her best friend, the man she had also fantasised about for ten years. "As you know we had quite a gun fight with the Nazis, and gave them a good bashing. Pierre managed to get an incendiary device beneath one of those bloody silly little tanks they used. I picked each of them off as they leapt from the stupid thing. Unfortunately there were several more tanks just around the corner. It was time to leave, you and Yvette should have been well away, so we pulled back towards our vehicles.

143

Remember that lorry Albert had, the one you guys left in pieces at the farm? That's the one we were using. Alain and myself were giving covering fire as the boys got in. We were to jump on as it sped past us towards a glorious retreat. A speciality of we French!" Jacques laughed. "I had one foot on the bumper, about to swing myself aboard when the bullet hit. I went flying, it just knocked the stuffing out of me. Next thing I knew, two rifles were pointing in my face." She stopped, intending that to be an end to the story.

"Don't think you'll get away with just that. Then what happened?"

"Gestapo. Black Mercedes, 84 Foch Avenue."

"And?"

She raised her eyes heavenwards, she was not going to get away with it. "They were okay. After what happened to Yvette I was expecting the worst. Beatings, rape and all that." The words she chose were light-hearted, but her eyes were darkening as she remembered. "A doctor removed the bullet and dressed my wound, along with all the scratches and cuts I sustained falling from the lorry. Then they put me in a cell, in some ways that was the worst time, wondering what they were going to do to me. Anyway, about two hours later they came and took me to another cell. This one contained some pretty horrid looking contraptions and manacles laid into the wall. I felt better. Would you believe that? I felt better. I could see what they had in mind for me. The fear of the unknown had gone."

Jacques sat riveted. Sophie was there in the cell once again. She had never before been so serious in his presence, and even now she was making jokes of it all.

"Two men, one with those silly spectacles that they wore and one without, entered the room. At first they were nice, polite and respectful. They did not know my name. That was good, whoever had betrayed us, I assumed Henri, had not given them my name or description. I knew I stood a chance of convincing them I was just a minor member of the Resistance."

Jacques needed to know. He was back with Yvette, her dress torn and her body violated. "Did they....?"

"No, Jacques. They didn't." She knew what he was thinking. "They are not all sadistic bastards and perverts. It was as if they were ashamed of what their colleague had done to Yvette. Sure, they tortured me, but I told them nothing. I'm not even sure if they tortured me that badly. They seemed happy to accept I had no importance. Their cruelty was aimed at my conscience more than my body, they threatened reprisals against both our people and innocent civilians unless I gave them names and plans of future operations." Suddenly she nudged him in the ribs. "See these baby-blue eyes, you could never imagine how many tears they are capable of producing. The poor little blonde, she's too sweet to go around killing good wholesome German boys!" The last part she offered in a whining tone. "It was enough, and I think the one without glasses fancied me."

Jacques laughed. "I'm sure he did."

"So they treated me alright. I stayed there about a month. They fed and watered me and things were fine."

Jacques sensed a change in her. "What then?"

"The one who fancied me came to apologise that I was being taken to Buchenwald the following day. I could see in his eyes that he knew what that meant, and I had heard the stories about such camps." She suddenly giggled. "I cried and begged not to be sent there. He took me in his arms and kept saying he was sorry but it was out of his control. He was genuinely sorry, the fucking shit!"

"Do you want to talk about Buchenwald?" Jacques had seen first-hand the horrors that such places had witnessed and the toll they had taken on human life.

"Not really, what's the point?" She looked at his endearing, caring face. "Oh, all right, why not? One last purge, for the sake of my soul." She gave him a look that was intended to show her spiritual connection, but looked more like a spooked owl.

"Bloody hell, Sophie. Don't you take anything seriously? Doesn't anything scare you or get to you?"

"You do. Both, actually." He just shook his head.

She giggled, then continued, "Seriously, Jacques, what more can I say? You know as well as anyone what it was like in those camps. You walked into Belsen on the 15th April, the day it was liberated and visited many more of them with Yvette. You saw the full extent of their evil. I was lucky, I was only there for nine months. It was better than most, a holiday camp for resistance fighters and political activists! It never plumbed the depths that Belsen did, and I was not Jewish. I was tall and blonde, more Aryan than the vast majority of their vaulted master race. That helped me to survive, and there were guards who favoured me. Had I been taken at the beginning of the War, I may not have survived. Had the War continued, I'm pretty sure I would have been put to work in a brothel, servicing the pride of German manhood. Luckily for me they were on the run and no longer had time to amuse themselves with French whores." She paused. "I was there, and you bore witness to the atrocities. Other people will make sure the world never forgets what happened there. It is not for you or I. We have dealt with it in our own ways and we must move on."

Jacques had heard her story, and he was not going to press the point. "What happened when you were freed? Why could we not find you? We tried, you know. We were not sure if you were alive or dead, but thought you may be in one of the camps and searched the records in each one we visited."

"It was chaos, Jacques, and I was sick. I was malnourished and suffering from a virus, probably mild typhoid. The Americans put me in one of their field hospitals. They were good to me, but it was still six months before I was well again. They told me I weighed just eighty pounds when they took me to the hospital. Now look at me." She prodded her perfectly flat abdomen as if it were an obscene gut. "One hundred and twenty pounds of obesity!" Jacques looked at the gorgeous girl at his side, trying to imagine her as skin and bone, but couldn't get past the curves he had always admired. "They healed me in every way possible, first physically and then a lovely married doctor actually administered to my mental state as well!" Jacques watched for a telltale sign of any misdemeanour that may have taken place, and sensed the slightest dilation of the pupils in her eyes. She didn't expand on the married doctor. "I ended up working with the Americans, reuniting the lucky few who survived the camps with their family and friends, as you tried to do for Yvette and her family. It was good for me, and part of my healing process. The fact that we never met, or were unable to get in touch was just fate. We worked for different people and in different camps, but some of our aims and goals were completely different." She wished she had not said the last part, it was not meant to be judgemental but may have sounded so.

Jacques nodded in recognition of her final statement. She was right of course, their lives had taken different paths in the aftermath of the War. Those paths having been carved by all that had happened during it.

"Don your parachutes, Madamemoiselle et Messieurs. Fifteen minutes to the drop zone." The instruction heralded the end of their conversation.

Sophie wanted to say one last thing to him. "I know you hated what she did, Jacques. Don't, they deserved it." She kissed him on the cheek and said, "Come on, mon brave. We will fight together one last time."

Sophie jumped first, followed by Jacques and the rest of the 6e Bataillon de Parachutistes Coloniaux. It was 10:35 am, and they fell through the moist morning air towards the jungles and hills of Dien Bien Province in the northwest corner of Vietnam, close to the border with Laos.

Jacques positioned himself by her side as they plummeted

towards the ground. She was smiling, and probably laughing too as the air rushed past her. On landing she skilfully gathered her parachute and ran to the cover of the trees by the opening of their landing zone. Within seconds he was by her side. Others joined them and they quickly regrouped to secure the area.

Sophie shadowed Jacques. Although armed like the rest of the Battalion, she also carried a camera. When their guns were raised in anticipation and fingers pulled the triggers, her camera took it's own shots.

Fascinated, Jacques watched her in action. He was sweeping the enemy enclave with the patrol he commanded, whilst she took photographs. Not of the enemy or where they might be, but of him and the French soldiers. It was their expressions, their fear and their bloodlust that she wanted to capture.

They met little resistance. They did not expect to, the drop had been well planned and the secret well kept. They suffered casualties, but not many. Sophie's camera paid particular attention to these men's wounds. Jacques's patrol encountered the enemy just once and had four kills. She took a few photos of the dead Vietnamese, but it was a nineteen-year-old French boy who had his throat slit during an all too brief burst of close combat that her camera concentrated on. Jacques shot the perpetrator, but it was too late for the young soldier. She used two rolls of film on the dead boy and the blood-covered weapon that had killed him. She also took pictures of the perpetrator, he didn't look a day over sixteen. Jacques had to drag her away to allow the medics to attend to the dead boy's body. The camera became part of her, an extension of her eyes.

It did not take very long to make the area secure. That night they set up camp on the perimeter of the airfield, along with the other patrols that had all secured their sectors. The next day they would take the airfield, it was now isolated and vulnerable after waves of French parachutists had been dropped into the Province.

In the camp, Sophie once again sat beside Jacques. It had been a long and hard day. "Your photographs are nearly all of dead Frenchmen." It was a simple statement from Jacques.

"Yes. That is what France must see. What the world must see if it is all to stop. It must see its children dying on the other side of the Earth, just to claim a piece of worthless jungle." She was looking straight ahead of her. "This is what I do now, Jacques. This is my new war."

"It is a good battle, Sophie. I hope you can win it." She could hear the doubt in his voice, then he laughed. "It's not exactly the glorious homage to French Colonialism the Generals had in mind when they said that I could bring you here."

She laughed as well. "No, it's not is it? But you said it, they are fools and they are fighting a fool's war. Can I win my war?" Probably not, but I will try. I know the sword does not work, so I will remove the S and try the word." She turned to look at him, his handsome face still camouflaged. She could smell the sweat on his powerful body, and sensed the raw strength of a natural hunter. A hunter totally at ease with the hostile environment his prey inhabited. Here, in this place he was a lion. The most beautiful thing she had ever seen. She shuddered as she imagined him taking her.

Jacques noticed her almost imperceptible movement. "Are you alright, Sophie?"

"No. I'm not. Here I am preaching about the horrors of war, and the fucking thing just turns me on! I feel as horny as hell, and I just want to rip off your clothes and let you fuck my brains out!"

"Everything's fine then?"

"Yes, but stop those bloody eyes twinkling at me!"

At first light they took the airfield. They just marched in and accepted the white flag offered by the token force that remained, which no longer had an appetite for the fight.

Later in the day the heavy engineering equipment arrived

with engineers who proceeded to repair and lengthen the runway. The entire command structure was flown in under the leadership of a Brigadier General. Several other support regiments, including a number of loyal Vietnamese arrived and by November the 22nd a fair sized army was in place at the outpost where the generals believed that the Vietminh would be drawn into a pitched battle they could not possibly win.

They worked late into the night setting up and fortifying the new air base. There was little fighting apart from a couple of snipers they had failed to mop up the day before. Jacques took a small patrol into the surrounding hills to nullify these insurgents. Sophie begged to go with them and despite Jacques protestations she marched through the air base entrance with the patrol, fully armed with both rifle and camera. She did not use the rifle but the camera had a busy day, mostly taking photographs of Jacques and later, of the two dead snipers. Jacques was good, better than she remembered and he had been one of the best in the Resistance. Now he was even more ruthless as he professionally neutralised his targets. She observed him as she had the previous day, a walking block of male testosterone, muscles and stubble. But from his camouflaged face his caring eyes watched out for her here in the hills of Vietnam, just as they had done in France.

It was all too much for Sophie, she could bear it no longer. That night she took Jacques to her private quarters and made him fuck her brains out. He did not object. Neither did he object when she returned the compliment.

The next morning she awoke in his arms. The reality had been every bit as good as the fantasies she'd had over the years. It was done, they had possessed each other, each desperately desiring it. Though with that knowledge came sadness, a sadness that it would probably never happen again. They had something very special, a friendship that went far deeper than any sexual relationship, a friendship that must never be threatened. What they had done, had to be done, and it would add to their bond.

150

But it must never be allowed to threaten it. For now she would just enjoy the moment.

"Hello, Sophie," he said as he kissed the top of her head. Good, she thought, there was no regret in his voice.

"Hello, Jack!" She turned and kissed him, pressing her breasts to his firm chest. "That was lovely, thank you."

"I'm glad you enjoyed it. I certainly did." They both laughed.

Jacques sat up and pulled the sheet from her body. "What are you doing?" Asked Sophie.

"Taking my own photograph in my head, so I will never forget." His smile told her that he understood the way it had to be, and that he accepted it.

"It was wonderful though. Better than I ever imagined. We will have it forever now, Jacques, and it will not spoil everything else we have."

"No, it won't. But as we are here, and we are already naked, why don't we...?"

"Yes, one last time." She giggled and pulled him to her.

It was unsaid, but they knew it was almost certainly the last time they would have sex, so they made sure it was special. Something neither would ever forget in the years ahead, and something they could relive whenever their eyes met. It was a union that would never spoil what they had, a real friendship.

"Now that was a better day, Buster. Proper memories." Buster was glad, there would be an early lunch.

Thirteen

There was a chill in the wind and the man pulled the collar of his anorak around his neck in an attempt to keep it out.

Buster liked the wind. It tickled his fur, and in particular the fluffy bits behind his ears. He positioned his head to maximise the ear tickling.

Usually the man did not stay on the bench too long when it was windy, but today he looked particularly wistful so Buster wondered how long he would have to wait for lunch.

Jacques was back in Normandy. After leaving Honeysuckle he had gone for a cup of tea with his parents and told them about the baby and Yvette, then he rode Daniel's motorcycle back to Tempsford from where he returned to Normandy.

Pierre and Alain met him and instantly fired questions at him about Yvette. He was able to say she was comfortable but still deeply traumatised, but she had finally spoken. They both took this to be a good sign.

Within hours he was blowing up a bridge. It felt quite therapeutic after what he'd been through, and he was glad to be involved again.

The invasion was just months away and they were all immersed in preparations. As a cover he still supplied wine to the merchants in the region, but very little was delivered. Pierre, Alain and Albert had relocated to their friend's farm. The arms cache had been lost to the S.S, along with most of Albert's scrap yard. All they had managed to retrieve was the lorry that once again lay in pieces in their friend's barn.

Three weeks later Albert received a message to meet an agent who would be dropped that night at location 'Five.'

He went with Jacques to collect the agent. They flashed their torches and saw the solitary figure jump from the Lysander, the parachute silhouetted against the moon.

They would have to get away quickly, the parachute could be seen for miles as it opened against the milky night sky.

The agent made a perfect landing, gathered their parachute and ran towards them. Not stopping the figure continued running to where they knew the vehicle would be. "Hello, boys," the cat's whiskers smiled at them as she passed.

"Fucking hell," Albert said, as he went off in hot pursuit. Jacques was silent, he stood for a second in disbelief then followed them.

In the van she appeared perfectly normal, the old Yvette, as if nothing had ever happened. She even kissed Jacques before asking how the preparations were going.

At the farm she hugged Pierre and Alain, then turned to her new host, Denis, and kissed him on the cheek. Jacques was dumbstruck. What had happened to the wreck he had left behind just a few weeks previously? In just three weeks where had she found the strength to deal with the loss and hurt that he believed had destroyed her? Jacques was almost in shock.

That night she simply lay in his arms without making love.

There was no question that they would not be together. As she snuggled against him and allowed him to hold her, finally in the privacy of their room he was able to talk to her alone.

"Yvette, are you alright? Are you really ready for all this again? It's been such a short time."

"I need to, Jacques. It is the only way I can deal with it. I need to kill them all." That is all she said, and she said it with an unnerving calm in her voice.

Jacques shivered. He heard the Arctic malevolence in her voice. He knew she had not dealt with her ordeal at all and her hatred was tangible, just a bandage over her wounds. He was afraid for her.

The weeks that led up to the allied invasion were manic. They lost far too many good men and women, but their lives were not lost in vain, France would be liberated. However for every Frenchman killed ten Germans would die, a great many of them at the hands of Yvette.

Each night The BBC would broadcast their instructions for the next day, all delivered in pre-arranged code, and all acted upon with devastating effect. The enemy's command and control were crippled, much of it by the simple act of cutting telephone lines.

One of the Resistance's most notable successes was to prevent the German reinforcements from reaching Normandy. They either attacked them directly, or gave co-ordinates for the allied aircraft to strike the desperate German forces that were striving to reach Normandy to defend its coastline. The net result was that the Allies were to gain a foothold in the region after commencing their landings on the beaches of Normandy on June 6th 1944, D Day.

During the next eight weeks allied soldiers, artillery and supplies flooded into the region. Whole ports were built from scratch to replace the ones the Germans destroyed as they retreated. During that time the Resistance continued to be an irritation to the German High Command. In particular the S.S. Panzer Division, Das Reich took enormous casualties as it struggled to get to Normandy from the south to launch a counter-attack on the Allies bridgehead. Due to Yvette and the rest of the Resistance it failed to get there in time. The Allies could now advance on Paris.

The Resistance were not yet finished. In advance of this push, Operation Cobra, the Resistance continued to rain down a storm of destruction on the retreating German army. The Allies would often find empty fortifications and dead soldiers where they had expected to have to fight.

The Germans did put up some sort of a fight, but many lives were lost and within a few short weeks, on August the 25th Paris was free. The shopkeepers, barbers and solicitors who took up the arms supplied by the Resistance, rid their city of the occupying force. Even the police force finally turned on their puppeteers!

During this time Jacques fought at Yvette's side, She was inspirational to all around her. Her bravery in battle became legend. Jacques was the only one she allowed to see the soul that was destroyed within her, the soul so cruelly dismantled by the Nazis. The scarred and broken soul she no longer had a use for that guided her along this path of revenge and destruction.

It broke Jacques's heart to watch her. In their time alone together he attempted to rebuild their more intimate moments and tried to rekindle the flame of hope and love he had seen when she was carrying their baby. But the flame had been extinguished. The outside world saw the same old Yvette, but Jacques knew she was dead inside, and no matter what he tried he could not bring her to life.

They kissed and they slept together. She promised that one day she would want sex again, but asked to be given time. Jacques understood, and did all that he could to help her come to terms with her loss. Some days there were good signs, on others she was in deep despond. To Jacques, she seemed most animated when she took the life of a Nazi soldier. But even that satisfaction was short-lived, there would have to be another, and then another. At times it just become indiscriminate and gratuitous killing. He tried to get her to see reason, but reason does not exist in a dead soul.

Paris was liberated. They could have stopped the killing, and many did. They returned to their homes and their families in Normandy, Brittany and beyond. Yvette was unable to stop, she continued east towards the Fatherland with Jacques. There was still work for the Resistance. Now they had joined up with the allied forces, plans and orders were far easier to obtain and they continued their guerrilla war against the crumbling army of the Third Reich. When that was finished there would be one last thing she needed to do.

In his arms, the arms that had protected her and stayed by her side, she said, "Jacques, I know what you think of me and how you have tried to save me, and I will always love you for it. I don't think I can ever put all of this behind me and be the person I was once was. More importantly, the person you want me to be." Jacques tried to interrupt. "No, listen, my darling. You have been the one good thing in my life, and I have given you very little. You are a wonderful man and deserve far more than I can give you." He tried again. "No, don't speak. There is one last thing I would ask of you. I need your strength for this. With you there, I will be able survive it."

Jacques knew exactly what she was going to ask. "Of course, Yvette. I will help you to look for your parents and sisters." He also knew that when that was done, whatever the outcome they would part, their relationship having run its course.

It was early 1945 and the German army was all but beaten. The Allies were now operating inside Germany. The Russian, Red Army were crushing them on the Eastern Front and had liberated parts of Poland. With that liberation came sketchy reports of extermination camps being discovered. Slowly the authenticity of the reports began to gain validation.

It was Yvette's worst nightmare. Throughout the War there had been rumours of such places, but never any confirmation of their existence. The people sent to them did not return to tell their tales. The Russians found six camps, the last one they liberated was called Auschwitz.

By this time Yvette and Jacques were working closely with The Allied 21st Army group and were deep inside Germany. The Americans had already liberated a number of camps in the west of Germany, Buchenwald being the one where Sophie had been incarcerated. Although they were not death camps, they were concentration camps and were places of appalling suffering that often led to death. The Germans merely incarcerated the inmates here; political and religious prisoners, criminals, deserters, shirkers and Resistance fighters. Rather than exterminate them, people were just left to die. Living visions of hell, packed with starving, dehydrated, disease-ridden prisoners.

Belsen was all this and more. As the Russians continued their advance towards Auschwitz and the other Polish extermination camps, a great number of the Jewish inmates were marched or transported by train to camps within Germany by the Nazis. Belsen received an extra 60,000 of these poor souls in a camp that was built for 8000 inmates.

On the 15th of April 1945, Yvette and Jacques entered the camp along with the Allied 21st Army Group, not really knowing what they would find. The first sights were disturbing, but not unexpected. They were greeted enthusiastically by hundreds of under-nourished, thin, but otherwise generally healthy prisoners. One man even ran over to Yvette and hugged her. He had been rotting in the camp for nearly two years, and until his capture had fought courageously with her Resistance group. They both cried.

157

It was a typical Nazi detention centre and they had been treated quite humanely compared to what they were about to witness.

The Nazi, Joseph Kramer, who was handing the camp over to the allied commander did not even have the decency to looked ashamed as he took them deeper into the complex.

There was a camp within a camp. In this inner complex the full horror of Belsen became apparent. About 60,000 tormented Jews either existed in appalling conditions of starvation with no shelter or sanitation in a cesspit of humanity, or they were dead.

The camp authorities had long since given up trying to bring the inmates any of the basic needs to sustain human life. Disease was rife, typhus, dysentery, tuberculosis and many other diseases were at epidemic proportions and taking life at an alarming rate.

As Jacques approached the inner camp his senses told him what was coming. He could smell the sickly sweet stench of decomposing bodies mixed with the foul smell of excrement and urine. He turned to look at Yvette. She was implacable, taking in all around her until she saw the human detritus. She fixed her eyes on some of the living first, the vast majority barely able to move, their ribs protruding through glass-like skin, distended bellies, like pregnant living skeletons, they barely moved. All heads shaven, they sat or lay on the ground in their own filth. Their lifeless, bulging eyes stared unseeing into a hopeless future.

Slowly amongst the living she started to see the dead, almost indiscernible from those who still drew breath, they just lay where they had died.

Every person who witnessed it was speechless. There was a ghostly hush within the camp, those dying were unable to make a sound, and the liberators were in deep shock. Jacques looked at the men around him, many were silently crying, others just stood, mouths agog.

He turned again to Yvette; she was down on one knee stroking the baldhead of a woman of indeterminate age. Her other hand held the arm of a dead girl, her fingers stroking the tattooed number on her stick-like wrist. Yvette was not crying.

After what seemed an age the Commanding Officer finally snapped into life. "Water, give them water. Now, jump to it!"

The next few days were the worst days of Jacques's life and they would forever haunt him. They found 20,000 dead bodies. While the camp authorities could still cope with the vast scale of the dead, they had stacked them into piles. Those who had died more recently just lay unmoving amongst the living.

It was a medical nightmare. Everyone became a nurse in an attempt to keep alive the 50,000 survivors they had found. Those that had a chance of survival were washed, deloused then disinfected with D.D.T. powder. Makeshift hospitals were set up within the camp, where the inmates were given fluids and food whist attempting to treat the plethora of illnesses that were rampant. 13,000 did not survive. Many had starved for so long they were incapable of digesting food.

Jacques watched a small girl eagerly take a biscuit from a soldier. She took one bite, but the shock to her body was too great and she died instantly. The soldier was distraught, he had simply wanted to help the poor child.

Yvette worked like a woman possessed to save all those she could. She did not sleep or eat for three days. Eventually one of the doctors insisted she take a sleeping pill and rest. Five hours later she was back in the ward, willing the dying to live. Soon she found yet another way to help.

In order to contain the spread of typhus, 20,000 diseased corpses needed burying. She suggested to the C.O. that the surrendered S.S. guards be made to carry the bodies to the mass graves that the British bulldozers had dug, as punishment for their crimes. There was not a man in the British Army who did not think it a good idea. The Nazi guards were not allowed any protection, and consequently a number of them contracted typhus and died.

Yvette left the hospitals to help oversee the process.

Jacques observed her throughout. In the hospital she was in pain, caring and hurting. Seeing the fear in the eyes of the S.S. guards who carried the decomposing, diseased bodies to their graves took away that pain.

As each mass grave was filled, Isaac, a senior British Army Jewish Chaplain held a service for the deceased. Yvette attended every one.

The strongest of the survivors were relocated to houses commandeered from German civilians. At Yvette's suggestion all these civilians were taken to the camp to see what evils had been committed in their name. Jacques would not let her attend these tours, he was afraid of what she might do.

Isaac Levy had also been watching Yvette, and he came to Jacques to voice his concerns about her state of mind. "Jacques, Yvette is a lovely girl with a good heart. I have watched her in the hospitals and seen everything she has done for her people. But there is something else there.."

"I know. It is hatred, Isaac. It has kept her alive since her family were taken. And all this has made it worse," Jacques interrupted.

"What can we do?" Asked the Chaplain.

"I will help her to find her family. If they are alive, it may make a difference. But if they are not, then I will do all I can for her."

"You are a good man, Jacques. I will pray for her, and for you."

"Thank you, Isaac. We may need it."

That night Jacques said to Yvette, "We have done all we can here, let's try and find out what has happened to your parents and sisters. We can start in the camp, there must be records of people who have been incarcerated. The Jews have only been brought here in recent months, so we can ask some of the survivors about their former camps, Auschwitz or any others in which they may have been held."

"I know what has happened to them, Jacques. I've seen it here." She looked desolate.

"And we've seen thousands of survivors too. Many are quite well now. It's not hopeless." He lifted her chin and smiled at her.

She managed a weak smile. "Okay, Jacques. We'll try."

The next day they extricated the chief administrator from the lock-up in which the captured guards were being held and made him take them through the few records of inmates which had not been destroyed. Three other guards and administrators were commandeered to go through the records, one a female guard called Helga who spoke French. Unfortunately Helga was an arrogant anti-Semitic, dull of mind and totally lacking in charm.

Helga was at best, unhelpful and at worst, obstructive. She made no attempt to hide her contempt for Yvette and her family. Jacques watched and waited for Yvette's reaction. She smiled at Helga and gave her a cup of tea.

They spent three long days searching the records, but there was nothing of any use.

At the same time they asked the inmates if anyone knew of her family's whereabouts. Yvette's old friend from the Resistance was useful, pointing them in the direction of anyone he thought may be able to help.

One day Jacques heard Yvette asking the inmates questions about Helga. "What was she like?" She asked a woman about her own age that was making a good recovery.

"A bastard, a real bastard, one of the worst. She would beat us and shoot women for fun. She must have killed dozens of us, but maybe they were the lucky ones!"

Jacques later heard her getting confirmation of Helga's crimes from other prisoners. That night, in front of him and before he could stop her, Yvette put a bullet in Helga's brain.

He leapt towards her when he realised what she was about

to do. "No, Yvette you can't. It won't help!"

She holstered her pistol. "Oh, but it does, Jacques." Then she left the room.

Jacques looked at the dead woman. The door opened about two minutes later, it was the C.O. with two other officers. He looked at the body and then at Jacques. "Jacques, my friend, this War is still going on, so she will get away with it, but when it is over you must rein her in." He turned to the other two. "Get some of the men to get rid of this!"

What Jacques did not know was that Yvette had left the room with the intention of executing the Camp Commandant, Joseph Kramer who would later earn the epithet 'the Beast of Belsen.' She was unable to carry out that intention, as when she arrived at the quarters in which he was being held he was gone, along with the rest of his staff. Ironically he would later be caught and tried for his crimes against humanity and subsequently executed. However that day, the female guard called Helga was the first victim of Yvette's one-woman execution squad, and whatever Jacques said or did he was unable to stop her.

That night he tried again, but Yvette just said, "She deserved to die." It was an answer with which he found it hard to disagree.

Despite their investigations they were unable to get any leads as to her family's fate. Yvette's surname was a common one and a great many of the inmates could identify people with that name, but none appeared to be related to her unless they had been split up, which by all accounts could be a real possibility.

They remained at Belsen for three weeks doing whatever they could for the people, while the majority of the Allied 21st Army continued their push towards the final defeat of the Third Reich. Many of the inmates had lost their entire families along with their homes and the lives they had once lived. Within this group a dream was born of the possibility of a new life in Israel, a place in which they would be safe and be free of persecution and hatred.

On May 8th 1945 Karl Donitz formally signed the surrender of Nazi Germany, after Hitler had committed suicide on April 30th. But Yvette's war was far from over. She and Jacques returned to Paris to try and trace her family's journey from Drancy Internment Camp, where they had first been taken.

Back in Paris the heady excitement of liberation still filled the air and the Boulevards thronged with Parisians enjoying their freedom. It appeared to all that the summer had brought the finest weather for years. There were dark spots in the general bonhomie, not everyone was happy, revenge was in the air as there were collaborators to be dealt with. But for Yvette and Jacques it was the last time there was any real intimacy between them, fuelled by the hope that the great city radiated.

Jacques insisted they spend a few days enjoying their freedom from the rigours of war. He hoped that normality might weaken her appetite for revenge, and for a few days it did. They were young and if not in love, they were still in lust with each other's bodies. They ate and drank in the bistros of the Rive Gauche and walked hand-in-hand along the Champs Elysee. They talked about their adventures with the Resistance, the friends that were now bad farmers once again in their farm in Normandy, and the friends they had lost or had disappeared. For days Yvette was almost the happy girl she had once been, the girl that had seduced him and the woman that was to have given birth to his child, but it did not last, it could not last. Once again the dark clouds began to build around her as the pain of losing their child began to eat at her anew, and she was consumed by guilt at being alive whilst so many had perished. She grew restless, and anxious to find her family. In short, she was uncomfortable with being happy, she did not deserve happiness.

Four days after arriving in Paris she walked into Drancy

Internment camp, with a purpose to her step and menace in her eyes. She had never been in the camp before, it would have been too dangerous for her to visit her family. Initially her friends had been able to take them some small luxuries, but that had soon ended when one day her friends returned saying her family were no longer being held there.

Yvette inspected the ghetto that had been home to her beloved parents and cried at the conditions they had been held in. Her fingers caressed the pieces of cheap furniture and she imagined them being there. One room had two beds in it. Their guide told them it was a typical family room. She could see her two little sisters curled up together in the smaller of the two beds. Everywhere she looked there were ghosts. But there were records too, here they had not been destroyed so there was hope.

It took a while but eventually there they were. Judith and Samuel Hayek transported to Auschwitz September 3rd 1942. The one place she had prayed it would not be. As she closed her eyes she suddenly panicked, where were Laila and Esther, her beloved sisters? Their names were not there. She frantically searched through the lists of names. If not Auschwitz, where? It took another hour, then with forty other children there they were. On August 2nd 1942 they had all been ripped from the protection and love of their parents and put on a train and taken to Treblinka, situated just to the south of Warsaw.

When Yvette had been walking around the ghetto she had cried, but as she stared at her sisters' names there was cold steel in her eyes. Jacques knew he had lost her again.

"The girls first. They will be nine and eleven now. Will you come with me, Jacques?"

Jacques knew she did not need him anymore, but he had promised and he would keep his word. "Of course, Yvette."

She smiled at him. "Thank you, Jacques. I know what you think, but it will be easier with you there."

The next day they boarded a train to Treblinka.

"Well, Buster, not the most pleasant of memories, I'm afraid. Tomorrow, weather permitting, I think some thoughts about Honeysuckle would be in order."

Buster knew the name Honeysuckle well. He wagged his tail.

Fourteen

It was three more days before they found themselves back on the bench. The thunderstorms had started the night after Jacques had been remembering Belsen and all of its horrors. Jacques thought it rather apt that such dark memories should culminate with the heavens and gods raining down their wrath on the Earth below. He felt for Buster though, he hated the thunder and would physically shake at the anger the skies were showing.

Slowly the storms abated and the angry gunmetal skies gave way to clear blue again. Secure in the knowledge that shaking and barking at the thunder had frightened it away, Buster set off at a pace to the Warren and the bench.

Jacques finally caught up with the revitalised dog and sat down next to him, producing the chew that Buster knew he had in his pocket.

"Lovely day, old boy. The rain has washed all that summer gloom out of the air. Look, we can see Studland Bay." He pointed at the horizon, still half-expecting Buster's eyes to follow the direction he was pointing in, but as always his stare never left his fingers, expecting another chew to appear. Jacques ruffled his ears and kissed the top of his head. "More interested in food, as always."

"Honeysuckle today, old boy. At least a lot of it is about her, so I'll enjoy that part, anyway." At Honeysuckle, Buster wagged his tail. 'Good, there would be smiles.'

Jacques was back on the train with Yvette. It was a long journey to Treblinka and they had fallen into a companionable silence, having already relived the days they had spent in Paris.

Jacques was idly turning the pages of the newspaper he had purchased at the station and was vaguely aware of Yvette studying him. He looked up and returned the smile she had on her face, then returned to the paper.

He sensed she was still watching him and was about to ask why she was staring at him, when she said, "I met her you know, I met your little next door neighbour. The one who stowed away on your boat to Dunkirk. The one you used to talk about all the time, and who now, you never mention."

Jacques looked up abruptly from his newspaper with an obvious look of shock on his face.

Yvette laughed at his perplexed look. "She came to see me in the nursing home. Marched up to the bed and introduced herself in perfect French with a Normandy accent. It could have been you talking." She was enjoying his reaction. "I was expecting a little girl with pigtails and grubby knees. Not a siren with the smile of an angel." She giggled, Jacques looked distinctly uneasy.

Jacques had not been in touch with Honeysuckle since his last visit. He had managed to write her a couple of quick letters but had no idea if she had ever received them. His life had been itinerant, to say the least, and he had never expected to receive any replies from Honeysuckle. "Why didn't you ever say anything?"

Yvette just shrugged, but continued to smile at him. "Little Honeysuckle is infatuated with you, you know."

It was Jacques turn to shrug. He did not know how to deal with the conversation they were about to have. Yvette realised his predicament and knew how much she owed him so was not about to cause him further embarrassment. "You all looked so shocked when I arrived back in France. I would probably never have returned if it were not for bloody Honeysuckle!" She looked more serious now.

"Go on," encouraged Jacques.

"As you know I was in a catatonic state, or at least pretending to be. I did not want to talk to anyone. I had nothing to say and there was nothing anyone could say to me. A stream of well-meaning do-gooders traipsed in to tell me everything would be all right and I would have another baby. I wanted to tell them all to fuck off, but it was easier to say nothing. Then Miss English Rose appears and tells me not to be such an idiot and that I owe it to you to pull myself together. Then she gave me that bloody smile. The one it's obligatory to smile back at." Yvette was smiling warmly at Jacques now. "Don't worry, she is not that perfect. She was also there for another reason." Jacques cocked his head and looked puzzled. "She came to see what her opposition was like."

The look on Jacques's face encouraged her. "At least I hope she was there for that. If she was only there for me, then she really is an angel! She sensed I was a fighter and would compete for my man, that it would be my natural reaction. She made no attempt to hide the fact that she adored you, almost goading me to react. It worked, for the girl to fight she had to speak to her adversary. So eventually I spoke to little Honeysuckle." She couldn't hide the irony in her voice, as that is how Jacques had always described her. "Anyway, I'm sure her perfect eyes were twinkling as she goaded me."

Jacques still did not know what to say. What had Honeysuckle told her?

"So little Honeysuckle, with the body of a goddess, did the trick. I knew I would never be able to keep you, but I sure as hell wasn't going to give in easily. If I can defeat the entire German army by myself, I was not going to let bloody Honeysuckle trample all over me."

Jacques was laughing now as he tried to imagine the pair of them together. Yvette was smiling too.

"The trouble is she is far too nice to hate. You are peas in a pod and made for each other." Now she was looking affectionately at him. "We know we will part company, Jacques. We have already discussed it. I hope she will be there for you."

"Thank you, Yvette. We didn't...."

"I know. You are both too perfect and too damned English to have done anything. If I had been in her shoes, you would not have been allowed to be so noble. I would have had you, even if I had been only sixteen." She surreptitiously stroked his inner thigh to emphasise her point.

"What did you talk about?" Jacques was no longer afraid of anything they may have discussed.

"After my dressing-down, you mean?"

"Yes, I suppose so."

Yvette laughed. "Apparently you could not win the War on your own and I should stop being such a prima donna and get out there and help you. She was a clever little minx; she knew exactly how to get me to react. Then she told me off for being so self-indulgent."

"What did you say?"

"I was about to give her the full extent of Yvette's vocabulary usually reserved for the Nazis, when she bloody well smiled at me. Christ, when you two are smiling at each other the whole world must glow!"

"And…"

"I said I was sorry, and I cried. But I spoke. I finally said something. She held me and I didn't stop talking for over an hour to someone who was a complete stranger. I talked about my family, I talked about our baby and I talked about the Nazi pig that had murdered her. She sat and listened whilst stroking my hair, just as my Mother had done when I was a small child. I told her about my hatred and demons and I told her about the love I have for you" She was quite serious now. "I do love you, you know, but I will let you go. When we have finished my search , you must go to her. She is delightful and perfect for you".

"Are you sure…"

"Yes, Jacques. I have been blessed to have you in my life and to be part of yours. In spite of all I have done you have been there for me, but you belong to Honeysuckle." She said it as a simple matter of fact. Then added, "But I still have you for now and will use you!" Her eyes displayed the mischief that had once been there all the time and had briefly returned whilst they were in Paris.

Jacques leaned across and hugged her, wondering how someone who could at times be so sweet could be such a devastating force majeure.

Yvette continued, "Miss Perfect stayed for two days. Caused mayhem. Every male doctor in the place fell madly in love with her along with every patient, and I include myself in that." She tipped her head to one side to emphasize the point. "She is like an English Sophie." Her thoughts obviously turned to her great friend, and absently she added, "I wonder what happened to Sophie? We can't find any sign of her anywhere?"

"She is a survivor, Sophie, she will be fine," said Jacques, hoping it was true.

"So is little Honeysuckle." Yvette's thoughts had returned to Honeysuckle. "She told me that she would join us in the Resistance, she would have been unbelievable, what strength she

170

possesses!" Admiration was written all over her face.

Jacques did not like the thought of Honeysuckle fighting as they had done. In his mind she was to be protected and put on a pedestal, but he understood what Yvette was saying. He could vividly remember Honeysuckle with the soldiers at Dunkirk, her compassion and her fortitude. Yes, she would have been remarkable.

"What did you talk about for two days?" Asked Jacques, slightly apprehensive again.

"You." She laughed at the alarmed look on his face. "Don't worry, it was all good. Little Honeysuckle thinks you are a saint. I had to fight the urge to shatter her illusion with tales of your sexual prowess. But we were honest with each other and she made me talk. As I said, it's very difficult not to talk to her. I liked her enormously and I think she probably liked me, despite me taking her dream away." She paused, "I'm sorry the bitch in me did not leave her with a promise to return you when I have finished with you!" She smiled at him. "I know all about your childhood and your special places, the mill and the Warren. She very cleverly let me know that I would have to fight for you and I'm afraid I left her thinking that I would. She was too perfect, Jacques, I couldn't resist it. But we are friends of a sort and she did me an enormous favour, she gave me back my fighting spirit."

Jacques was imagining the pair of them, two protagonists, Honeysuckle in her way every bit as strong as Yvette. She was not the killing machine Yvette was, but a powerful force that could change destinies and shape events. He could see Honeysuckle cajoling Yvette into regaining control of her life, all the time taking stock of the woman he had made pregnant. For her part, Yvette would not allow this young woman to see her weaknesses and her guile would have clicked back into action within minutes of meeting her. Yes, Honeysuckle was the perfect person to get Yvette to snap out of her melancholy. In one way they were adversaries, but they were similar in so many other ways. Seeing them together would have been quite something.

"What are you smiling at?" Yvette already knew the answer.

"The pair of you sizing each other up."

"Two feline predators preparing to fight over their prey?"

"Something like that," he replied.

Yvette laughed. "You'd have been scared stiff if you had been there. If little Honeysuckle hadn't been so civilised and nice, I'd have tried to scratch her eyes out." Then she added, "But it would not have been easy, she would have put up one hell of a fight. So our sparring was verbal and much of it was left unsaid with a raised eyebrow or knowing look. She was good, your Honeysuckle." Yvette gave him a respectful look. "I'm sorry for my sarcasm, but this goddess was sitting by my bed, and I'd been led to believe she was a scrawny little child. Men!" The respectful look gave way to a withering glance.

"We never did any...."

"I know, I asked her, and little Miss Perfect wouldn't know how to tell a lie, would she?" She raised an eyebrow and waited to see the relieved look on his face, then added, "That's if you don't count the kiss at the mill!" She delighted at the look of horror on his face. "She was probably a minor then, wasn't she?"

"I, I suppose...."

Yvette was revelling in his discomfort. "Mind you, if you had been completely French it would not have stopped you, you would have taken her. Don't worry, darling, I know you'd never cheat on me. You are too much of an English gentleman, and little Honeysuckle would never have let you anyway!" She took his hand, suddenly more serious. "Jacques, she is lovely and good. You will be perfect together." She leaned across and kissed him on the lips. It was not a platonic kiss, it was sensual and full of promise. "I am French, and I do not have your silly hang-ups. So, as I said, while I still have you I will use you."

She stood up and pulled him to his feet, then led him

through the carriage door into the corridor and started to walk towards the rear of the train before stepping into the tiny bathroom and pulled him in with her. True to her word, she proved that she had no inhibitions. Like a wonderful cameo from an old film they both climaxed as the train entered a tunnel, the sudden change in air pressure and noise masking Yvette's scream.

Once back in their carriage they were silent. Yvette read a book and Jacques sat with a smile on his face. At first he was smiling about Yvette. She was an incredibly sensual woman and their sex-life had been thrilling from the first time they had made love. He remembered days in Paris, nights in small inns and auberges where they had made love and experimented, often after laying plans to destroy a nearby depot or bridge. Woods where they had lain in wait for a passing convoy or train, had witnessed their passion for each other. And the farm where the brothers had been bad farmers had played host to their carnal desires, as had the fastest lorry in France! They had been good times and the sex unbelievable, but he knew it was coming to an end and part of him was sad.

Then his thoughts turned to Honeysuckle and he had an overwhelming desire to see her. It had been ages since their last short meeting. How was she? What had happened with her boyfriend Simon? He couldn't help it, but suddenly it was Honeysuckle who had been with him in the tiny bathroom.

Yvette watched his face and thought his expression was the result of their passion. She was glad that he looked so happy, but sad that they would soon part.

The train finally rolled into the station at Treblinka, a loud blast on its whistle announcing their arrival. Yvette had enjoyed the long ride and part of her did not want it to end, realising it would be one of the last times they could be totally relaxed together. As she stepped from the train onto the platform she shuddered as she imagined the fear and trepidation her little sisters were feeling as they had stepped from another train a few years earlier.

The train's billowing smoke symbolically descended to engulf them, once again her life enveloped within a dark foreboding cloud. She knew this place would bring her heartbreak and her life would change yet again, but she was ready, and that dark side of her soul welcomed it.

"Well, Buster, I have just had imaginary sex with Honeysuckle in the toilet of a train. And not for the first time, I might add!"

Buster did not think imaginary sex was anything worth eating so showed little interest in the man's revelation. However his rustling in the carrier bag did get his attention, and the appearance of cheese and onion crisps, his devotion.

Fifteen

It was another wonderful late summer day. The man had taken the opportunity to walk up to the memorial on Tennyson's trail. It was a short but steep climb and the views quite fabulous from the top. When Buster was young he would not have been brought up here, the chalk cliffs dropped two hundred feet into the angry surf crashing against the rocks below. Rabbits found sanctuary in the cliff face from any pursuing dogs and more than one poor hound had taken the chase a step too far. The young Buster, being a rabbit chaser extraordinaire, was not well suited to the terrain. So it was only in his advancing years that Jacques had brought him up to the top of the Down with its threatening cliffs.

He had left his car at the farm in the valley, which boasted the finest cream teas on the Isle of Wight. Something Buster had been looking forward to on their return to the farm, and something Sophie had come to love too over the many years she had visited the island.

Back in the small garden by the farm's teashop, Jacques picked pieces from his scone and fed them to a drooling Buster.

"Another month or so and the cream teas will be over for the winter, old boy." He slipped the last piece into the expectant dog's mouth.

He liked the farm tearooms. They had proper bone china, and the delightful fresh-faced children who lived on the farm served homemade scones and cakes. He had known the family all his life and their Grandpa had been one of his closest childhood friends. Little Rosie brought him a fresh pot of hot water with which to freshen his teapot and squealed with delight as Buster licked her knee. Her whole face burst into a smile that reminded him of Honeysuckle when she was about seven years old.

Sophie had sat at the exact same table with him less than two years ago and devoured three of the tantalising scones along with a generous slice of almond cake and an impossible amount of Earl Grey tea, as full of life in her dotage as she had been in her youth.

"I think I must have some English blood in me," she had said many years before, "I like it here too much."

Armed with his fresh supply of tea, Jacques decided to stay in the garden to reminisce about Sophie.

Buster was more than happy. Every table had people sitting at it now and each table appeared to have food on it, and Buster knew just how to look half-starved!

Sophie had written her article for Paris Match and was now persona non grata with the French military establishment. This was a position she relished, but a position that was making it very difficult to return to Dien Bien Phu to do a follow-up about a number of the young soldiers she had met there, and previously written about. She had learned from Jacques that at least two of them were dead, and that the occupation of the airfield was not going well for the French.

Jacques sat opposite her in the club, Saphine's voice keeping her audience spellbound from the small stage. He had returned to Hanoi to report back to the High Command about his reconnaissance of the build-up of heavy artillery that the Vietminh had miraculously managed to facilitate, along with the insurgent aspects of the battle about to be played out at Dien Bien Phu.

"The fools got it completely wrong. There is going to be a blood bath. Somehow the Vietminh have managed to get a bloody arsenal of big guns on the ridges surrounding the airfield. All of them pointing down at the poor French below, and now they have anti-aircraft guns so it will be difficult to evacuate the troops. These dick-head generals still think they can defeat them in a battle. It will be carnage." Jacques was angry.

"I have to be there, Jacques. Can you take me back with you? I have to be on the front line. I'm a war correspondent. How can I report it if I'm not there? Please, Jacques, promise them I won't slag them all off. Please, Jacques," Sophie implored. "I'll make it worth your while!" She added mischievously.

"I'll see what I can do. I'm flying back the day after tomorrow. To be honest, if you show the boys your scar again they will just take their Resistance heroine back there anyway, regardless of any permissions." He paused. "It will be dangerous, Sophie. I mean it, we will take a spanking from the Vietminh. They are bloody good."

"Shut up! You know the more dangerous it is, the more I want to go, and the photos will be really powerful. With the right words I could really make a difference."

"Okay then, it's a deal. I'll just pick you up. We won't ask anyone's permission. I'm quasi freelance anyway." He smiled at her.

Saphine finished her set and came over to join them. Jacques poured a large glass of Chenin Blanc and passed it to her.

He watched rapt as her luscious red lips sought out the goblet and swallowed gently.

He was brought back to reality by Sophie's giggle as she watched the effect Saphine was having on him. Jacques looked at Sophie and offered a Gallic shrug by way of explanation, which resulted in a more resounding laugh from Sophie.

Saphine watched them both, once more baffled by their unspoken conversation, but no longer surprised by it. "Is he taking you then?" She asked Sophie.

"Of course, he can't say no to me, cherie!"

"Be careful, Sophie. Jacques says it will be very dangerous." Saphine was serious now.

"He will protect me as always. That is what our Jacques does." Mockingly, Sophie pinched his cheek.

"Let's hope I can this time," Jacques retorted a little grumpily, sensing the start of an onslaught from the pair of them as they teased their favourite man, as always treating him like a small boy.

The onslaught did not come, Sophie was too busy planning her trip back to Dien Bien Phu and the pictures she would take when she got there.

After a late supper, Jacques found other things to do with Saphine's sensual lips in the privacy of her apartment. They also spent the majority of the next day in bed, because Jacques needed the physicality of her welcoming body before he went back to the heat of the battle.. He was uneasy about the coming weeks, he was used to being the predator and the hunter did not like the idea of being hunted. And now Sophie was going to be with him, but he did not mind that. There had usually been a girl at his side when he went into combat. It felt right that way, and they were the best fighters he had ever known.

He called the loadmaster to tell him there would be an extra piece of cargo on the flight to Dien Bien Phu. He was more than happy to accommodate Mademoiselle Sophie, who he remembered well. For her part, Sophie undid an extra button on her fatigues to facilitate a smooth passage through the boarding process.

As the plane approached Dien Bien Phu they started to attract some anti-aircraft fire. Jacques was back in his Lysander over the fields of Normandy searching for the faint flares on the ground. He saw the runway lights appear several thousands of feet below them as the Flying Boxcar spiralled down over the airfield in an attempt to avoid the flack.

"I saw the anti-aircraft guns on a patrol, but they weren't using them then. They bloody well are now!" He shouted to Sophie as an explosion rocked the plane.

They landed safely and disembarked from the plane. They were shocked by what greeted them and it proved to be a precursor of things to come. By the end of the runway was a makeshift hospital with over a hundred wounded, and several hundred dead bodies.

"What has happened?" Jacques asked a medic carrying supplies into the tented morgue.

"These guys have been evacuated from Lai Chau. They were taking a battering from the 316th Vietminh. 2,100 left to come here, only 185 of them are still alive and most of them are in pieces, fucking carnage!" He hurried through the flap with his supplies.

Jacques turned to Sophie. "That's what happens when we expose our troops to them in their environment. They have lived, worked and fought in these monsoon lands for centuries. It's madness."

A distant voice called to him. "Jacques, when you've dumped your kit can you come to my office. I've got a job for you." It was Colonel Castries, the commander of the camp. Jacques nodded to him.

When Jacques returned from the meeting Sophie was alarmed at the look on his face. "What's the matter?"

179

"We've lost two complete patrols, good men, trying to gain intelligence on the exact location and numbers of the Vietminh. Apparently there has been a big build-up in the few days I've been away. They want me to take a patrol to try and find out what we are up against."

Instantly Sophie said, "Can I come?"

"No." He said it sharply. "Sorry, no, Sophie. It really is too dangerous. Your job is to report this war, not die in it. I want you alive to tell the world what a fuck up all this is."

Jacques was right of course, so she did not argue. "Be careful, cheri."

"Don't worry, I will. I want to read your articles." He smiled at her. "Going tonight, under cover of darkness, just four men. Don't know what we'll find."

Sophie busied herself piecing together the story of the survivors from Lai Chau and taking photographs of the wounded men. It was not a pretty story. Hundreds lay rotting in the jungle, others had been captured and a good many appeared to have deserted. The final option being one Sophie found hard to argue against. It kept her busy though, as she watched the clock waiting for Jacques's return listening to the rain of a tropical storm pounding like a machine-gun on the corrugated tin roof of her billet. Not that she would have slept much anyway as she lay awake pondering the depth of her feelings for him, and wishing a certain Honeysuckle did not exist.

The morning light brought an end to the incessant rain and the return of a very tired and very wet Jacques. As soon as she saw him, without thinking she ran towards him and threw her arms about him.

"That's nice," he said as he hugged her back. "Better stop though, they will all get jealous."

Sophie giggled. "Sorry, Jack. Public displays of affection are frowned on aren't they?" She feigned a mock embarrassment at her actions before hugging him again, this time adding a kiss and

180

saying, "I'm so glad you are safe. What was it like?"

"No scraps luckily, but the enemy is all around us and there are a hell of a lot of them just sitting in the hills around this valley, guns pointing at us. There are probably 50,000 men, at least 5 divisions. They are well armed with some bloody good artillery. How the hell they got it here, Christ alone knows! This could be a massacre, we only have about 16,000 men, tops." Jacques had a troubled look on his face. "What will happen now?" Asked Sophie.

"I don't know. I am going to make my report to the C.O. with a recommendation that all the men he has set up in positions around the valley to form the anchoring point of this 'fortress' are brought back and the whole lot shipped back out by Transport Command. Then they can find a battle they stand a remote chance of winning!" He suddenly laughed. "The guys tell me that he's called the seven fortifications we've dug in after his mistresses, names like Beatrice, Gabrielle and Dominique. Oh! and I particularly like Claudine. I think Sophie would be nice too wouldn't it? Except I'd hate to think anyone called Sophie would have an affair with that prick! Just think, when the shrapnel blows their leg off the boys can take heart from the fact that they are being slaughtered in a place with a nice name!" He almost spat the last words out.

"Will they listen to you, Jacques?"

"Of course not. I'm just the bloodhound that sniffs out the prey for their sport. I'm convinced they think it is all a game. Fucking idiots!" He suddenly relaxed and smiled at Sophie as his hand took hold of hers. "Don't worry, I'll look after you. If the Nazis couldn't kill us, I'll be damned if I will let the bloody French do it."

Sophie laughed. He had a huge smile on his perfect face and she knew he really believed he would look after her. "Actually I ... "

"I know. You'll look after me. Either way, we stick

together." He squeezed her hand. "You do know it's not too late for you to…"

"Oh shut up, Jacques. You know I love a fight. I'm as bad as the French generals. I am staying right here. There is one hell of a story about to unfold right in front of my eyes." She paused, not knowing whether to say the rest. "And you are here, Jacques. For now we are meant to be together."

His reaction made her heart leap. He took her in his arms and whispered in her ear, "I know, Sophie."

She held him tightly and fighting back tears, managed to say, "Go and talk to the fucking idiots!"

The reaction of the C.O. was exactly what Jacques had expected it to be. No thought given to retreat. He would take the fight to the enemy. That night the shelling began.

The next day patrols were sent to engage the enemy and diminish it's firepower. All returned bloodied. As Jacques had warned, they were completely surrounded by the Vietminh.

As the siege commenced Sophie recorded the events and observed the troops at the disposal of the French Command. It seemed to her that 'disposal' was the perfect description of the men, who were mostly French, but included many Algerian and Vietnamese. The fighting machine even included two Bordels Mobiles de Campagne, mobile field brothels, where Vietnamese and Algerian prostitutes attended servicemen. These girls fascinated Sophie. She had no problem with the oldest profession in the world and had no time for the moralising of her generation. After all, her best friend and Jacques's girlfriend had been a whore. What fascinated her was the way the girls' attention to duty naturally moved from pampering to the delights of the flesh, to caring for that same flesh as it became scarred and burned. Almost seamlessly they began to nurse the men they had pleasured. The brothels became hospitals and the beds used for healing not whoring. It was a natural progression, not driven by the authorities, but by the girls themselves.

It was a story she could not wait to write and her camera worked overtime on the fallen angels that cared for the men.

Another angel had found her way to the camp, a real nurse whose plane had been damaged during a medivac flight. Shortly after her arrival the runway had been bombed to such an extent that escape was impossible. Not that she would have left anyway, and under her direction the fallen angels worked wonders with the production line of war-ravaged bodies that were carried broken and bleeding from each of the seven fortified emplacements. The mistresses, Beatrice, Gabrielle and Anne-Marie witnessed the mutilation of hundreds of young French soldiers as shelling was followed by wave after wave of Vietminh attacks on the entrenched and battered French battalions. The French fought back though, and on one day, Elaine, mistress number five, changed hands a number of times as fierce trench warfare, reminiscent of the First World War, sent hundreds to meet their maker. Both French and Vietnamese.

The airfield was out of commission so any supplies had to be dropped by parachute from planes desperately trying to avoid the anti-aircraft fire expertly being delivered from the Vietminh. Supplies became sparse, but so did their intended recipients.

Throughout the siege, which lasted over three months Jacques fought courageously with his men. They conducted clandestine ops, in a vain attempt to locate the positions of elusive artillery that seemed to vaporise from known positions, and reappear on another hilltop. On a couple of occasions he was able to neutralise some guns, but he would often find wooden guns masquerading in place of the real things. They would sit there totally benign, yet more menacing than the real guns that appeared to have an itinerant life of their own.

Sophie had wanted to come with him on one of these forays into enemy territory, but he would not allow it. "This is not your fight, Sophie. You shoot your pictures and win a bigger war," he repeatedly would say to her.

Again, she knew he was right. She was gathering a portfolio of pictures and the written word that was compelling, but she desperately wanted to be at his side. Throughout the months their bond grew greater and they spent time together whenever they could. Often no more than five minutes at a time, but they were five precious minutes.

When Sophie was not gathering her ammunition she would help the medics as best she could, and became firm friends with the angels, fallen or otherwise.

After the first six weeks everyone in Dien Bien Phu knew what the outcome of the battle would eventually be, everyone except the Generals. It was a matter of survival and praying that their Commanding Officers would concede to the ever-increasing strength of the Vietminh. On May 7th 1954 the final assault took place. As each of the mistresses had fallen and the central positions captured, those who were able had fallen back on Isabelle where a garrison of sorts, still remained. Within their number were Sophie and Jacques.

From Isabelle the C.O. radioed the Generals in Hanoi and said, "The Viets are everywhere. The situation is very grave. The combat is confused and is going on all around us. I feel the end is approaching, but we will fight to the finish."

Jacques heard the voice on the other end of the line say, "Well understood. You will fight to the end. It is out of the question to run up the white flag after your heroic resistance." He shook his head in disbelief and knew he would either die, or the plan he had made for escape months previously would have to be put into action.

In reality neither actually happened, at least not according to his plan.

"Well, Buster. I think three scones is enough, don't you?" He handed the last piece to him, which Buster devoured with his usual enthusiasm. "You won't eat your dinner when we get back home." A statement the man knew to be untrue, as Buster was a Labrador and would only stop eating when he'd drawn his final breath.

At the word dinner, Buster ran to the car and sat waiting patiently for the man to let him in and take him home for some food. He felt quite peckish and could remember the aromas of the casserole the man had put in the oven before they had left the house.

Sixteen

"Come on Buster, let's visit the old mill before we go up onto the Warren."

There was a lovely walk along the old railway line that had once passed behind the mill. Now it was a cycle path with walks off into the woods that lined the banks of the Yar estuary. At the end of the line in Freshwater, a cup of tea and a teacake would await them.

Jacques loved to come here occasionally. It was still their place. The place she had first kissed him. He was not so keen that the path and cycle way had brought a glut of people to their special pool, which once could only be reached by rowing boat. But it was still beautiful and people had to walk through the trees to find it. The last time he'd been there someone was sitting by the water's edge and he was quite piqued that they should be there. 'You silly old fool,' he'd chided himself. It was a happy place, a place that others should enjoy. But he had not been back since, until today.

The mill's wheel no longer turned, but the building still played host to a number of happy families during the summer months. As they walked by, two children cast off in sea kayaks from the wall that manfully held the tide at bay at the side of the mill. A boy of about ten, and a girl with curly black hair perhaps five or six, hung on his every word as he gave her instructions. Jacques smiled.

It wasn't far, perhaps half a mile, and they left the hard-packed surface of the path for a narrow, dried mud path which wound it's way beneath encroaching ferns and through the trees to the water's edge. Ducking beneath overhanging branches and round the roots of a sapling that had not endured the winds of the previous week, they stepped out by the hidden pool. Good, there was no one there.

Buster watched the man sit on the rock and throw a small stick into the crystal clear water for him to retrieve. In his day, Buster had been something of a champion retriever, so knowing his role he stepped gingerly into the water, albeit without quite the same enthusiasm he once possessed.

The man watched the look of semi-indignation on Buster's face and laughed. "Okay, how about this then?" He produced a bone-shaped biscuit from his pocket, which a rejuvenated Buster relieved him of.

Buster could hear an audible sigh from the man, and knew it was time to settle at his side and wait for lunch.

Honeysuckle had her head on his shoulder and she was crying. Through tears she half-whispered, "I'm so sorry, Jacques."

Far too long had passed since he had seen her. When the fighting was over he had managed to write a number of letters, most of which she had received. In turn, she had replied to each one, most of which he had not received as he was constantly travelling. The ones he had received contained nothing of the news she had just given imparted. It could not be written. She had to tell him to his face.

He had finally arrived back unannounced the previous evening. He'd knocked on her door before going to see his parents, and had left six hours later. He did not see the floods of tears that engulfed Honeysuckle after he had gone.

It was a further three hours before he went to bed after he had caught up with his parents.

At ten o'clock in the morning he had met a strangely subdued Honeysuckle who, armed with a picnic and oars, had rowed him to their pool.

The previous evening and all the way back from Poland Jacques had felt like an excited schoolboy, his heart fluttering at the thought of finally seeing her again and palpitating when he did. At first he couldn't speak when he saw the look of sheer delight on her beautiful face. Quite naturally she had stepped into his out-stretched arms and pressed her head to his chest without saying a word.

Still holding her Jacques said, "I have so much to tell you, Honeysuckle," and without waiting for a reply or seeing her reaction, he started to explain all that had happened since he was last with her.

He described Yvette after she returned to France and explained how her remarkable recovery was down to a certain English girl who had visited her in hospital. How they had prepared the way for the advancing Allies, and taken Paris from the retreating Nazis.

Honeysuckle listened intently, enthralled by his news whilst dreading having to tell him hers. When he described the concentration camps and what they had found there she completely forgot about her own predicament, and simply sat in disbelief and shock at all he described. But what he told her about Yvette made her agonise even more about what she knew she had to tell him. The woman she thought had taken the most precious of things from her, was now a woman she could not help but feel compassion for.

"When we got to Treblinka it was as if she had taken the final step into the hell that had been awaiting her. Her mood changed and I knew the previous days had been the culmination of our journey as a couple, and so did she." Jacques had said.

"What happened there, Jacques?"

"At the camp it was remarkably easy to find out about her sisters. One of the survivors showed us the record of their deaths, then took us to where they had been murdered. From the main camp, where they were stripped of their clothing and had their heads shaved, he led us up a short hill that the S.S. cynically called Himmelstrasse, road to heaven. It was still lined with barbed wire. At the top they were marched into the gas chambers, where hopefully they will have died before their bodies were dragged out and thrown into pits full of burning bodies. The man displayed no emotion when he showed us these places, and neither did Yvette. She spent two hours kneeling by a temporary memorial at the site where we think they were buried. Initially I held her hand then stepped back to allow her time to grieve. I watched her, wanting to take her in my arms and tell her they are safe now, but I did not. Yvette was no longer there. Her spirit had gone."

"It must have been terrible." Honeysuckle touched his arm.

"Yes, but we had seen so many terrible things. What was terrible for me was knowing that the last spark of life in what had been a vibrant girl was flickering and dying." He paused. "The next few days Yvette spent gathering names of all those who had worked there. She hardly spoke during this time. When she had all the names she thought she could get, she turned to me and said, 'I still don't have them all. You can't help me any more. When I have them all, I will make them pay for what they have done. You must go now. Go to Honeysuckle and thank her for me.' I could not leave her like that and we still hadn't tried to find her parents, so I stayed for a while."

"What happened next?"

"She shot two known collaborators. One a local dentist who pulled out the gold teeth of the dead, and another who made the victims hair into jerkins for U-boat crews."

"What about her parents?"

"After Treblinka we went to Auschwitz in the vain hope that they may have survived. They had not, but three more collaborators met their maker. One of them being the man whose company installed and maintained the ovens that had gassed her parents along with thousands of others. More names were gathered and added to her death list, hearing of the deaths of the collaborators many others fled, fearing they would be next. I begged her to stop her indiscriminate killing and to try and pool resources with others who saw themselves as avengers. There was a man called Tuviah Friedman, a Polish Jew who had escaped from one of the camps. He was starting his own quest to hunt down any Nazi who had been involved in the extermination programme. I managed to get him to come and talk to Yvette. He was a good man and had managed to fight off the red mist that still engulfed her. They got on, united by their hatred. He was about to be appointed as Chief Interrogation Officer at Danzig Jail, where his role was to gain information from Nazis who'd been involved in the death camps." Jacques half-smiled to himself. "He even got Yvette to laugh when he described what his role would be. He was good though, giving her some direction for her hatred. He offered her a job with him in Danzig and a promise that together they would make them all pay. And privately to me, he promised he would look after her and address her need for revenge. I believed him." Jacques was thinking about what to say next and Honeysuckle waited as he found the words. He added simply, "So she went to Danzig with him and I pray that she is well."

Honeysuckle could see the affection he still felt for Yvette and she understood. "Don't worry, Jacques, Mr. Friedman sounds a good person. She will be fine." She knew Jacques had shared a life with Yvette that she could never be part of and what they had witnessed and done together must make it feel like several lifetimes.

"When she left, she kissed me one last time and said, thank you, darling Jacques, for everything. I will always love you, but you deserve more. You deserve Honeysuckle."

At these words Honeysuckle almost broke down. She had pulled him to her and lent her head on his shoulder, fighting back the tears.

Now, here by their pool, it was Jacques's turn to fight his emotions.

"I'm so sorry," she said again. "You know I love you more than life itself and nothing will ever change that, nothing can ever come between the way we feel about each other."

"Will you marry him?"

"I don't know yet." She moved her eyes away from his. It was too much to bear.

"How bad is he?" Jacques knew he had to be strong for them both.

"Pretty bad. They have been experimenting with a new surgery putting skin grafts on his face from other parts of his body. It has been going on for months and I know it must be agony." She looked at him, "You do understand, don't you, Jacques?" She was almost pleading with him.

Unfortunately Jacques did understand. It was so typically Honeysuckle, part of the reason why he loved her and why he would always love her. And he felt sorry for Simon. It was every pilot's worst nightmare, being trapped in the cockpit of a burning aeroplane.

Not waiting for his reply she continued, "He asked me to marry him just as he was about to get on the ferry back to the mainland and report for duty, then he handed me the ring. 'Think about it, just think,' he said. I didn't give him an answer. If only I had said no then. But now, how could I refuse him after what has happened?" Her eyes again pleaded with him.

"I understand, Honeysuckle. I know it must be awful for you both. This damned war has ruined so many lives."

All he wanted to do was to take her head in his hands and kiss her passionately and beg her to change her mind, but he did not. They were so much alike that they may just as well have been one person. He would have done exactly the same thing, and in a way he had done with Yvette. "I love you. You know that. I will try and be there for you."

"I love you too. I'm so sorry." Finally she resumed the tears of the previous evening, this time in his arms.

"That was a shit day, Buster!" Jacques tickled the old dog's ears.

Buster perked up and made a theatrical production of sniffing the lunch bag.

"You and your stomach, old boy! Come on then, lunch."

Seventeen

Jacques stepped out of his front door with Buster by his side, and noticed the wind had brought the first leaves down from the old oak tree by the garage.

Buster sniffed a couple of leaves before re-acquainting himself with the trunk of the tree, then trotted off down the drive to the gate.

The wind had abated and it was a pleasant early autumn day. Not many leaves had started to change their hue, but a few of the older trees had given up the fight to keep their foliage.

As they walked up the chalky path towards the bench, the man watched the sailing boats in the Solent down below, which had arrived too late to capture the wind that had been blowing the evening before. Those boats had now migrated to other parts.

He noticed Buster was lagging a few yards behind instead of his usual habit of leading. "Come on, Buster. Keep up, we won't stay too long today."

At the bench Jacques stroked the lettering on the plaque, lovingly tracing the O, an E and the H. He always did this whenever he arrived and also when he left, then he sat down after lifting Buster's back legs onto the wooden seat.

"Where to today, old man?" Answering his own question, "Oh yes, we have unfinished business in Vietnam, don't we?"

Vietnam sounded a bit like ham to Buster who looked questioningly at the man.

Another shell slammed into the earth about fifteen yards away bringing a shower of debris down onto their heads.

"Jesus, Jacques, that was close! So what's the plan?" As always Jacques could see Sophie was not scared, in fact she found it thrilling.

"Tonight, under cover of darkness we go on our holidays to Laos."

"What should I pack?"

"Some light fatigues to travel in and something for the evening when we get there. Don't forget your bikini for the pool." Another hail of debris covered her animated face.

"What about the rest of us, can we come?" A mockingly plaintive voice asked from across the bunker.

It had never been part of Jacques's escape plan to include a whole platoon, he had anticipated making the journey when the battle was virtually over. He had no desire to be a prisoner of war and there was Sophie to consider, she must never suffer that again. The next morning would surely see the final push by the Vietminh to take the last of the mistresses. There were still several hundred survivors and, unbelievably a good many of them wanted to fight. Others were not so keen, and many could not. Jacques had fought beside these brave soldiers for months and those who wanted to escape deserved a chance to avoid captivity. They deserved their chance of freedom rather than just raising a white flag. Jacques had the skills to offer them that

194

chance. "Okay, how many want to come with us on holiday?"

Four hours later the main body of the garrison that guarded Isabelle, the 5th mistress, made an attempt to break out. Only 68 troops, an Englishman and a French woman succeeded. They did so because of Jacques's ability to move undetected through terrain which although he had grown to hate, he had also learnt to understand and make his friend.

Once through the enemy lines he had them move in small groups, each group led by men with whom he had done his reconnaissance. He took five troops and Sophie, who had taken the weapons he'd given her and used them to stunning effect during their push for freedom. Once through the enemy lines they met no resistance. It seemed that the Vietminh were happy not to pursue them. They had their prize, which included well over 10,000 prisoners of war.

Once in Laos, Jacques and Sophie were easily able to return to Hanoi where they learnt of the scale of the defeat. On May 8th 1954 the Geneva Conference began, one day after the Garrison had finally capitulated in Dien Bien Phu. The conference had been arranged to negotiate the future of Indochina. Ho Chi Minh walked into the conference with reports of his troops' victory in all the newspapers. The French were humiliated and Vietnam partitioned, the communist Democratic Republic in the North and a French supported State of Vietnam in the South. This temporary partition was supposed to end with elections, which would unite the country. After their ignominious defeat the French withdrew all their troops from Vietnam within two years, however the election never took place and the Americans replaced the French support for the South in an attempt to stop the spread of communism.

Of the 10,000 captured troops in Dien Bien Phu, less than 4000 survived to be repatriated, and the Vietnamese fallen angels were sent for re-education!

Saphine saw her future in the South and moved to Saigon

where Sophie and Jacques also relocated for a short while. After the war they had a few good months together during which time Sophie produced some of her most incisive journalism. She wrote articles illustrated with photographs that, in part may well have hastened the French withdrawal from Vietnam, and most certainly altered the French people's perception of colonialism.

Though in a different club, but still as loved in the South and as big an icon as in Hanoi, Saphine's voice filled the room. Sophie looked at the man she knew she loved and idly wondered what it would be like to live with him in a small fisherman's cottage and cook his meals. She quickly put the ghastly thought out of her mind. She was quite happy to have lived another life with him.

"Will you go back and see Honeysuckle now, Jacques?" Lifting the gin and tonic to her lips. A drink she now loved because she associated it with Jacques.

"I don't know if I can. I tried it for a couple of years and it was hell." He was perfectly serious.

"What then? There is no work here for you anymore."

"Isn't there?" He had a wicked grin on his face.

"What are you up to, Jack?" She put the glass gently back on the table and gave him an almost threatening look. "Come on, tell me."

Jacques loved that he'd kept a secret from his best friend all this time, but had decided she should know after all they had been through together.

"Come on, spill the beans or I'll..."

"You'll what?"

Grasping for a threat she said, "I'll make you come to bed with me and Saphine. You know you couldn't bear it!"

"Okay, you win. Do you really think I've been working for the French all this time?"

"What? But you have. You take orders from them." She was incredulous.

196

"Yes I do, but I take orders from someone else too." He was enjoying this.

"I can't stand it, you bastard. Tell me!"

"Okay, okay, I'm British. Am I not? I work for the British government."

"And..."

"Being near Honeysuckle and seeing her all the time was unbearable, and the situation, ah well, you know the situation. Anyway, after the War the people who set up the Special Ops Executive asked if I'd work for them within the Secret Intelligence Service. I declined, wanting to be near Honeysuckle. When that didn't work out, I thought, what have I got to lose? It seemed there was still plenty of intrigue in the World and battles, predominately against communism, to be fought."

"More!"

"The British Secret Intelligence Service wanted my unique skills to be put to good use. The Cold War was brewing nicely with the Russians, but I didn't speak Russian. I did speak French though, and the powers that be believed Indochina would develop into another front against the threat of communism from China. My job? To assess that threat on the ground and assess the ability of the French to deal with it."

"You are still a spy? You bastard, why didn't you tell me?" She was really rather angry.

He leaned across and took her hand. "I was not spying during any of the stuff that we went through. I was fighting for the French and for our survival. All I've done is write a couple of reports. Actually, I used rather a lot of your material in them! If I was a spy, I was not really spying on the French, it was the Vietminh that I was directing my energies against." He waited, then added more seriously, "This is not over, Sophie. The Americans will carry on this war against the Vietminh and I'm not sure they will be any better equipped to fight them than the French. Some of what I have learned in the past couple of years may just save some lives on both sides, who knows?"

"Will you fight with the Americans then?" She was calm now.

"I don't know. It is not a battle I want fought at all. These are good people, they do not deserve to have their country turned into killing fields for other peoples' political ambitions." He looked over towards Saphine. "She does not deserve it."

"What will you do?"

"After I return to London, I am to go to Washington and liaise with the U.S. military. After that, I don't know."

"And Saphine? Do you love her?" It was not a jealous question.

"Yes, in a way, but I love you even more."

"But not as much as Honeysuckle." She looked away. Why had she said that?

"In a different way, Sophie. I'm sorry, I can't explain it." He desperately did not want to hurt Sophie. Saphine was not a problem, Sophie had never been bothered by their sexual relationship. He knew that, but he also knew that Sophie was more in love with him than her demeanour ever showed, and increasingly Honeysuckle had become the object of a caustic comment or barbed remark.

Sophie had gathered herself together again. "You don't have to, Jacques. I should not have said that. You belong to Honeysuckle. I have always known that. I am being childish."

Wanting to change the subject, Jacques asked, "What will you do next?"

Sophie was fine now. "I shall return to Paris and be civilised for a while, then I will probably come back here to report on the war you think will come. Who knows? If you are also here we may be able to have sex again in the jungle!"

They both laughed and each of them was taken back to the night they had spent in each other's arms in Dien Bien Phu.

"It was good wasn't it?" She said, knowing exactly what he

was thinking.

"Yes, it was. It was the best night I have ever had." He smiled at her.

"Better than Saphine?" One eyebrow rose as she spoke.

"Yes, better than Saphine." He knew what answer to give.

"Thank you." She had a smile on her lips, and perhaps a tear in her eye.

Saphine was suddenly by their side and saw the tear that had now appeared in Sophie's eye. "Are you alright, cherie?" Throwing Jacques an accusing look.

"I'm fine. I will be going back to Paris for a while and am just a bit sad at leaving." She wiped the tear away and threw back the rest of her drink. "More G and T, Jack old man!" Pushing her empty glass across the table to him.

"I'll be right back. The usual for you, Saphine?"

"Mmm, please." Saphine sat down next to Sophie and put her arm around her. "You'll be back soon." Jacques could hear her words fade as he walked to the bar.

Three weeks later Jacques boarded a B.O.A.C aeroplane in Kuala Lumpur bound for London. One hour earlier Sophie had stepped aboard an Air France flight for Paris. It had been a sad moment. Neither had wanted to leave the other, to walk away from the perfect relationship that could have been so much more and at times had been so intense. It felt to them both that their parting would mark an end to the remarkable bond that they had formed during their time in Vietnam. But it was not an end. They promised to stay in touch and half-hoped that Vietnam would see them reunited again one day.

Onboard the plane the airhostess handed Jacques a copy of The London Times. Hearing her English accent, he felt as if he was   back in Blighty. He realised how little he had spoken English since his arrival arrive in Vietnam. He had missed it.

"A cup of tea, Sir?"

"Yes please, that would be lovely. Thank you."

He found himself pondering how sad he was to be leaving Sophie and to be leaving his exotic sex kitten, Saphine. And under the circumstances he and Honeysuckle had found themselves in, how much was he really looking forward to seeing her again?

"Well, that is what I was thinking, Buster. I couldn't help it. They were two astonishing women you know, quite beautiful, both of them."

Buster looked up at him. 'What was he talking about now?' But talking usually meant remembering was over and he was hungry, so he arranged his position to accept the soon-to-be proffered food.

Eighteen

The man pulled the collar of his Timberland jacket together in an attempt to keep the cold wind out. It was the coldest day yet. Autumn was definitely on the way.

Buster seemed quite chipper today, leading the way past the barrows and along the path through the gorse bushes towards the bench. He stopped suddenly in his tracks and looked aghast.

Someone was sitting on the bench where his lunch would be served. Nobody ever sat there, it was his bench. If he could have been bothered he would have growled at them, instead he turned and looked beseechingly at the man with a 'do-something' look on his greying face.

The man laughed at Buster's indignant look and said, "Good morning," to the elderly couple sipping the steaming liquid they had in a cup and flask. "It's a good day for a hot drink. Winter's not too far away now."

"Good morning. You're right, the wind is quite bracing. We

thought we would take a rest before we do the next part of the coastal walk. This is a beautiful spot, quite perfect, we have saved the best till last. We just got to get back to Yarmouth now, and we will have walked all around the island."

It was the lady who did the talking. She was perfectly dressed for hiking and even had a wonderful old knotted wooden staff by her side.

"It's a beautiful walk if the weather is kind to you. I did it many years ago with my wife and still take this old chap on the parts I loved the most," replied Jacques.

Buster was not happy. Why was the man talking to these usurpers in a friendly manner, so he grumbled his displeasure.

"Would your dog like a sandwich? We have far too many," the woman asked.

"Oh yes, he likes sandwiches a lot!"

Buster knew the word sandwich and he stepped towards the lady in anticipation. There followed a rustling in her rucksack and a huge doorstep of bread appeared with ham hanging out of it.

Buster couldn't help himself. He sat up and begged. He hadn't done it since he was little older than a puppy. How demeaning he'd thought, but for such a prize he would do anything.

Jacques laughed. "He hasn't done that in years. You are honoured."

"No, we are honoured," and she handed the perfectly balanced dog the finest sandwich he had ever seen. Who, to Jacques's surprise, took it gently from her hand before devouring it in three bites! "My, he likes his food doesn't he?"

By now Buster was sitting on the man's lap, who had still not spoken, and was positioning his head on the lady's thigh with pleading eyes.

"He's quite a character. What is his name?" She asked.

"This is Buster. He seems to like you. I'm sorry. Get down,

202

Buster." Jacques went to pull his collar.

"It's okay, we love dogs. Had one like him ourselves once." It was the silent man, who was scratching Buster's back. "Anyway, this must be his bench. I saw the look on his face when he first spied us sitting on it, and we must be on our way, so we will leave you two in peace." He smiled at Jacques, and for a second Jacques was reminded of Simon's face before he was so grotesquely burned.

Buster was trying to lick the face of the lady, who obviously loved his attention. "You have Buster's approval now."

"So it seems, but we must love him and leave him. Come on Jim, we should make the four o'clock ferry to Lymington if we get on. It has been a pleasure meeting you both."

"And you. Enjoy the last part of your walk. It's particularly nice by Fort Victoria through the woods that border the edge of the beach."

Buster scrambled to the floor and they were gone. He took a few steps after them in case any more sandwiches fell out of her bag, but they failed to materialise so he returned to the bench and unaided sat himself down next to the man with his head in it's customary position.

"You were a lucky boy, weren't you?" Buster didn't know what lucky was. He assumed it was the same as being an exceptional hunter with the good sense to recognise some very nice people sitting on his bench who were easy prey!

Jacques was still thinking about Simon's face. He had been back on the island for about four months. Simon was about to return from the Burns Unit in East Grinstead where Sir Archibald McIndoe was treating him.

Simon was now a fully paid up member of The Guinea Pig Club, a title chosen after the Battle of Britain when the unit was first established. It typified the humour and backbone of those who had been treated there. Guinea pigs, because that is quite literally what they were, pioneering the way in plastic surgery.

The club contained patients, doctors and nurses along with benefactors. All notes taken at the meetings had to be short because the secretary had his hands seriously burned and could only write slowly and badly. Any incumbent in the position of club secretary always had to have burnt legs so he could not run away with the money!

Honeysuckle had visited Simon once a week and each time had stayed overnight in a nearby hotel. She had told Jacques that they were doing a fantastic job with him, but he had not actually seen Simon for himself. He had seen burns and knew all about suffering, but he sat on his Father's fishing boat thinking about what Simon would look like. Would this reconstructive surgery leave him as handsome as he had been before? He was pretty sure it would not, but he really had no idea what he would look like. All that he did know was that he had enormous respect and compassion for the man who had suffered inside that burning Spitfire, and for the woman who visited him each week. The woman he loved.

It had been an awkward four months. Honeysuckle lived next door, but it was as if she went out of her way to avoid him. Whenever he did see her, his stomach became knotted and he often found it hard to find the words that had so readily been available between them all of their lives.

For her part, Honeysuckle longed to be with Jacques but avoided him as best she could in an attempt to ease the pain. Whenever she saw him all she wanted was to hold him.

Jacques started to fish with his Father once again. It filled the days and after the horrors of war gave him just about enough excitement to stop him going insane. His parents knew the misery both he and Honeysuckle were experiencing and Big Jacques tried his hardest to make each day onboard the boat as much fun as he could. When he was not entertaining his son he sat and listened in awe to the stories Jacques told him of his exploits during the War.

They were good days, but the nights were not. It was as if the two households who had loved each other and virtually coexisted for nearly thirty years put up a barrier to stop their children suffering. Jacques decided to put an end to it. It was madness, Honeysuckle and he had to find a better way to deal with what had happened.

He knocked on the door and Honeysuckle answered. It had become the norm for her to panic when she saw his face. "Bonjour, Jacques, how are you?" Delivered, as always in French.

"Bien, Honeysuckle. We must talk."

"I know. Come in, Maman is at the Church." She held the door open and followed him into the living room.

"We have to find a way of dealing with this. It is eating me up inside." Jacques stood with his back to her by the fireplace; he was looking at the photograph of her Father, seeing the resemblance to Honeysuckle for the first time.

"Me too, I can't bear it, Jacques." She stepped forward and wrapped her arms around him.

Jacques closed his eyes and held her hands against his chest. He knew there was more she wanted to say, so waited as his heart raced.

"I will marry Simon when he comes back, just as soon as we have made the arrangements. I don't love him, but I believe I will grow to. He is a good man and the way he has dealt with what has happened to him is inspiring. The hospital and the poor members of the Guinea Pig Club are incredible. Being there with them has opened my eyes to what people are capable of enduring with humour and camaraderie. When Simon comes home he will need me. I don't see his scars anymore, all I see is a remarkable man. But others will see a mutilated and scarred monster and he will not have the support of his friends in the hospital. I know it bothers him, though he would never say anything."

Jacques always knew that is what Honeysuckle would do and he screwed his eyes together forcing back the tears.

"There is something though, my darling Jacques." She hesitated.

"Go on." Jacques was almost whispering.

"I love you and always will." Still searching for the right words, she continued, "I always thought we would be together one day, even when I found out about Yvette, but now I believe we probably have different destinies. I cannot give myself to you, but I can give you something I have kept for you. Something that is yours, and has always been yours."

Jacques turned to face her and saw the look on her face, the look he had first seen in their pool the day she had kissed him like a siren.

"I am a virgin, Jacques. If you take my virginity you will always have a part of me that I want you to have. Now, come."

Without saying another word or waiting for his reaction she took his hand and led him up the narrow staircase to her bedroom. The room where, as children she had shared everything with her hero and as a young woman had shared her secrets.

When she turned and faced him by the side of the bed, Jacques thought no woman had ever looked so beautiful.

They made love, clumsily at first but slowly growing accustomed to each other's needs. Though an accomplished lover, Yvette had seen to that, Jacques treated her like a porcelain doll. Honeysuckle, though scared and naive in the art of lovemaking gave herself to him with total abandon.

They both knew it was not perfect, but it did not matter. Their lovemaking was almost spiritual, each offering them self to the other. It was the natural and necessary culmination of all that their lives had been until that day. They were one, each part of the other and always would be, regardless of other partners.

Unknown to them, Audrey, Honeysuckle's Mother came in

206

when they were making love. She did not stay, aware of what was happening, but went round to see Jacques's parents where she stayed for several hours to give them time together. All of them were aware of the significance of the moment and were happy for their children. It would probably be the only time they knew physical love with each other and they would not deny them that communion.

Eight days later Simon stepped off the ferry to be greeted with open arms by Honeysuckle and with a kiss on his cheek. She always kissed the side that had suffered the worst of the burns. It was her way of letting him know that she didn't find his disfigurement abhorrent.

Audrey was also there supporting her daughter and greeted Simon in the same way she always had.

Jacques watched from inside the tearooms in the High Street. He felt like an interloper with no part to play in the drama that was about to unfold. He found himself thinking in exactly those dramatic terms. Was it to be an uplifting tale of one man's fight against adversity, or a tragedy? From his vantage point he found it hard to think of it as anything other than the latter.

They didn't see him as they walked past the tearooms heading towards Honeysuckle's cottage, but Jacques saw them. It was impossible to see any expression on Simon's discoloured contorted face, but he could see concern on Honeysuckle's as she noticed everyone staring at Simon.

Jacques deliberately made no attempt to see either of them for a few days. Not because he was feeling any antagonism towards Simon, but because he thought Simon needed some time to adjust to his new world, and for Honeysuckle to adjust to his being there.

Simon's parents were both dead. He had said that it was a blessing that they should not see their new mutant son. So he stayed for a week with Honeysuckle and Audrey whist making plans to return to Farringford House and arranging for some new staff to attend to him there. During the War it had become run down, particularly since his Father's passing and even more so during the months that he had spent in hospital receiving numerous agonising skin grafts.

After the first few days had passed, Jacques decided it was time to go and face them. Tea and scones were served by the fire in the living room of the house where just a couple of weeks previously Jacques had experienced the most intense moment of his life. But now, to his surprise all that tension had gone. The object of his desire was still there and just as desirable as she had ever been, but it was sadness not jealousy that he was feeling.

"Simon has a plan, Jacques," Honeysuckle said excitedly.

"Go on then, tell me," he said it as if he was her older brother once again, and he noticed it in his tone. Was that to be his new role? He dismissed the thought and decided to revisit it later.

"A hotel. He wants to make Farringford into a hotel and we shall run it." Honeysuckle was still excited.

"Return the old girl to some of its former glory, poets and posh-totty on the lawns. What do you think?" Simon's voice had not changed one iota. The mask had contorted into a strange shape that in time Jacques would come to recognise as a smile.

"It sounds a fantastic idea." Jacques was finding it difficult not to stare at Simon's face.

"Right, first rule, old boy. If we are to be friends you have to get used to this porridge of a face. So have a good look now, crack your jokes and we can get on." The face contorted once again into a 'smile.'

Simon's words took Jacques completely by surprise. "Was I.."

"Yes. I don't care, getting used to it. Best meet it head on though, and get it over with. Mind you, I only want good jokes.

Ones I can use myself." The smile appeared again.

"Do that smile again."

Honeysuckle was watching the interaction intently.

"What, this one?" One side of his face sagged.

"Yes." To Honeysuckle's surprise, Jacques managed to mirror the exact movement. Simon roared with laughter, which moved the face into another impossible contortion, which Jacques tried to mimic, but with less success.

Audrey watched aghast as the two of them sat gurning at each other like two four-year-olds. Honeysuckle just giggled.

Eventually they managed to gain control of their laughter and their faces. Simon sighed and took a sip of tea, which heralded another bout of hilarity as Jacques copied him yet again.

"Come on you two, calm down. It's like having small children again." It was Audrey.

"Sorry, Audrey." Jacques winked at Simon who tried to wink back, the result being tea spluttered everywhere as Jacques tried to fight back another laugh.

The bond was formed. Jacques and Simon were to become good friends especially when they were alone together without Honeysuckle. When she was with them there was a strained atmosphere between the two of them that hopefully Simon never picked up on. To each other it was obvious that they felt the same sadness at the loss of what might have been, and it was hard to move beyond it.

Jacques watched Honeysuckle's relationship develop with Simon, often from afar as he did not seek out their company, and it became obvious that they were becoming closer. It was also obvious that Honeysuckle genuinely did not find Simon's deformities repellent. Jacques became convinced she did not even see them, as was the case with all in West Wight who saw him on a regular basis. Simon dealt with his disfigurement with such good humour he rapidly became loved by everyone.

It was when Jacques was alone with Honeysuckle that the

problems arose, which happened rarely. Jacques made sure of that. He was not jealous of Simon as his relationship with Honeysuckle did not seem to fit any of the accepted norms. Given Honeysuckle's caring nature and Simon's incredible strength of character it seemed to work quite naturally and Jacques accepted it. Although in accepting it he discovered it did not alter the way he felt about her.

Five months after Simon's return he married Honeysuckle in the Church in the middle of Yarmouth. It was an extraordinary affair. The Guinea Pig Club turned out in force, along with the majority of the town.

On the Thursday before the wedding Jacques met the Club members in the George Hotel, where they were staying for Simon's stag night. It was the funniest night of his life. His sides hurt from laughing from the humorous way they described their tragic exploits. All of them were heroes who showed humility in the face of suffering and amongst them, Simon was a star. No, Jacques was not jealous nor did he begrudge Simon a prize. If only that prize could have been someone else.

The wedding took place on a perfect summer day. The congregation was a mixture of salty fishermen and an alien species, which formed a moving Guard of Honour as Simon walked out of the Church with Honeysuckle on his arm. Jacques's Father, who she had asked to give her away, escorted Honeysuckle up the aisle. His son stood at the back of the Church agonising at the irony of the gesture.

The reception took place on the lawn by the water's edge at The George. Fuelled by the spirit of the Guinea Pig Club members, it was a lively affair and the most joyous wedding Jacques ever attended, and Honeysuckle, what of Honeysuckle? She glowed radiantly as the centrepiece to it all. Jacques constantly found himself staring at her, wondering at her beauty and what might have been.

Did Jacques enjoy it? No, but nobody would have known

and he could have coped with it, had it not been for one unexpected moment.

It was late, and he was alone with Honeysuckle in the garden. Jacques had asked her to go for a stroll. His intention was to wish her happiness in her marriage and begrudgingly yet in a magnanimous way relinquish his claim on her. A gesture he knew to be both childish and churlish.

"It's done then, Honeysuckle." He stood staring across the Solent.

"Yes, it's done, Jacques."

He turned towards her to deliver his carefully prepared speech, but before he could start she put her arms around his neck and kissed him. A proper kiss, a lover's kiss, pressing her whole body against his.

She pulled away and said, "I still love you, Jacques. Don't ever underestimate me or doubt my ability to love you." She turned and walked back to her husband.

Jacques stood watching her as she walked towards the hotel, he was in total shock. Whiter than white in her wedding dress, the perfect and angelic Honeysuckle had fragrantly accosted him. Was it the alcohol she had consumed, or had she meant what her tongue and body had said to him?

It was the last time they talked to each other that evening and it was two weeks until they saw each other again. Honeysuckle and Simon had taken a honeymoon in London and visited the theatre and museums. They stayed at the Ritz and attended the ballet and the opera, they went to some of the finest restaurants and danced in the hotel. Later Honeysuckle told him that it had, in part, been an assault on society to see how it would accept Simon, as well as being their honeymoon.

Jacques did not ask, nor did Honeysuckle proffer how their honeymoon had been, but she told him the assault on society was a success and no longer held any fears for them. Neither did she make any attempt to kiss him again, even though every fibre of his body wanted her to.

The refurbishment of Farringford was gaining pace, and Honeysuckle immersed herself in its organisation. The money was available to develop the hotel, but for Farringford to survive as a country house the project had to be a success.

After their return from London Simon and Honeysuckle moved into Farringford. They had their own rooms on the ground floor, but the rest of the building was converted into a hotel. Jacques visited several times and worked with Simon in the grounds creating paths and plantings. The stuck-up child that Jacques remembered no longer existed. Simon was not afraid to get his hands dirty, and worked tirelessly to create what had now become Honeysuckle's dream as well as his own.

During all of this Jacques never spent more than a few moments alone with her and she never referred to the kiss on her wedding day. Jacques wondered if she even remembered.

Farringford was progressing ahead of schedule and it's opening had been planned for the following spring. But by Christmas enough refurbishment had been completed that Honeysuckle decided to open the hotel to the public for two weeks as a trial and to get the name known in the correct circles.

The home of Alfred Lord Tennyson was advertised in The Times and the finest periodicals. Within days the bookings began, within a week their limited rooms were full. From the 23rd December to the 2nd January, Honeysuckle played hostess to twenty romantics, all of whom were enthralled by their hostess and her welcome.

Jacques played no part in any of this and at first neither did Simon. "Best keep me hidden," were his words, "I'm not really front of house material," but in fact he was, the ultimate romantic in an age that needed romance and it's heroes.

On New Year's Eve they had a Ball for their guests and a number of invited local residents. Well over a hundred attended, it was a triumph and it had all been orchestrated by Honeysuckle.

Jacques exchanged his fisherman's overalls for a dress suit and black tie, and then along with his parents and Audrey attended the first of Farringford's New Year Balls.

Big Jacques's moustache twitched with pride at everything his surrogate daughter had achieved. Jacques was equally proud of the woman he loved. She was radiant as she greeted them in reception with Champagne and canapés, a goddess in her heaven effortlessly charming all in attendance.

Jacques enjoyed himself, and the romantics seemed to enjoy him. Honeysuckle had made sure they knew all about the French Resistance fighter who would be there. Jacques's natural charm did the rest. One couple had brought their eighteen-year-old daughter with them who at that tender age found Jacques particularly exciting. It provided hours of amusement for both Honeysuckle and Simon as they watched him try to extricate himself from the snares she kept laying for him.

"You're encouraging her," Jacques said a little brusquely to Honeysuckle.

"I might be, but it has been a long time since you've had a kiss, isn't it?" Honeysuckle looked at him with desire in her eyes. "Perhaps you need one."

She was doing it again. All she had to do was look at him that way and he was powerless. Months had passed and he was dealing with the situation as best he could, then she would say something, or say nothing, but with a look that left him defenceless.

He didn't have time to reply, she was gone. The rest of the evening was ruined for him, all he wanted was to kiss her. He did not. Instead he kissed the eighteen-year-old who, despite her romantic leanings had not yet learnt how to kiss.

What Jacques did not know was that Honeysuckle was as desperate for his kiss as he was for hers and that she had fully intended to rectify the situation that night, had she not witnessed him kissing the said eighteen-year-old.

A few frosty months followed as Honeysuckle tried to deal with her own self-acknowledged jealousy. As winter thawed, so did the reception Jacques received and by April the hotel was ready to open and Jacques was forgiven.

A Grand Opening Ball brought eighty socialites from London, and Jacques from Yarmouth. The evening started with poetry readings and ended with fireworks.

While the fireworks entertained her guests Honeysuckle took Jacques's hand, and led him away from the house to the stables. Once there she took the kiss she had been agonising about since New Years Eve, the kiss he'd denied her.

During the kiss their tongues made love and neither wanted it to end. They stayed longer than they should have done, but it told Jacques that the kiss at her wedding was not driven by alcohol but by her heart.

"I love you, Jacques. Please forgive me and try to understand, darling." Honeysuckle was nearly crying.

"I do understand and it is why I love you too," Jacques replied.

After that they were able to talk more openly with each other. It seemed that these stolen kisses were confirmation of their feelings. However infrequent they were an affirmation of their unspoken vows, the vows that were exchanged the day she had given herself to him.

Another summer passed and Farringford House Hotel became legendary. The pull of Tennyson brought people in their droves to the idyllic house nestling at the foot of the chalk downs that led to the Needles. Running it was hard work, but rewarding both spiritually and financially.

It became a huge part of Honeysuckle's life. In one way she loved Simon, but it was not in the way she loved Jacques and she never wanted it to be. The passion she felt for him ate away at her. She would plan a kiss for months knowing that is all she could physically have of him, and knowing it would never be enough for them. She thought of him constantly, and it seemed the only time she was not thinking of him was when she was immersed in hotel business. She recognised this and it became the weapon she used to cope with her obsession. Though not the same way, the hotel became her passion and she devoted herself to it.

Jacques watched with admiration as she built then ruled over her empire, whilst Simon worked tirelessly to help her. What was Jacques's input? Fish. Jacques and his Father supplied them with fish. The best French fish caught in English waters! For Big Jacques it was enough, he was content. Jacques was not.

A life spent catching fish and a kiss once every six months from the woman he idolised was just not enough for Jacques, after the adrenalin-filled world he'd been part of for so long.

It was on the boat one day that his life changed. They had just checked their lobster pots on the way back into port when Big Jacques said, "This life is not for you, son. I see it in your eyes. You don't love the fish like I do and what you do love, you can't have." It was a statement of fact, and exactly right.

Jacques looked up at his Father, the man whose nationality had shaped his own life. "I know."

"Then you must go, mon fils. Find a life that will make you happy."

"What about you, Papa?"

"Ha! How do you think I got on before you were born and during the War?"

"Okay, okay, point taken. I will think about it, Papa."

"Pass me that pot. You are a terrible fisherman anyway." The moustache rose to tickle his ears as he grinned.

Two more visits to Farringford without being able to take Honeysuckle in his arms and the decision was made.

When he was demobbed, as part of his final debrief he was

offered a job working for the Ministry of Defence in MI6, which had amalgamated with the Special Operations Executive. He had declined, but now it seemed the perfect escape from the hollow life he found himself living. The life that was slowly drowning his spirit

He telephoned his old handler, Vera Atkins and left for London seven days later.

Before he left there was one thing that he had to do, something he found as hard as anything he had ever done. He telephoned Honeysuckle and asked her to meet him where, as children, they had watched the dogfight between the Spitfire and the Messerschmitt.

When he arrived she was already there. Standing with her dark curls blowing in the wind that whistled up from Alum Chine below. She wore a tweed skirt and tight-fitting sweater that hugged her figure. It wasn't cold, yet exposed on the Warren she looked vulnerable as if she'd rushed out without picking up her coat or a hat, anxious to get there as quickly as she could.

When he'd called she was in her office thinking about him. When he spoke she knew instantly why he wanted to talk to her. Instinctively she knew that he was leaving, he didn't have to say anything. She almost ran from the office to her car, and drove as fast as she could the short distance to the Warren.

Jacques stopped about five yards away and watched her, as always his heart accelerated. She hadn't heard him approach, tears were rolling down her cheeks when she turned and saw him.

"How long have you been watching me?" She half-whispered.

"All your life," he replied. He raised his arms and she stepped forward into his embrace without speaking. There she cried until there were no more tears.

Eventually she managed to say, "When?"

"Tomorrow."

216

"Where?"

"London."

Then the question she needed to ask. "Will you ever come back?"

"I don't know."

Her tears started again. She had pushed him away; she had always known that she would.

"That was another shitty day, my dear Buster. Some might say bitter sweet. I finally knew that nothing had changed between us, yet there I was about to change it all. It happened right here exactly where this bench is."

Buster looked up. The man was obviously going mad. After remembering, he always seemed to want to engage him in conversation instead of getting out the sandwiches.

Nineteen

"Come on, fella, no lunch unless you move your backside. We won't stay long but we haven't been out for days, it never stops raining. Come on!"

The mention of lunch made Buster stir his stumps. He didn't much like wet and windy anymore, but the man obviously missed the bench so he ambled over towards the door.

The man put his arms into the old jacket and donned his favourite hat. It was a surfers' hat that Lissette had given him some ten years previously as a joke after watching him hanker after being sixteen again whilst he was watching the kids surf at Brook Chine. He seriously considered buying a windsurfer before Sophie and Honeysuckle pointed out the possible shortcomings in his ability to handle it. So Lissette did the next best thing. She bought him a beany knowing he would love it because a seventy-year-old should not be wearing a beany, and Jacques did not like being conventional.

Lissette was Honeysuckle's daughter, attractive but not as striking as her Mother. She had been born in 1955 and conceived while Jacques and Sophie were fighting their way out of Dien Bien Phu.

With Lissette had come a puppy. Two more followed and dogs became a much-loved fixture at Farringford. Part of the experience of staying there was to be greeted by at least one wagging dog when you arrived.

As he pulled the beany over his unfashionably long thick grey hair, he smiled as he thought of Honeysuckle and Lissette surrounded by their dogs.

Outside the wind was raw but it wasn't raining and he'd missed the walk to the bench, not to mention his time sitting on it.

"Come on. Keep up, Buster."

He was half-watching the television attached to the wall behind the bar whilst also watching the small child approach each GI in turn, as they walked along the street with their chosen woman of the night on their arm. Some of them would buy a single red rose from the angelic child, whilst others, more mean spirited, came very close to clipping her behind the ear for bothering them.

Jacques had watched the child for several months and concluded that her sale rate was incredible, and had she been allowed to keep any of the profits she would be the richest child in Saigon. In reality, each time her basket was empty she was relieved of all the money by a thoroughly distasteful character who would almost certainly have the same child working as a prostitute the second she began to grow breasts.

Saigon had changed since he had left at the end of 1954. Now the American Dollar was king, and with it had come an American culture that the Vietnamese living in Saigon had embraced because it had brought them wealth.

The little girl stepped onto the curb and offered one of her roses to a heavily muscled Marine sitting at a stool next to him in the street bar. He was not a mean-spirited man, Jacques could see it in his eyes, and so he bought two and handed them to the girls that had been serving their beer from behind the bar.

"You a journalist, buddy?" The Sergeant turned and smiled at Jacques.

"No, I'm with the British Embassy. Boring stuff I'm afraid. I leave the writing to the clever ones." Jacques offered his hand, "Jack, how do you do?"

"The guys call me Mac." Mac took his hand and shook it. "Nice to meet you."

" Have you been here long, Mac?"

"Just finishing my extended tour, man. I'm going back to The Big Apple in a month's time. Can't come soon enough."

"I'll bet. Are you a Yankees or a Mets fan?" Asked Jacques.

"Yankees, of course! You know about baseball? Never met a Brit who knew anything about it."

"I don't know much, but I spent some time at the U.N. in Manhattan and went to a few games. It's great, but I've never played, it's hardly played in Britain." He smiled at the Goliath sitting next to him. "Who are you with, Mac?"

"1st Force Reconnaissance Company. I've been here eighteen months now."

Jacques knew why Mac was drinking quietly in a bar on his own. "You'll have seen some bad stuff then."

"Yeh." He instantly changed the topic of conversation. "You want another Tiger, man?"

"Sure, but it's my round." Jacques called in fluent Vietnamese for two more beers. They eventually appeared, lukewarm in front of them.

"Damn! You can't get a cold beer in this place. Cheers anyway, Jack."

Jacques had met a number of men like Mac since he'd been

220

in Saigon. The majority were decent human beings who had aged ten years within six months of arriving, just as he had once done in France. A large number of them were even younger than he had been. He'd seen boys who did not even shave blown to pieces and others killed, half-crazed on drugs walking oblivious into a waiting bullet. This war was everything he'd warned Sophie it would be all those years ago when they had left Saigon the first time. In fact it was far worse.

As he had expected, he had been sent to Washington a month after he'd returned to London, and over the course of the next year he worked with the Americans in the Pentagon imparting his knowledge and opinions about all things Vietminh. He made a number of friends in high places and impressed a lot of people. Unfortunately for him, those connections had resulted in a request for his services just as the bloody war was about to kick off, and now he was one of the very few British personnel who were actively involved in the Vietnam War, albeit in an unofficial/official capacity. And all as a result of being able to speak French fluently at the age of seventeen!

Jacques felt a tap on his shoulder and he swung round to have the lovely Sophie position herself between his legs and plant a hello kiss on his lips.

"Well it's been real nice talking to you, Jack. Looks like you got a prettier friend now. I can't watch, it reminds me too much of home!"

Jack laughed and introduced him to Sophie. Though now in her early forties, her smile melted the heart of the young Marine Sergeant who charmingly excused himself and left, leaving them alone.

"Nice guy," Sophie said.

"Yes. He's entering the darkest hour. One month of a nineteen month tour to go. You get twitchy."

"You don't seem to."

"I will when I've got a month to go, believe me."

Jacques actually did very little front line work these days. His role was more in the training of intelligence gathering, but just occasionally he would still step out with the boys. He'd never worked with the 1st Reconnaissance or he would probably already have known Mac.

"Are we going to see Saphine tonight?" Sophie asked.

"Why not, we haven't seen her for a couple of weeks have we? Come on, we'll get a bite there too."

Saphine came over as soon as they walked into the club and threw her arms around them. She was still staggeringly beautiful and was in love with a Cavalry Captain who had promised to take her back to Nevada the second Uncle Sam would let him.

It was not a hollow promise, David Spurnyak the 3rd was madly in love with Saphine and had been from the day he walked into the club and laid eyes on her. From that day he had followed her every move like a puppy.

Saphine had met him six months previously and liked him a great deal. She did not love him anyway near as much as she had loved Jacques, but Jacques had never asked her to marry him and she always knew that he never would. Not only had David Spurnyak the 3rd asked her to marry him, but he was rich, he was very rich or at least his family were. They owned a farm in Nevada that Saphine had worked out was three times the size of Saigon and a lot of land in the desert in Las Vegas. Saphine knew all about Las Vegas and it's potential. Yes, David Spurnyak the 3rd was a good catch, and though she was twelve years older than him she looked younger. So she was younger!

There was something else, another reason why she could not have Jacques. Sophie had Jacques, and Sophie was the best friend she had ever had so she was happy for her.

Jacques and Sophie made a handsome couple. They were right for each other. There had never been any talk of marriage and Sophie suspected there never would be, but she did not care, she had Jacques. At least she had 95% of him and that was enough, and when they were not together she ached for that 95%.

It hadn't happened suddenly, in fact it had taken years but her wait had paid off. After they had returned to Europe he had written her a number of letters and she had replied to them all. They talked on the telephone, often for hours on end. Then he wrote from America where he was working and told her what life was like in his temporary posting to the United Nations in New York.

Quite by chance, and after a great deal of lobbying by her, she persuaded her editor to allow her to do a piece on the U.N. and it's effectiveness/ineffectiveness in solving the world's problems and disputes. One week later, armed with a ticket to JFK she went to see Jacques. She vowed that they would either end up as lovers, or she would finally consign him to the list of people she would always love but never have. To date, it was a list of one. It was a fine sentiment, but in reality she knew she could not walk away from him.

Jacques met her in a chauffeur-driven black limousine and they were driven into town where again, quite by chance she was staying at the same hotel as him!

Her plan to finally become his lover was not that difficult. Jacques had decided that a life of occasional six-monthly kisses with Honeysuckle did not qualify as a sex life. He deserved more, some happiness and a proper relationship. So he had decided a long time before he'd booked her into his hotel, that he and Sophie would become lovers.

Within seconds of getting into the limousine they were back in the comfort zone of their previous relationship with it's charged sexual tension. That evening he took her to his favourite restaurant in Greenwich Village and that night they made love as if they were in back in the jungle.

Since that time work had kept them apart for long periods which only heightened their need for each other, and now they were back once again in Vietnam where it had all begun, still doing the jobs they had been doing all those years ago.

Saphine's core audience had changed from her Hanoi days. Western faces, mainly officers and embassy staff, occupied over half of the seats. The grunts found their entertainment in the houses where Saphine had grown up and where she had become a woman. Vietnamese society still came to see her, but not in the numbers that they once had.

If Saphine had not worked in the club, Sophie and Jacques would probably not have frequented it. They liked their own company when they were able to be together, not wanting to share each other with the world. But when they were there they enjoyed it, it was always lively and Saphine's voice was still spellbinding, and Saphine herself always a delight to be with.

However, on this particular night Saphine was not her usual effervescent self. Sophie picked up on it immediately. "What's wrong, Saphine?"

Saphine smiled weakly. "David has only one month to go before he can return to America and they are sending him up-country. He says all the paperwork for my visa is coming soon, but I am scared. It is just a month, what if something happens to him?"

Jacques interjected, "He will be fine, Saphine. Do you know where he is going?"

"Phuoc Tuy Province, I think," Saphine replied.

Jacques wondered at the wisdom of anyone telling a Vietnamese person plans of a military action. Sure, Saphine was safe and he trusted her completely, but she only had to tell one other person and all security is breached. The problem was that half the U.S. army had girlfriends and my, how they like to boast about their exploits!

He knew instantly what the operation was about. He was party to all such planning. It was to be a U.S. search and destroy mission intended to lure out the Viet Cong D800 Battalion, a

224

crack unit of highly trained insurgency troops that were wreaking havoc in the South. He did not know who would be assigned to the mission, but it would appear that the 1st Infantry Division, 2nd Battalion 16th Infantry, Rangers in which David commanded Charlie Company, had drawn the short straw. It was a mission that Jacques was not at all happy about, but one that his new employers thought essential. If the Vietminh had been ruthless, then the Viet Cong, who fought a guerrilla war in the South, had taken ruthless up a notch. They did not fight by the rules, they even made the French Resistance look like amateurs.

"He should be fine in that one, Saphine. Don't worry," he said to Saphine with an encouraging smile on his face, but with an uneasy feeling in the pit of his stomach.

Saphine perked up. "So, how are you two love-birds?"

"Very well." Sophie kissed Jacques on the cheek, whilst he turn put his arms around her waist and playfully nibbled her neck.

Saphine giggled as she watched her two favourite people in the world at play. "What are you working on, Sophie?"

"I'm doing another piece on the Viet Cong and their increasing use of terrorist tactics and assassination to achieve their goals. Like the My Gonh Restaurant bombing and the medical centre they attacked last week. The targets are increasingly becoming civilians, and any government official seems fair game. Innocent people going about their business just get caught in the fall-out. They have taken terror to another level, we never targeted civilians in The Resistance, and it is a scary development. Even poor farmers are held at gunpoint and their crops stolen to feed the guerrilla army, and if they resist their fellow countrymen shoot them. I want to find out more about these people, is it a political doctrine that motivates them or a hatred of having their country occupied by foreigners? I'm trying to set up a meeting with them and get some interviews."

Sophie was excited.

"And I'm not happy. What if they kidnap you or worse?" Jacques was cross.

"Then you will come and save me. Like you always do, my English hero." She felt his biceps as if he was Popeye, than added, "But they won't do any of that. They want their story told and their propaganda printed in the world press." She hesitated a second before she turned to Jacques, and knowing what his reaction would be she said, "Actually they contacted me and have already assured me of my safety." She winced waiting for the backlash.

"What? They said come and talk to us and we promise you will be all right. What the hell do you think you are doing?"

"I'm a respected journalist who is published worldwide. They need the power of my pen to get their message out there. If it is a good message, I may write it, if it is not then that is what I will write. Don't treat me like a little girl."

"You are a little girl."

"No I'm not."

Saphine exploded with laughter. It stopped their argument in its tracks. They did not argue much but when they did it always developed into a childish squabble, which they would both soon recognise and laugh about. They were strong characters, life had made them so, and disagreements happened. The disagreements were very often about Sophie's safety and Jacques noble, but unnecessary desire to protect her. "Don't be so stupid," she would say. "I can look after myself," a fact he knew to be true. Other than Honeysuckle it seemed that all the women Jacques associated with were nigh on being Amazons, and if Honeysuckle had been two years older she would probably have become the most formidable of them all.

He and Sophie were totally compatible and they had spent good years together as a couple. Very few men could understand what drove Sophie, or would be able to live with that drive. She often thought that Jacques was the only person she had ever met with that ability, and privately she loved his old-fashioned insistence on being her protector, provided he never actually did it!

"When is the meeting then?" He managed to say through gritted teeth as she now poked him in the ribs with unnecessary force an attack that, in private would have resulted in them having a wrestling match followed by sex.

"Thursday. They will pick me up at the station and take me to see someone high up," she paused, "I think it may even be, Giap."

"Vo Nguyen Giap?" Jacques was startled. Giap was their top man, he had commanded the Vietminh troops twelve years previously in Dien Bien Phu. If he genuinely wanted to get a Western journalist on side then they must believe that things were not going well for the Viet Cong. Jacques knew that recently the Viet Cong had taken some devastating losses, as he had a hand in some of the planning. There were over half a million U.S. troops in Vietnam along with nearly a million other allied fighters. That is why the terror campaign had escalated. The American generals had taken this as a sign that they were getting the upper hand. The development with Sophie indicated that they might well be right.

"I don't know for sure, but I know that it is a very high ranking official who wants to meet me. I know what you are thinking, Jacques. I will not be the bait in some sort of trap. I want this meeting, it is the written word that will finish this conflict, not guns. If you capture or kill him, another will just appear, you know that. You said yourself that for every V.C. you kill five more appear!"

Jacques did, and as usual Sophie was right. "Just be careful, that's all I ask." The conversation was over.

Sophie turned to Saphine. "When does David go up-country?"

"He has already gone, he went today. Last night may have been our last night together, so I sent him away drained and exhausted." Saphine giggled.

Jacques was well aware what that would entail and was grinning uncontrollably to himself.

"You can stop smirking, Jack. I know what you are thinking. Come on, take me home and exhaust me!"

They both embraced Saphine; Jacques's embrace was slightly longer than Sophie's. It was Sophie's turn to smile as she dragged him away.

On Thursday evening Jacques was anxiously waiting in their apartment for Sophie to return. It was past midnight before he heard her slip the key into its lock. Relieved, he jumped up to greet her as she stepped in to the cloying heat of the poorly-ventilated room, with it's single ceiling fan whirring slowly above their heads.

"Well? Are you alright?" Jacques shot at her.

"Of course, cheri. It's nice to know you care!" She kissed him on the lips. "It wasn't Giap, one of his top men though. He was most charming and said he had read all my work. He particularly enjoyed the piece about our escape from Dien Bien Phu, and implied it was unfortunate that we hadn't met twelve years ago! Apparently he led the final assault on Isabelle, so it was his platoon that we had the altercation with as we left on our holidays!"

"Where did they take you?"

"Always the spy, my darling Jack! I really don't know, I was blindfolded and we drove for well over an hour, but I fancy it was round in circles. It sounded noisy outside as if we were still in the city. They all wore civvies and did not bother with any unnecessary military forms of address."

None of this surprised Jacques and he knew there would be no more intelligence to be gleaned from Sophie's liaison.

"What did they want to talk about?" He asked.

"That was interesting. I half expected the, 'it is useless to resist' stuff, but it never came. We had tea, and a civilised conversation about the futility of war and the pain it inflicted on people. He told me heartrending stories of his own people's suffering, families torn apart by civil war and children turning their back on childhood to fight their oppressors. He actually said, "It is the same as when you fought for your country after the Nazi invasion." He knew all about me, Jacques. They had done their research." She waited, "And they know all about you. He asked how my English boyfriend was, the one he nearly met in Dien Bien Phu! But he was not threatening, it was as if he was telling me there was nothing they did not know about the people who occupied his country."

"So he was saying, 'it is useless to resist,' but in a rather more subtle way." Jacques smiled.

"Yes, I guess he was."

Jacques was thinking, then smiling at her said, "So, are you going to write their propaganda?"

"Of course, but there will be the usual liberal smattering of my own propaganda which will totally neutralise it. Thus leaving the thinking reader as confused about what is happening in Vietnam as he was before he read the informative article. Just as confused as the writer!"

"The usual then?"

"Yes, the usual." Changing the subject she said, "I need a G and T, a large one. Then I need you." She kissed him more passionately.

There was a loud knock on the door. Although it was one o'clock in the morning, this was Saigon. It never slept and Jacques often received visitors at all times of the day and night.

"Damn, I was looking forward to the rest of that kiss." He walked to the door and unlatched it.

Still wearing her stage frock and in full stage make-up that was now smudged down her cheek, stood Saphine. When she saw Jacques her dried tears started again and she flew to his arms.

"What is it, Saphine?" Asked Jacques, holding her as Sophie came to see what was happening.

"David is dead. They have killed David." She could hardly get the words out.

"Cherie, come and sit down." Sophie took her hands and led her to the sofa. "What happened?"

"His friend, John came to the club and told me that Charlie Company had been ambushed and David was dead. I don't know much more."

"My poor, Saphine. Come, have a drink, and you must stay the night with us." Jacques poured her wine and his heart went out to Saphine. David had been her future, her rescuer from the hell that Saigon was slowly becoming.

Jacques promised he would find out the details the next day from the high command. He knew it would help her, knowing always did. He also knew that Saphine was a strong woman, not a fighter but a survivor. In time this tragedy would be just another stumbling block in her quest for survival through a difficult and turbulent life.

That night, like a small child she came to their bed and climbed in. She lay between Sophie and Jacques, they tenderly held her trying to share and ease the pain of the child whose world had just fallen apart.

It turned out that Charlie Company had encountered sporadic fire from the Viet Cong as they moved through a rubber plantation. Soon they were isolated and surrounded. The plan had been to use them as bait and the other Companies would attack the Viet Cong, but the other Companies did not arrive in time to stop Charlie Company taking huge casualties. Vietnam had defeated them again, its jungle once more proving impenetrable. A 'friendly fire' shelling they received from their own artillery did not help the fact that Charlie Company took huge casualties. During the night their defences were breached and several men had their throats slit. David was one of them, already injured and with inadequate medical care he would probably have died anyway.

Five days later Jacques and the two girls attended a ceremony at Tan Son Nhut airport as David and another fifty servicemen were repatriated to the United States in body bags. It was the closet to Nevada Saphine ever got.

That night the three of them celebrated David's life and hoped his death at the age of twenty-seven was not completely in vain.

As Jacques poured them each another shot of cheap brandy an explosion shook the walls of the street bar. None of them even flinched, partly because the cheap alcohol numbed them, but also because it was becoming commonplace, just another attack in a rotting city.

The following night Saphine was singing in the club once again, and another dream began in the company of two admiring young chopper-jocks who had just arrived to start their tour of duty.

Later that week something else happened that took Jacques totally by surprise. He was getting tired of the war, tired of watching young men like David sacrificed for reasons he could no longer discern.

He was in the same bar where he had met Mac, and hoped he was able to survive his last month in Vietnam, unlike poor David. On the wall behind the bar the television was still flickering away, and the little girl was still walking the streets selling her roses.

As she smiled up at him, he took a swig from the nearly empty beer bottle and as he did so he raised his head and glanced briefly at the flashing television, something he rarely did. The bottle had barely touched his lips when he removed it as his jaw dropped.

There was no sound on the TV but there was a caption that said in Vietnamese, 'Nazi Hunters get their man.'

"Jesus," he whispered to himself. The person being interviewed had a face he knew so well. "Turn it up, turn it up!" He yelled at the startled barmaid.

The face was gone and the picture returned to the newsreader in the studio. "...The lawyers who successfully prosecuted Adolf Eichmann, the architect of the Holocaust, have successfully brought another Nazi war criminal to justice. And now for the weather."

"Jesus," he said again. It was her, Yvette, with grey hair and spectacles. "It had to be her."

"Are you alright, Jacques? You look as if you've seen a ghost." Sophie had just stepped into the bar.

"Yes, I think I have!"

"Blimey, it's cold isn't it, Buster? Sorry that all took a bit longer than I'd expected."

He rustled in his coat pocket and produced a biscuit. "Come on, let's have lunch at home. It's too cold out here."

The man stood up and set off down the hill with lunch still in the bag. A puzzled Buster eased himself awkwardly from the bench. Had he really been dragged all the way up here for no lunch?

The man had never let him down before, so he set off after him. How he was expected to walk all the way home without nutrition? He was not sure. Maybe another biscuit would appear. Yes, that would help a starving dog!

Twenty

"It's warmer today, old boy, and the wind has gone. I promise we will have lunch on the bench today."

Jacques had not forgotten the look Buster had given him the previous morning when he stood up without giving him his food. The silly dog had sulked all afternoon and it had taken lemon drizzle cake at three-thirty in the afternoon to change his mood.

On the walk up to the Warren he thought of Yvette's picture on the television, but that story would have to be another day. Today was a Honeysuckle day. The day she met Sophie.

As usual once they had arrived at the bench his fingers traced the letters of the name, and he sat down.

By way of an apology to Buster he had prepared two lunches, a small one now, and the main feast to follow later.

To Buster's delight the unexpected sandwich appeared with great ceremony, and was devoured with equal aplomb.

After New York Sophie and Jacques had become an item. Still spending long periods apart, their relationship was often carried on down telephone lines or through the written word.

In some ways Jacques preferred the latter, or at least he delighted in reading Sophie's letters, if not in writing his own. After all she was a writer and managed to pen smut and filth just as well as she corresponded on war and politics. The smut and filth stimulated his groin as much as the serious writing stimulated his brain, and the beauty of her written word was that he could read it over and over again. He would often find innuendoes he had missed on several occasions previously, or unwritten words that could change a meaning. She was brilliant at making her readers think, and he was her most avid reader, both journalistically and privately.

He had been back to the Isle of Wight a number of times before he had cemented his relationship with Sophie in New York. Despite his pathetic threat to Honeysuckle, he could not stay away, of course he had to see her. When he had said that he did not know if he was ever coming back he instantly regretted it. She did not deserve that cruelty and he had written to her and apologised, promising that he would see her soon.

He had gone to see her just before he left for Vietnam on his first mission as a MI6 officer. It had been just as agonising as the years he'd spent there before. There was not even a kiss. His being there seemed to depress Honeysuckle, so much so that embarrassingly Simon asked him one day what he thought was the matter with her. "She is usually so full of life," he'd said.

He soon came to the conclusion that he had been right to leave. They appeared to be much happier apart, so he had left for Vietnam. Less cruelly this time, with a vow to return and a promise to write, which he had done.

His letters contained no mention of his real business in Hanoi, but were informative of other things and of life in general.

They were the letters of an older brother, as hers were of a young sister.

Saphine had satisfied his carnal desires and that night in the jungle so had Sophie. However, through all that time he never stopped desiring or loving Honeysuckle.

When he returned the first thing he did was go and see her. He went to his apartment in London first, had a good night's sleep then got his old MG out of storage and took it for a long overdue service whilst he went for his debrief.

The following day he set off for the island with the top off the car. He enjoyed the cool air on his face, a face he thought would never be cool again after life in Vietnam.

Honeysuckle knew he was coming and waited on the pier for him in Yarmouth. As the ferry steamed out of Lymington he wondered how he would react to seeing her. Would his experiences in Vietnam make it easier, and more specifically would his knowing Saphine and Sophie? He was older now, would that help?

As the ferry approached Yarmouth she stood on the pier and waved at him. A headscarf held her hair back, but it still cascaded down her shoulders, much longer than he remembered. She looked like a film star standing there. Nothing had changed, that familiar fluttering in his stomach as the butterflies reawakened.

"Bugger!" He muttered to himself as he waved back. "No change there then."

His parents stood by her side. He hadn't even seen them at first, all he could see was Honeysuckle.

They went straight round to his parent's cottage and had tea. Audrey came round from next door and it seemed that the conversation had not changed from when they were teenagers, and for that afternoon they were teenagers once again. All talk was of the past, happy times before the War. There was no mention of Simon or Lissette, the daughter Honeysuckle had failed to mention in her letters.

It was like being in a marvellous time warp, when everything was still possible, when it was preordained that Honeysuckle would marry Jacques.

The next day he went to Farringford where time had not stood still. His Mother had told him all about Lissette after Honeysuckle had left. She had asked her to, begging her forgiveness for not telling him herself.

As his Mother explained Lissette to him, Jacques found that he did not mind and was happy that Honeysuckle had someone by her side that she loved, someone who would not leave her as he had.

Like all good mothers Elizabeth had bought her son a present to take to baby Lissette. So armed with a teddy bear the size of a small house he set off for Farringford.

The hotel was obviously thriving. Rolls Royce cars, Jaguars and Daimlers littered the drive, and the grounds he'd helped to sculpt were immaculate.

Simon stepped out of the front door to greet Jacques and the bear, which was sitting proudly in the passenger's seat.

"That for me? Thanks."

"No, you handsome beast, it's for your ugly daughter. How are you, Simon? It's good to see you." Jacques jumped from the car and shook his hand.

"And you, old boy. Missed your face round these parts."

"Where is she then? This ugly monstrosity you have sired.

With that Honeysuckle appeared at the door flanked by a puppy. She was holding the baby in her arms and a look on her face that said, 'isn't she beautiful, but she should have been yours.'

Jacques leapt up the three steps to where she stood. "Well done, Honeysuckle, she is gorgeous, you clever old thing. Both of you, well done."

He took the baby and all he could see was the tiny

236

Honeysuckle who had been passed to him when he was a small boy. He gave Honeysuckle a smile that made her want to cry.

He stayed a week on the island and on balance enjoyed the visit. Now it was definitely easier to be near her than when he left, but all the old feelings were still there. It was wonderful to see his parents, who in turn were happy to see a more relaxed Jacques.

"Will you be coming to the New Year's Eve Ball, Jacques?" Simon had asked one day.

"No, Simon, I have to get back to London. I'm to travel to Washington soon and will probably be there for about a year. Unfortunately there is much to do before I go. I would have loved to." Seeing Honeysuckle in her goddess role did not appeal to him, he remembered it too well.

Honeysuckle's heart sank. He was leaving again. She would not see him for at least a year. But worst of all, she knew she was happier when he was not there and that Jacques was too, yet she could not bear to think of him going.

"If you are leaving us again so soon, you must give me this afternoon to reminisce about our childhood. Walk with me onto the Warren, Jacques, and remind me about those innocent days."

If Simon ever suspected they were more than surrogate brother and sister he never showed it, not then or at any time during their lives. "Go on you two, she is always much happier after you've been chin-wagging about your youth. When she came home the other day she was like a little girl again."

"Okay, after lunch, the Warren it is then."

They spent two hours walking the chalk paths and sitting on various rocks before settling for a lengthy period on the stone near where the bench now stood. They were two good hours, for once alone and comfortable in each other's company.

"Are you happy, Honeysuckle?" Jacques tossed a piece of chalk into the nearby gorse.

At first Honeysuckle did not answer, but stared out towards the Needles. Eventually she said, "Yes, I am. I have a beautiful daughter and a good husband. The hotel is a huge success and I have a good life. Yes I am happy and I am lucky." She turned and looked at him. "With the passing of time I have grown used to not having you by my side, but you are here, always here." She held a fist to her chest in the form of a heart. "The War took so much from so many, but it spared us our lives and we still have a love that can never be replaced." Then almost as an afterthought and to gain an affirmation of her words she added, "Don't we?"

"Yes we do, it can never be replaced." He smiled at the woman he so obviously adored.

She smiled back at him. "What about you, are you happy, Jacques?"

"I suppose so. As you say, we are luckier than thousands of others and I have friends who bring me a great deal of happiness."

"Would any of these friends be considered a girlfriend by any chance?" She raised her eyebrows. She had often wondered, but he had never talked about girlfriends. She couldn't believe that there would not be a stream of girls wanting her handsome Jacques.

Jacques smiled at her raised eyebrows. "Yes, I had a girlfriend in Hanoi. She was a singer and very beautiful. She was half-French and half-Vietnamese."

"Now I'm jealous. I know I shouldn't be, but she sounds very exotic." She tried to inject some humour into the words, but was angry with herself for actually feeling a pang of jealousy when he said yes.

He laughed. "You have no need to be. It was fantastic, but it is over. They were good times, though." He sensed her true feelings and was not going to let her off too lightly.

Honeysuckle sat thinking about an exotic singer and smoke-filled rooms, about her naked body draped over Jacques who was lying in her bed. The picture disturbed her more than she would have liked. She thought about what to say next and decided to take the plunge. She would have to say it, she could not help herself and it hadn't been said for ages.

"That is the one thing I yearn for, Jacques. The only thing that makes me unhappy."

"What is?" Jacques was not sure what she was talking about.

"You, your body, your tongue. Some nights I lay awake remembering, imagining. I'm still young and I want you. I know I'm wanton and I shouldn't, but...."

"You are not alone, darling. My fingers caress you body every night and I constantly relive the day we made love. Some times with Saphine, her name was Saphine, it was you I was inside."

Honeysuckle's eyes were closed as she took his hand and held it to her breast. She took a sharp intake of breath as his hand made contact through her thin blouse. She opened her eyes. The look that haunted him was there once again, the look that said, 'Take me.' It was a look that could easily destroy her life and ultimately her very being, because she would not be able to live with herself if she did what her look was asking him to do.

"One kiss, darling. I have waited so long, one kiss that will have to last me a year and maybe a lifetime. Please, Jacques." She was almost begging him.

It was the most passionate kiss they had ever had. Their hands clawed at each other's bodies but slowly the realisation of where the kiss was leading dawned on them and they hesitatingly and reluctantly withdrew.

Honeysuckle was trembling, but she managed to say, "Thank you. I'm sorry if you think I tease you. I don't, these moments are like life's blood to me. I need them and I'm sorry if I am being selfish."

"You are not selfish, Honeysuckle. You are anything but

selfish, and did I look like I was complaining?"

Honeysuckle laughed. "No, you weren't complaining." She was in control of herself again and she giggled. "This Saphine has taught you well. Your tongue has learnt new tricks which I shall dream about on cold winter nights." She gave him a wicked smile. "Come, we should get back, I have to feed Lissette. Do you like her French name?"

"Yes, it's lovely and so is she, just like you when you were tiny."

Jacques suddenly realised that their whole conversation had been conducted in French, just like it had always been. Since Simon had come back from the hospital all those years ago, they had naturally reverted to English. Partly because it would have been rude to talk French in his presence, but also because subconsciously it had marked an end to the relationship they had known until that point. Even when they had spent short periods alone together they had spoken English.

As always Jacques left the Isle of Wight totally confused, but happy. Yes, remarkably happy.

* * * * *

Washington was a very interesting place to be, the most dangerous city in the States, but one of the most exciting to be in.

He was close to the seat of power of the most powerful man on the planet. He even met the incumbent President once, albeit very briefly. At a reception in the Pentagon he shook Dwight D. Eisenhower's hand before the President was introduced to other alien workers seconded to the Pentagon.

He loved their use of the term 'alien' to describe foreigners visiting their country, and by the end of his year there he realised

240

why someone had once described Britain and the United States as being one country divided by a common language.

The sheer scale and potential of their military power staggered him. His brief was, of course, preparing for conflict in Vietnam, but some of the scenarios planned for that conflict amazed him. His personal battles had been small scale compared to some of the more extreme scenarios proposed by the Pentagon planners. Despite this, his was one of the few voices that cast any doubt on their ability to succeed against the, 'godamn-commy-bastards.' Some pen pushers were unbelievably myopic in their assessment of the enemy's capabilities.

Whether he managed to get them to understand what they actually faced in Vietnam he was never really sure, but at least they had been told and all he could do was wait and see what transpired.

During his time there he made up his mind that he must get on with his life. His love life, that was. Those two hours with Honeysuckle had been precious, but they were not enough, nor would any subsequent stolen moments be enough to sustain him. The longer he was away from Sophie the more he realised he missed her. He was about to get her to visit him in Washington, when the call came for him to go to the U.N. in New York where he was to be an adviser to the British delegation on Vietnam. More particularly he was to give them an insight into the possible American intentions and capabilities in that region.

If he'd liked Washington, he loved New York, and after Sophie had visited he loved it even more.

She stayed two months to write her piece for Le Monde. She could easily have done it in ten days and still seen New York, but she had an incentive to stay!

They were two fabulous months. Months without war and terror, months they could totally relax in each other's presence, months they could do what normal people did and enjoy everything that New York had to offer. They had never been together without a war raging around them or the threat of capture or death. They were both on a high, the drug giving them that high, normality.

Sophie had never been as happy. Honeysuckle was a presence, she knew that, but she was not a threat. Jacques had been totally honest and told her all about their kisses and how he realised he could never have Honeysuckle. But it was enough for Sophie, she had the kindest, bravest man she had ever known.

After that visit she returned twice more to New York and he took his leave in Paris where their romance flourished.

Only once did he visit the Isle of Wight and it was to tell Honeysuckle about Sophie. He had mentioned her in his letters but never the extent to which their relationship had blossomed. It was right that he should tell her to her face.

He agonised about where he should do it, he felt both the Warren and the pool were wrong. They were their places, places he should not convey such news to her. He remembered how wretched he felt at the pool when Honeysuckle had told him that she would marry Simon. He would not do that to her. He decided on the pier, it was somehow symbolic of their partings and meetings and in their convoluted life it was yet another of those occasions.

He asked her to lunch with him in the George hotel on the pretext of 'catching up.' He was sitting at the bar when she entered. If he'd had any preconceived ideas that it would be easy they were blown away at that point. The damned butterflies swarmed the second he saw her.

"Bonjour, cheri, it's lovely to see you," she said.

They kissed on both cheeks and looked at each other, searching for any changes that may have occurred during the two years they had been apart. Some laughter lines perhaps, Honeysuckle's hair slightly shorter, but in essence they were the same.

During lunch the talked of New York and Washington, Lissette and the hotel; their parents and their past, but never of the future.

After lunch they walked to the end of the pier and leant on the rails, looking across the Solent at the sailing boats.

"What is it you want to tell me, Jacques?" Honeysuckle suddenly asked.

Jacques was surprised. "How do you know I want to tell you something?"

"I know you, Jacques. I can sense every tension in your being. This is why we are here, isn't it?" She touched his arm.

"Yes, it is." He hesitated. "There is a girl...."

"Sophie, the girl in your letters."

"Yes, how did you know?"

Honeysuckle just smiled. "You silly man, I read every word you write over and over and the words you don't write."

"Oh!" Jacques was wondering if it were possible to have any secrets from her. "Well, we are together, I suppose you would say." He no longer had any use for the words he'd prepared to say to her. He waited for her reaction.

Honeysuckle was still smiling on the outside, though inside her selfish heart was crying. She couldn't stop herself from asking, "Do you love her very much?"

"Yes, I suppose I do." He looked away. He could not bear to hurt her or look at her as he said it.

Honeysuckle knew she had no call over Jacques, yet it was a blow, but a blow she had experienced before with Yvette during the War when she was still a child. She had grown used to knowing she would never have him.

"Will you marry her?" She managed to ask without her voice trembling.

"I don't know, Honeysuckle. We live strange lives and don't even see each other that often, but we are good for each other." He genuinely had never thought of marriage.

Honeysuckle did not speak at first, but stood lost in thought, her arm linked with his. They remained stationary for an age, each wrapped up in their own thoughts.

Honeysuckle was trying to work out the ramifications of the revelation he had just made, the revelation she had half-expected. Jacques just waited for her reaction and when it came, as always it surprised him.

Eventually she turned to him with that look in her eyes and asked, "Does this mean I won't get my kiss anymore?" A mock look of pain appeared on her face, but her eyes showed total confidence as to what his answer would be.

Jacques burst out laughing. She smiled. "You minx, you know we will always have the kiss. After all, we belong to each other don't we?"

"Yes, Jacques. That's right." There was authoritative tone to it, like a mother affirming a lesson learnt by her small child.

He burst out laughing again and she threw her arms around his neck and they hugged.

Both still laughing, they parted and Honeysuckle said, "I must meet her. You have had to accept Simon all these years and have been wonderful. It is only fair that I should meet the woman you have chosen. It will be my punishment, and your revenge," she added with a small giggle. "Can you bring her to the Ball on New Years Eve? I really would love to meet her and make sure she is worthy of you." The last said in a more serious tone.

Jacques smiled. "She is worthy, Honeysuckle. She is more than worthy." Jacques suddenly realised that part of this whole process was to gain Honeysuckle's approval. "I will see if she can come over from Paris."

"Good. If she can't, then I will go to Paris." It was a statement, not an idle threat.

Honeysuckle never had to go to Paris. The second Jacques told Sophie of the invitation, there was no doubt where New

Year's Eve would be spent. She had to meet the woman who meant so much to Jacques, to meet the one woman who could steal Jacques from her.

Before she left for England she spent more money on one dress than she had probably spent on all the clothes she had ever bought. If there was to be a battle she had to be well armed!

Jacques had spent Christmas with his parents and on Boxing Day they had gone to the hotel and spent the day with Honeysuckle's family. The whole process was as easy as it had ever been. Lissette was a delight and still slept each night with her teddy bear, also called Jacques.

"A bloody common name round here," Simon had said.

One night Lissette had dragged teddy Jacques into bed with Mummy and Daddy and cuddled up with them. Honeysuckle couldn't help it, she slowly relieved her small daughter of teddy Jacques and took over cuddling duties herself.

Sophie arrived on the 30th and was greeted with open arms by Big Jacques.

"At last, a French woman in my house. Come in, please come in." His moustache was twitching.

"May I take your coat, dear?" Elizabeth gave her an altogether less Gallic greeting.

Of course Big Jacques was instantly in love with the French beauty, whilst Elizabeth warmed to her in her own English way.

By the time Sophie had helped Elizabeth pick out a dress for the Ball and helped with her hair and make-up, warming had moved to like.

"She is lovely, Jacques," she whispered to him as they awaited Sophie's appearance in the living room for a glass of Champagne, before they left for Farringford.

The door opened and in she walked. The three of them had been chatting, but now there was silence. It was Big Jacques who spoke first. "Mon Dieu, you are beautiful." He stepped towards her and took her hand, then led her into a twirl with his hand above her head so all could see this epitome of French beauty.

Elizabeth clapped her hands in delight. Jacques just stood there staring at the sensational woman in her Dior gown and eventually managed to say, "You look absolutely stunning, Sophie." His eyes were almost popping out of his head.

It was exactly the reaction she had wanted. She could go into battle.

Jacques dropped them at the main entrance to the house and parked the car. The doorman took the ladies' coats as they walked into the reception.

"I'm scared," Sophie said to Elizabeth.

It had remained unspoken why Sophie had come to the Ball, but Elizabeth was well aware of how she must be feeling.

"Come on, let's check our make-up before we go in," said Elizabeth, "you'll be fine. Honeysuckle is very nice."

By the time they had completed their toilette, Jacques had returned and was already standing talking to Honeysuckle by the ballroom entrance where she was greeting her guests.

Sophie had never felt as apprehensive as she felt at that moment. Neither the Nazis nor the Vietminh scared her the way the thought of meeting this girl did.

Suddenly she saw Jacques talking to Honeysuckle. Sophie stopped in her tracks and held Elizabeth's arm. "God, she is striking." It took all her courage not to turn around and flee.

"Yes she is, Sophie, but so are you. Come on, stiff upper lip." Elizabeth gave her an encouraging smile and the words made her giggle. She had heard Jacques say them so many times. "Come on, I will introduce you." She took Sophie's arm and pulled her towards her Nemesis.

"Honeysuckle, I'd like to introduce you to Jacques's girlfriend, Sophie." She wasn't sure why she had brought Jacques into the equation but ridiculously, she felt for this French girl and mentioning him somehow helped to redress the balance between the girls.

Honeysuckle turned and seamlessly offered her hand and a smile that would melt anyone's heart. She had known that Sophie had been standing there but had deliberately not looked at her. "Hello, Sophie, I've heard so much about you. Welcome to Farringford. You look stunning, I love your dress." Honeysuckle delivered it all in perfect French.

French! The bastard had never told her she spoke perfect French. Unfazed, and in perfect English, albeit with her wonderful accent, she replied, "It is very kind of you to invite me. I have heard a great deal about you too. Jacques's description of you does not do you justice, you are very lovely." The first riposte was over, and Jacques had been drawn deep into the battle.

Honeysuckle smiled, but before she could reply Simon appeared. "Ding dong! So this is the famous Sophie that Honeysuckle keeps talking about. I hear you have tamed our Resistance fighter."

Still smiling Honeysuckle offered, "Simon, my husband. He likes a pretty face." This was by way of explanation.

"Nice to meet you, Simon. But I don't think anyone will ever tame, Jacques, he is a rare wild species." So far it was going well.

Every bone in Honeysuckle's body wanted to fight this woman and reclaim her man, the man she knew she could tame with just one look or a single kiss. But it was not about that; it was about getting to know the woman she was conceding her man to.

Sophie waited for the next salvo. It did not come. Elizabeth watched with interest. It was good, Sophie was prepared to fight for her son, and it appeared that Honeysuckle would do exactly as she had expected. Honeysuckle was like a daughter to her and actually she knew her better than she knew her son, after all she had spent far more time with her. Honeysuckle was the strongest character she had ever known, and Elizabeth knew that if Honeysuckle so wished she could beat Sophie in any catfight to get what she wanted. But she also knew how Honeysuckle's moral code had shaped her life, and that same moral code would give them her blessing, albeit after a brief skirmish. Not disappointed, she watched Honeysuckle take a step back from the fight.

The two boys watched on, oblivious to any posturing or atmosphere between the girls.

"Come, let me introduce you to some of our guests. They are all romantics in love with art and poetry. I have already told them of your heroics in the Resistance and they can't wait to meet you. In years gone by they found Jacques almost irresistible." She threw him a smile and a look that told him not to worry, it will be all right and we will get on. But I have not forgotten the eighteen-year-old!

Elizabeth was happy how things were developing, as Honeysuckle took Sophie's hand she watched them walk away like two teenagers about to get up to mischief at a dance.

Having introduced Sophie to a gaggle of admirers she went to seek out Jacques. "No young girls on your arm yet?" She said as she approached.

"That's not fair."

"Poor little thing, you probably ruined her for life you know, like you ruined me."

"Who ruined who? That's what I'd like to know." They teased each other.

"She is a beautiful girl, Jacques. For a blonde!"

"Do you like her?" It was a ridiculous question, they had only just met.

"I will tell you after tomorrow. You must come for lunch with us in the restaurant and hopefully by then I will know her better." She laughed. "I have never seen her fight, but I can see she would be formidable."

Jacques had absolutely no idea how she would know, or

even say that. He innocently replied, "She is."

Between pandering to other guests Honeysuckle spent as much time with Sophie as she could that night. Sophie soon saw that she was not going to have to fight for her man and that Honeysuckle was everything that Jacques had described.

It was at midnight, after they had all sung Auld Lang Syne and the guests were hugging and wishing each other a Happy New Year, that finally Honeysuckle uttered the only threatening words she ever said to Sophie.

As she hugged her she said, "Happy New Year, Sophie. I know we will be great friends, but if you ever hurt him the way I have, we shall be mortal enemies."

Before Sophie could answer, Honeysuckle had moved on to the next guest. She felt small. Insignificant against the aura and power that oozed from the most beautiful woman she had ever encountered. She also felt a little sad, once again she knew she would never have all of Jacques. She had won her battle, but in victory there had been defeat.

Lunch the next day was delightful. After the meal the boys were dismissed to play billiards while Honeysuckle got to know Sophie.

Honeysuckle did not mention the threat she had made the previous night and the afternoon passed with the pair of them assessing and liking the other's qualities. They were very similar in a number of ways; both fiercely loyal and proud; both were full of the joys of life, yet they possessed a practical side; they were both compassionate and caring, and both of them were in love with Jacques.

Honeysuckle was completely open and told Sophie her side of the story that had ripped Jacques and her apart. It was almost identical to Jacques's version, but Jacques never realised how close Honeysuckle had come to taking the path that would have led to him. Sophie felt for Honeysuckle, it was the first time she had seen vulnerability in her.

Sophie found herself questioning if she would have done the same. She had always thought Honeysuckle stupid for giving up the most precious thing in life to her, but now she had met her it seemed so right. The girl she was rapidly growing to like would have been a shadow of the person she had become if she had taken that other path. She had always believed Honeysuckle's actions to had been so typically English, devoid of passion, 'stiff upper lip' and all that. But now she understood. Honeysuckle was not devoid of passion, she was the most passionate person she had ever met and it was that passion which guided her. Sophie had been around English people too long, she understood them now and she realised she was like them.

"I will never hurt him, Honeysuckle. I promise." She suddenly said, completely out of context.

Honeysuckle smiled. "I know," then she laughed. "Before you leave I have to give my report about you to Jacques. Do I like you?" She made a serious face.

Sophie waited, wanting approval like a small child.

Honeysuckle saw the look that reminded her of Lissette. She took Sophie's hands and squeezed them. "I do, Sophie. I like you enormously."

"Thank you." Sophie embraced her. She wanted to cry. How had this woman become so important in her life in such a short time?

They stayed till the sun went down and had a cocktail before returning to Yarmouth to spend their last evening with his parents.

Jacques watched the girls giggling together before Honeysuckle came over and took his arm and took him to one side.

"She is delightful, Jacques. I really do wish you all the happiness you deserve." Then she took him slightly further away and out of earshot of the others. "I still love you though, and you owe me a kiss."

The terrible thing was that he wanted to give her that kiss right then, despite everything he felt for Sophie.

"We're completely messed up, aren't we?" He said.

She laughed. "Yes and it's lovely isn't it?"

"Yes. It's lovely."

They were quiet in the car driving home then Sophie said, "I can see why you have always loved her. She is incredible, I have never met anyone like her."

"Yes you have, you are like her. Far more like her than you think and you make love like a the goddess Venus, to boot!" He squeezed her leg.

Sophie smiled. Yes, physically he was hers, all hers.

"So that was the day they met, Buster. Once they had formed an alliance I never stood a chance!"

Talking again, that was good. It was lucky a dog had the good sense to eat a sandwich when it was offered, otherwise you could go for hours without a square meal.

Lunch number two found it's way into Buster's mouth. Yummy, the best so far!

"We've got that ghost to deal with next time, old man. It's getting too cold out here. Perhaps we will deal with the ghost in the warmth of the cottage. What do you say?"

The man did not wait for the answer, he knew what Buster was thinking.

"See you soon, old girl. Don't get too cold out here." He touched the letters and smiled to himself.

Twenty-One

The man settled into the wicker chair that sat in the window and looked out down the valley towards Totland. One of the island buses slowly made it's way along the road towards Alum bay, its top visible above the hedgerow. Buster ambled over and settled at his feet, his head uncomfortably perched on the man's left foot.

"The ghost then. It's the ghost story today." He made a spooky face at Buster who just ignored him.

Buster had already had lunch, dog food in a bowl, not proper food in a sandwich. But he was temporarily replete so decided a snooze by the man's foot would be a good way to pass the time until some proper food arrived.

"It was her, I'm sure it was her, Sophie. I just caught the end of it, but she was a lawyer who had just prosecuted a Nazi war criminal. I'm sure it was her." Jacques was excited.

"Calm down. Who was prosecuted? If we know that, it

should be easy to see who the prosecuting lawyers were."

"I don't know, but they said she had also prosecuted Adolf Eichmann. That should be easy to find out. Christ, I work for MI6! All it will take is a phone call."

Twenty minutes later they were in the British Embassy on the telephone to MI6 Headquarters in London. Fifteen minutes later the telephone rang on the desk in front of him, he grabbed the receiver and put it to his ear.

As he listened he scribbled a name on the pad in front of him.

Sophie slid the pad across the desk and looked at the name he had written. SARAH EHRLICH.

"They are faxing her file to me. Bloody hell, we have had a file on her all these years. I never thought..."

"Why would you? She disappeared off the face of the Earth. You tried to write to her in Danzig, but you never got a reply. This may not be her, Jacques. She is twenty years older now."

"It's her, look it's even her real first name. I know it is her."

They made a cup of coffee as they waited for the fax machine to burst into life.

"I should have thought to check our files."

"Stop beating yourself up, you didn't have a name to look up." She passed him the cup.

About an hour later the machine started to print page after page in a completely random fashion. After a while it went quiet and Sophie organised them into some semblance of order.

She pulled up a chair, put it next to his and placed the document on the desk in front of them. Jacques looked down at the name on the file; SARAH EHRLICH born SARAH HAYEK - FRENCH RESISTANCE - CODENAME - YVETTE.

"Christ, all her bloody names are there." He turned the page.

They both read the file. It read like a novel. The stuff about her life up to the end of the War they knew well. They had been part of it. It was what happened after that interested them.

It transpired that Yvette did not stop her killing when Jacques had left. '1945 - Suspected reprisal killings of known war criminals and collaborators.'

"Why was she never arrested?" Sophie asked idly.

"Perhaps she was just doing what the authorities wanted her to do," said Jacques.

'1946-48 - Known liaison with Tuviah Friedman, Nazi Hunter (see separate notes and file) at Danzig jail. Deaths of suspected war criminals under interrogation.'

'1948 – Recruited by Haganah.'

"What's Haganah, Jacques?"

"I think it was a Jewish paramilitary group that formed in Israel after the war, whilst the British still ran Palestine. I believe it became the core of the Israeli defence forces."

"So she carried on fighting."

"Let's see." He turned the page.

'1948-50 - Worked with Tuviah Friedman in Vienna in the documentation centre where they hunted down numerous Nazis.'

"At least she appears to have stopped killing," Jacques offered.

'1950 - Moved to Israel and attended the Hebrew University of Jerusalem to study law.'

'1954 - Attended Harvard Law (USA) - studied International Criminal Law.'

"We can see where all this is going. I knew it was Yvette. She is still very attractive..."

"Oh shut up!" Sophie poked him in the ribs.

'1957 - Joined Tuviah Friedman's Nazi Hunter team.'

'1962 - Successful conviction of Adolf Eichmann, on 15 criminal charges, including crimes against humanity and war crimes.'

"Look, he was caught by Friedman's team in Argentina,

then he was tried and executed in Israel"

It went on to list the other prosecutions and suspected dealings of Sarah Ehrlich. It appeared that she worked closely with MOSSAD, the Israeli Secret Service, in extracting known war criminals from various parts of the world. More recently she had been working in West Germany.

'1962-66 - Successful prosecution of a number of Treblinka guards.'

"Bloody hell, she got them. She said she would."

They sat in silence imagining the enormity of what those prosecutions must mean to the woman they knew as Yvette.

On the last page of the dossier was a note that read; Marital Status - married to Fritz Ehrlich, German, Jew, and Lawyer. Children - two female - names; Laila and Esther

"It's their names, her little sisters' names." They were quiet again.

Eventually Sophie said, "Do you think she is okay now? Look she is married with children."

"I hope so." He laughed. "I have to say, I find it hard to believe she has resorted to the law for her justice. I suspect anyone who gets acquitted end up floating in the Rhine!"

Sophie smiled. "We must go and see her. I would love to see her again. How come we did not know about her, she must be famous."

"Because we've been rotting in jungles or underground in bunkers in the U.S.A..!" He chuckled. "Yes, lets try and find her. I am due some leave and all you do is write." The last bit earned him a slap on the arm. "I will get MI6 on the case, about time they made themselves useful."

Two weeks later they flew to Bangkok and boarded a Lufthansa flight to Frankfurt, but not before Jacques had made a telephone call to make sure they would be welcome.

He dialled the number in Cologne that he'd been given, a female voice answered the phone and spoke in German. It was her voice, a voice he knew intimately, but it spoke in a language he knew she hated, or had once hated.

"Hello, Yvette. How are you?" He'd meant to call her Sarah.

"Jacques, is that you?" She fired back in French.

"Oui, c'est moi."

"Oh, Jacques, it is good to hear you. It has been too long."

Jacques explained that he had seen her on the TV and that he was a great friend with Sophie again and they would love to see her.

"Sophie, she is alive?" She sounded excited.

"Oh yes, Sophie is very much alive," he replied.

Without hesitation she invited them to stay at her home in Cologne. They didn't talk much, preferring to catch up with all the news personally, but she sounded well and did promise that she was more like the Yvette that he had once known.

Two pretty little girls stood one either side of their Mother as Sophie and Jacques walked out of the arrivals hall at Cologne airport.

Jacques could see a slightly plumper woman than he remembered, but it was still Yvette and she nodded in their direction as they appeared.

Sophie waved and Yvette removed her arm from one of the girl's shoulders, where it had been resting and waved back. She was smiling the smile Jacques knew so well, the smile that he had rarely seen towards the end of their time together.

As he approached he said, "Hello, Yvette."

Before she could answer one of the little girls said, "Who is Yvette?" And looked up at her Mother.

"She is someone I used to be. One day I will tell you all about her, I promise." She paused, "Laila, Esther, meet my two oldest and dearest friends, Sophie and Jacques."

Yvette pushed the girls forward to shake hands. As she did so her eyes locked onto Jacques. There was a look of affection on her face for him, but an even greater look of pride in her daughters.

Jacques couldn't help thinking that if she could she would have said, "Look I have brought them back, they are safe."

Jacques shook each of the little girls' hands in turn then embraced Yvette. "It is good to see you, you look so well."

"No I don't, I am overweight and grey, but I am the happiest I have ever been. And look at you two, you are stunning, Sophie, and Jacques as handsome as ever." She took the youngest child from Sophie's arms. "Come on Esther, you are too big to be asking to be picked up. We will take my friends to meet Daddy." She gave them both a wicked smile that in years gone by had meant something else to Jacques. "It's a little ironic that I should marry a German, don't you think?"

Having relieved Sophie of her small daughter, Yvette turned to her, the woman who had nearly perished trying to save her life and the life of her baby. She held her hands and said, "It is so good to see you again, Sophie. We have so much to talk about and I still have to thank you for what you did." She hugged her oldest friend whom she had thought to be dead. They both had tears in their eyes.

As they approached the house, Fritz came out to meet them and introduced himself. "It is a pleasure to meet you both. I have heard so much about you. Please come in, I will get the children off to bed while Sarah gets you settled in."

It seemed odd her being called Sarah. Sophie looked at Jacques then said, "Should we call you Sarah?"

"Don't you dare, I hate it. I always have. It just seemed right that Yvette died when the War ended, she was never real. But now you are here she will be alive again, I much prefer it. I was quite sexy as Yvette wasn't I?" She looked at Jacques as she said the last bit.

"I think 'quite' is something of an understatement." Jacques shot back.

She obviously liked the compliment and turned towards the house.

Yvette had prepared a meal for them. "A daube!" She announced as she removed the lid of the casserole. "For old times sake, before we go and kill the German bastards." She leant across and affectionately pinched Fritz's cheek. He just shook his head.

That evening Fritz excused himself to prepare an important brief he had to present to the court in the morning, but it was really to allow old friends to talk about killing Germans!

The second he had gone Sophie started chatting with her oldest friend, as if time had stood still between the apartment in Paris and this home in Cologne. "How did you meet him?"

They were off. "At university. I had calmed down a bit by then and ready to have a relationship." She looked apologetically at Jacques. "I was a lot older than most of the students, but so was he. We sort of gravitated towards each other."

"And the children? They are gorgeous?" It was Sophie.

Yvette smiled. "At first I was scared to have children. Hell, you know why, but my blood lust for revenge became less important with each one of them we hung or put in prison. The children just naturally happened, we weren't trying but I have been blessed with two beautiful little girls who no one will ever hurt." She smiled, a calm confident smile.

It was Jacques's turn. "I am so happy for you, Yvette. So often I've worried about you."

"I'm sorry, Jacques. You are the one person in my life to whom I owe a proper apology for my behaviour. Not for the killing, I would do it again, but my behaviour towards you. I know what I owe you and I have never forgotten it. I have often thought that I should try to find you and thank you, but assumed you would be with that bloody Honeysuckle and the last thing you needed was for me to turn up again. So I did nothing."

At bloody Honeysuckle, Sophie burst out laughing. "I'm

sorry, that's what I used to call her." Jacques looked hurt.

Yvette looked at them both, they were obviously a couple but had never actually said so. "You two, you always flirted, right in front of my face most of the time. What's the story?"

Sophie took great delight in taking Yvette through their life's story starting in a club in Vietnam. Yvette revelled in all of it. "So what happened to bloody Honeysuckle then?" She finally asked.

Jacques was not about to let them do a character assassination on her, so quickly took up the mantle of storyteller.

When he had finished, Yvette said, "I always knew she was remarkable." She was serious now. "Did you thank her, like I asked?"

"No I didn't, actually I didn't." Jacques looked thoughtful. Sophie looked at Yvette and both raised their eyes heavenwards in a plea for help. "Men!" They said in unison.

"Why don't you thank her yourself. One day we could all go to the Isle of Wight and see her."

The girls just looked at each other and shook their heads.

"What? What have I said?" Which heralded a round of hysterical laughter from the girls.

Honeysuckle was left in peace after that, both girls knew her importance in everything that ever happened to them.

Jacques wanted to know about Yvette's work so started to pump her with questions.

"Be careful, he is a spy you know," Sophie said behind her hand to Yvette.

"I know that now." She giggled, "I had MOSSAD pull his file. I have connections in high places you know." She raised her eyebrows at him. "Vietnam seems to be your thing. They like you in the Pentagon, I hear."

"Bloody hell. What colour underpants do I wear?"

"Black used to be your favourite," Yvette said, as Sophie

giggled.

"Don't worry. You are off their radar, to quote. Otherwise they would not have given me the file."

"Can I see it?" He asked cheekily.

"No you can't. Anyway I don't have it, I gave it back, and it has a terrible photograph of you."

"Okay, I give in, forget the file. What was your finest moment in court?"

Yvette was serious now. "There were two. That shit, Eichmann was the first. He orchestrated the whole thing, the logistical movement of Jews from the ghettos to the extermination camps. I was part of the team who extracted him from Argentina, and I saw it through to the end as part of the team who prosecuted him. I stood as close to him as I am to you now and stared him in the eyes and smiled as they tightened the noose around his neck."

"You haven't completely lost it then!" It was Jacques.

She looked at him and watched his cheeky little smile spread as his eyes twinkled till they shone, and she remembered why she had loved him.

She smiled back at him, the confident smile still there. "No, the hatred still burns within me. It was Tuviah who told me to make them suffer with the eyes of the world on them. It was he that taught me there was another way, a better way to humiliate them before they died. And a way to make sure the world never forgot what they did." The smile grew. "But even then there were some who didn't deserve to draw one more breath." Her eyes challenged him to admonish her and he could have sworn that her jaw raised a fraction.

Jacques knew better. That self-assurance had made her the remarkable lawyer she had obviously become, and had once made her an unstoppable force in his bed. He said nothing

"What was the other?" Asked Sophie.

"The guards at Treblinka who were only doing their duty."

260

She made a distasteful face as she said it. "Three hanged and the rest will think about what they did in a prison cell for the rest of their lives." She laughed. "If I had found them back then they would all be dead."

"They were lucky boys!" Jacques was in no doubt that she meant it, and would have executed each and every one of them.

Sophie watched them, the avenger and her voice of reason. She was taken back to France and another time when she watched the handsome young English boy skilfully rein in the Resistance's most fanatical fighter. He did it with humour and a guile that made Yvette look at herself, to question her motives and her methods. Without him Yvette would have perished in some dark and distant field in Northern France and there would not have been a new Laila and Esther to captivate the world.

He was doing it again, making Yvette laugh at herself and at her own fanaticism. He had been doing exactly that when Sophie first really noticed him. Not his body and face, she had already noticed those, but his being, the character that made him the man who she had grown to love. She suddenly wanted to be alone with that man, to shut out the world and love him.

She was brought back to the present by Yvette's laughter. She had stopped listening, she'd been in her own reverie with Jacques.

They stayed for two days. Two good days, which brought happiness to them all, a closing to what had been open-ended.

"Will you stay in Germany, Yvette?" Sophie asked just before they left for Paris.

"No, when our work here is done we will go to Israel. Fritz has one surviving uncle there. It is all the family we have left, apart from you." She held her dearest friend's hand. "Thank you for coming, Sophie. It has meant so much to me. And your man, look after him. Jacques is very special. If you don't you will have me to look out for and you don't want that!" She tried to look threatening.

"Why is it that all his ex-girlfriends threaten me?" Sophie tried to look scared.

"Probably because we all still love him."

Sophie knew that was the case with Honeysuckle, and looking into Yvette's eyes she decided she was perfectly serious. "I promise that I will cherish him, but I probably won't obey him. No one ever obeys him, do they?" They both laughed.

At the airport the little girls kissed them both and Yvette embraced each of them in turn. She made them promise to stay in touch and before they could walk through security Yvette grabbed Jacques again and gave him one last hug.

"Thank you, Jacques," is all she said.

They flew back to Paris and spent ten glorious days together. Sophie was not going to share him with anyone else, especially an ex-girlfriend!

She had to stay in Paris for a month to sell some of her freelance work through her agent, and to catch up with her editors at Le Monde and Paris Match. Jacques boarded a plane to London to see his bosses, and briefly visit with his parents in Yarmouth and of course, unsaid but understood, Honeysuckle.

"Just because I am not there does not give you carte blanche to sleep with any of your ex-girlfriends. They all seem to be in love with you still, and when you get back to Saigon I include Saphine in that. Just because she spends half her life trying to get me in her bed does not mean you are no longer desirable to her, so hands off!"

"Yes, Miss."

Sophie arranged his collar like he was a child going off to school, then kissed him on the forehead. "Now, get along, and behave!" She added as he turned to go.

"So that was the ghost, Buster. She is alive and well, and still haunting Nazi War Criminals. You'd have liked Yvette."

Yvette did not sound like food to Buster!

262

Twenty-Two

It was a slightly warmer day and Jacques wanted to be on the Warren, so he could remember the events he intended to cover that day.

He made some hot soup and put it in a flask, cut the sandwiches and took a handful of biscuits from Buster's jar and slipped them in his pocket, but not before giving a couple to the salivating dog who sat beseechingly in front of him.

He grabbed a blanket and stuffed it into a rucksack. It would be cold up there and even Buster seemed to feel the cold these days.

"Come on, young Buster, off we go."

At the bench he gave Buster two more biscuits and settled down with him, the rug tightly wrapped around them both.

Jacques stared out to the Solent, calm and benign unlike the day it had taken his Father's life.

His business in London had not taken long. All he had done was give them a verbal brief, which was basically the same as all the written ones, which had been posted in the diplomatic mail, minus a few expletives.

The ferry crossing had been quite rough with a strong westerly wind preceding a depression that was approaching from the Atlantic.

His Mum and Dad greeted him in their now long-accustomed fashion, with a wave from the pier before embracing him as he disembarked from the boat.

He spent a wonderful evening with them describing Vietnam and its people, but little about the war. He did talk about Yvette and the remarkable happenings of the past month that led to their reunion.

However the main topic of conversation was Sophie. Elizabeth had grown to love Sophie, partly because of her spirit and partly because she obviously brought happiness her son. Which was something she had prayed for all the years she had watched him agonise about Honeysuckle.

Elizabeth was not disappointed with the look on Jacques's face when he talked about Sophie. It was an evening she would never forget, her son happy and her silly old French husband at home by her side.

"And you, Papa. Maman writes that you only fish twice a week now," said Jacques.

"Oui, just fish for our own plates and some for the hotel. That is all. I am retired. So I bowl and now there is a French name on the clubhouse wall. Club Champion 1966, the old buffers don't like it, c'est bon, c'est tres bon!" He laughed, they all did, and it was obligatory.

The next day he borrowed his Father's car and drove to Farringford to see Honeysuckle. She had been waiting by the door and ran down the steps to meet him, excitedly followed by her dogs wagging maniacally. Then she hugged him as he got out of the car.

"I've missed you. How are things?" She was still hugging him whilst the dogs sniffed inquisitively at his ankles.

Jacques had been wondering what his reaction would be when he saw her. He had been so completely happy with Sophie that he had actually stopped thinking about Honeysuckle every day, just occasionally there was a day that he did not.

As she embraced him, he let his head settle on her mop of dark curls. As they touched his cheek the butterflies swarmed in his stomach, he was relieved, nothing had changed.

"I have so much to tell you, Honeysuckle, and I have to do something I should have done twenty years ago." He held onto her, his head not wanting to lose contact with her hair.

"I'm intrigued. Come in, there is a nice fire burning in the drawing room. I'll have some tea sent in and you can tell me everything. Simon will be back soon, he has gone to meet the architects to discuss the refurbishment.

Armed with a cup of tea, a Garibaldi biscuit and an admiring dog watching him, or the Garibaldi, he listened to Honeysuckle as she said, "I can't wait to hear your news, but first how is, Sophie?"

Jacques smiled, a smile of contentment. "She is very well. She is in Paris with her editors and will meet me back in Saigon in a few weeks."

The smile told Honeysuckle everything she needed to know. He was happy, Sophie made him happy. She fought back the pang of jealousy she felt.

"Good, I am so delighted for you both," she said, which was perfectly true.

"And Saigon, I keep reading about bombs. Isn't it very dangerous? I know you have lived with danger all your life, but I am just a parochial island dweller and I worry for you both."

"Ha! parochial island dweller, please! If you were in Saigon, the Viet Cong would have run away years ago!" They both laughed.

"Seriously, Jacques. What is it like?"

"Yes, it's dangerous, but you learn to live with it. It will get worse because at the moment, we are winning. To counteract that, Charlie, sorry that's the Viet Cong, will increase its terror war in the urban centres of the South." He paused. "This sounds just like my briefing in London." He smiled again.

"I asked because I want to know. You never told me anything about France and what you were doing there. 'Not for small ears,' you once pompously said to me." That last part she delivered with all the pomposity she could muster.

"Did I? I'm sorry. I always did underestimate you, didn't I?"

"Yes. But I knew your motives, so I forgave you." She smiled at him, assessing the man. "You look good, Jacques. Do you still have all those muscles?"

He laughed. "Are you flirting with me?"

"Probably. I still have to dream, don't I?" She looked questioningly at him. "Anyway, what is your news?" It was time to change the direction the conversation was going. She knew if she did not, she would be in great danger of straying into self-imposed forbidden territory. She put the thought out of her head.

"Yvette, I have seen Yvette. She is well, married to a German, no less, and has two children named after her poor sisters."

"Oh my! That is wonderful news, tell me everything." Honeysuckle put her tea down and moved to sit next to him on the sofa, touching his arm as she settled down waiting to hear about Yvette.

Jacques was aroused by her close proximity but made no attempt to move. He proceeded to tell her everything, from the television in Saigon to meeting the children, and Yvette's veiled threat to Sophie when they left.

Jacques knew about Honeysuckle's threat to Sophie the day they met, she had told him. When he mentioned Yvette's threat,

Honeysuckle just squeezed in tighter against him and gave him a sweet smile with her head half-cocked.

Jacques just laughed and hugged her when he saw the smile. "I love you, young Honeysuckle." It was a platonic gesture.

"I love you too," she replied and stroked his cheek, her gesture only half-platonic. To stop anything else from happening Honeysuckle asked, "You said there was something you have to do, what is it?"

"Oh yes, something Yvette asked me to do twenty years ago that I never did."

"Go on."

"To thank you, she asked me to thank you for giving her back her life when you visited her in hospital. She said that without you, Laila and Esther would never have been reborn."

"I think there was a bit more to it than me just visiting her."

"Yes, of course there was, but you started it, Honeysuckle." They looked at each other, a thousand words unsaid yet understood.

A door banged outside in the reception. "That will be Simon. You'll stay for lunch?" She reluctantly let go of him and stood up.

Simon entered. "Look, darling, we have Jacques with us, he is staying for lunch."

"Fantastic, good to see you, old man." He strode across the room and shook Jacques's hand as vigorously as ever.

"You two have a chat whilst I see Chef and arrange for something special to eat." Honeysuckle turned and left them together.

Simon took Jacques around the hotel explaining their plans for the alterations. Then they walked around the grounds, fighting the strong winds as they went, whilst Simon outlined his blueprint for a nine-hole golf course. "My new passion, old boy," he said, "do you play?"

Jacques laughed. "Not too many golf courses in Saigon, I'm

afraid."

"No, I suppose not." Simon had never actually thought about Saigon before.

They had a wonderful lunch and a bottle of one of Simon's best vintages. They were drinking coffee when Mary, the receptionist interrupted.

"Sorry, Honeysuckle, but there is an important phone call for you at reception."

Honeysuckle got up and left the dining room. She returned five minutes later with a look on her face that not even Jacques recognised.

"Jacques, come with me to our private lounge. Do you mind waiting here, darling. I'll explain later." She touched Simon on the arm gesturing for him to remain seated.

She took Jacques's arm and led him from the room into the private quarters.

Once they were alone, and without asking him to sit down she threw her arms around him and held him to her. "I'm so sorry, darling. Big Jacques is dead, he drowned whilst fishing this morning." At that she burst into tears, unable to keep her composure any longer.

Jacques did not speak at first. He had Honeysuckle wrapped distraught within his arms, and his first thought was for her. Big Jacques had been her Father just as much as he had been his. He had been the one to give her away at her wedding, and had always championed his beloved Honeysuckle, his surrogate daughter

"How?" He was eventually able to say, the first tear rolling down his cheek.

Through her own tears, Honeysuckle replied, "Your Mum doesn't know the exact details yet. Apparently he went to catch a fish for your supper." With that she was inconsolable.

Jacques knew what to do. He just held her until the tears stopped, his own tears mingling with her curls.

When eventually her tears ran dry she said, "Come on, we must go to her."

Honeysuckle broke the tragic news to Simon, who offered to go with them, but Honeysuckle declined. "Please don't be cross, darling, but at this time I think Elizabeth would just like to be with close family. Your time will come and your support will be invaluable." As always she used the perfect words.

Elizabeth was brave, the only thing that Jacques found difficult to deal with was when his Mother said, that she thought she had beaten the damn sea after his Father had retired. These words were too much for Honeysuckle who had now lost both her Fathers to that same damned sea, she was inconsolable.

Strangely, Honeysuckle's anguish helped Elizabeth through her loss. She had to help the girl she loved as her own daughter, putting her own grief aside.

Sophie arrived twenty-four hours later to help Jacques deal with his own loss.

The funeral took place a week later, a week during which relationships were strengthened. Simon behaved impeccably, making sure humour was not lost because Big Jacques was a funny man in any number of ways. His own laugh demanded that everyone laughed with him. He was a character who was larger than life and whose life should be celebrated. So that is what the week became, a celebration of Big Jacques's life.

During the week Jacques watched Sophie expertly care for his Mother, always using the right word at the right time. But there was something else, something he had not expected.

Honeysuckle was the one who was most devastated at his passing, Honeysuckle who would normally be there for everyone else. But now it was Sophie who stepped into that role, and particularly for Honeysuckle, becoming her personal counsellor. It was a role that previously Jacques would quite naturally have taken. Death was no stranger to either Jacques or Sophie and they were both well equipped to deal with it. On this occasion

Sophie was the better qualified, and she saw that Honeysuckle was the one who needed the most help. The woman she once believed was her adversary was now the woman she wanted to help.

Sophie's concern was genuine. She liked Honeysuckle, she had always admitted to it. By the end of the funeral she loved her, and the feeling was mutual.

On the day they were inseparable, never more than a few feet apart. "Look at those two," Jacques's Mother had said to him. "They are like sisters." The smile on her face on such a sad day warmed her son's heart.

They stayed on after the funeral to be close to Elizabeth, who after a couple of days was growing tired of their concern. "For God's sake, I'll be alright. I have an island full of friends and my best friend lives next door. We can be grieving widows together. Now get on with your lives, the pair of you." It was an instruction that was not to be ignored.

The night before they left they had dinner with Honeysuckle and Simon. It was a seal on the bond that the girls had forged. Over the meal Jacques watched the two of them, and it was quite obvious how close they had become. His Mother was right, they were indeed like sisters; two very beautiful sisters.

When they parted Honeysuckle hugged them both. To him there was no mention of a kiss, but there was something in her eyes that told him she had not forgotten. Her embrace with Sophie was something new.

Honeysuckle cried when they embraced, "I know what you have done for me, Sophie, and I will never forget it. Look after each other, I love you both." She waved as they drove away.

In the car, Jacques looked across at Sophie who was smiling to herself. "See, I told you that you'd like her."

"Oh, shut up!" She slapped his arm.

The man arranged the blanket on his knees again. Buster's wriggling had exposed one leg to the raw elements. He looked at the Solent below, the sheltered inland water that had so cruelly taken his Father.

His thoughts turned to his Mother. The woman everyone had loved, and none more so than Honeysuckle and Sophie. She had lived on, easily making her four-score years and had passed away peacefully in her sleep, in the cottage where she had lived in her entire life.

"They are like sisters." He could still hear his Mother's words.

He took a deep breath and rattled the paper bag full of sandwiches to awaken Buster from his slumber.

Instantly alert with his mouth open, Buster was hungry. He thought lunch would never come!

Twenty-Three

Jacques watched the snow flurries through the window, a cold winter the newspaper had promised. The forecasters had been right so far, although it was not yet Christmas.

He put the last of the baubles on the tree and looked across to Buster sleeping by the fire. The scene brought back happy memories of childhood Christmases, but that is not where he was going to visit today.

The fire looked particularly inviting, but first he had to get Buster's lunch. He'd completely given up on dog food by now. He couldn't stand the look of disdain Buster gave him each time he put down his bowl. He just cooked for two, whatever he had, Buster had. Today's lunch was beans on toast, a choice he knew he would live to regret!

Unaware and uncaring at the fallout that was about to invade their living room, Buster devoured the beans and the toast, unbuttered.

Outside the snow was getting thicker, and Jacques

remembered his Mother's saying, 'little snow, big snow. Big snow, little snow.' Today's was little snow, by evening it would have settled and probably be a couple of inches deep.

It did not matter. Buster had enough food in the house to last till spring.

Jacques put another log on the fire and watched it spit vehemently onto the rug in front of the hearth. He put his foot on the offending shard, which was smouldering on the rug and ground it out, adding another dark splodge to the evolving pattern.

He stared into the embers and was back in Vietnam. The war had taken several twists and turns, and several more lives.

After he had returned to Vietnam it was a couple of weeks until Sophie joined him. They were lonely weeks, weeks he consciously hoped would never happen again. He and Sophie had spent long periods apart, but the death of his Father had made him feel his own mortality. For the first time, he thought of death. He did not fear his own death, one day it would happen, but he did fear not living his life. And his life was now firmly intertwined with Sophie, regardless of his feelings for Honeysuckle.

When Sophie arrived he could hardly remember being so happy. She had probably been having similar thoughts because she cried when she ran to his arms.

The next year was fantastic, they lived each day as if it were their last and each night as if it were their first.

The war raged around them as they lived in their bubble of happiness, until one fatal day.

It was the 31st January 1968. Tet Ngyun Dan, The first day of the traditional lunar calendar and an important Vietnamese holiday. Jacques was working late with the Americans in the U.S. Embassy, which was situated directly opposite the British

Embassy. There had been a massive build-up of North Vietnamese troops, and supplies had poured into the South via the Ho Chi Minh Trail from Laos, whilst the increasingly irritating and highly effective Viet Cong escalated their activity. The intelligence they had collected suggested the biggest offensive to date, designed to destabilize the American-backed Saigon government and cause the people of Saigon to rise up against it, thus hoping to end the war with a single blow.

In the early hours of the morning Jacques was discussing the likelihood of its success with the Embassy staff when he heard gunshot from the yard outside. At the same time the Viet Cong hit five other primary targets in Saigon, including the airport and the Palace. The Tet Offensive had begun.

Jacques was not armed, so along with the others at the meeting they made their way to the arsenal of weapons kept at the Embassy. A gunfight was rapidly developing outside but as yet no one had gained access to the Embassy. Armed, Jacques took up a position at one of the windows, and returned the fire of the now entrenched Viet Cong who were shooting at them from behind planters in the courtyard.

"This is like the fucking Wild West!" He yelled to the man next to him just before the bullet hit him in the back, an unlucky ricochet from a wall.

At first it seemed surreal and he did not know what had happened. Then the realisation hit him, finally his luck had run out, he had been shot. The last thing he heard before he was passed out was a cry of, "Medic!"

Unfortunately there were no medics, but there was a man who had seen twenty of his colleagues shot and several die, but he knew just enough to keep Jacques alive. The bullet had not hit his heart, but had penetrated a lung, which had collapsed. He owed his life to that marine.

It was six hours before the Embassy was completely retaken by U.S. troops. During that time Jacques had been drifting in and out of consciousness. When awake he was coughing up blood, he knew the signs and he knew he had a chance. It was a matter of time, did he have enough? When he was unconscious he dreamt of Honeysuckle and Sophie, Saphine and Yvette. He preferred those times.

The last time he awoke he was on a stretcher with drips supplying him with blood and other fluids. An oxygen mask was being held to his face, and all he could hear was shouting.

The next time his eyes opened he was lying in a hospital bed with Sophie by his side.

Her eyes were red from crying and she smiled at him. "I leave you alone for one minute, and look what you go and do!" She stood up and gently lent over and hugged him. "I thought I'd lost you." There were tears in her eyes again.

Jacques wanted to talk but couldn't, he just mouthed through the mask, "I love you," and he was instantly asleep again.

He spent two weeks in the hospital with Sophie almost constantly by his side. She filled him in on all that had happened at the Embassy and elsewhere. How the Viet Cong were hitting town after town, with appalling loss of life, more innocent victims of the damned war.

To Jacques she seemed angry, angrier than he had ever seen her in any of the conflicts in which they had been involved.

One day she apologised and said that there was someone she needed to go and say goodbye to, but promised to be back in a couple of hours. Before Jacques could ask who it was, she was gone.

Four hours later she returned. She had been crying and she looked sad. "What's the matter, Sophie? You've been crying." Jacques was concerned.

"I can tell you now. I couldn't before, you weren't strong enough and would have insisted on coming. I told her why you couldn't be there, and she understood. I know she did." She was crying again.

He was really concerned now, "Come on, darling, tell me." He raised his free arm to console her.

Sophie looked at the broken man's attempt to comfort her, took his hand and kissed the back of it. "It's Saphine. She is dead."

Jacques took a while to digest the information. "Oh no! Not our Saphine." The look of pain in his eyes renewed her tears.

"Come on, Sophie, tell me what happened. It will help." Again he tried to stroke her face.

Through her tears, Sophie held his hand in both of hers. "The night after you were shot, the killing and the bombing started. Restaurants, bars, it seemed anything with U.S. servicemen was fair game. Saphine's club was targeted, a bomb. They said she was on stage singing at the time." She paused, "Oh, Jacques our beautiful, Saphine. She never hurt anyone in her life. It's not fair."

It wasn't fair, but neither was war. That day altered the course of their lives.

Five days later he was discharged. He wasn't really ready to be but he wanted to visit Saphine's grave, and the hospital was in dire need of his bed, so the doctors agreed to let him go as long as Sophie looked after him.

The next day she took him to say goodbye to Saphine. The woman who had helped to mend his broken heart after Honeysuckle married Simon. The woman he owed so much.

It was a simple grave, non-secular with it's inscriptions and was surrounded by a sea of flowers, some laid very recently.

The words on the stone said, 'Saphine, loved by all who met her and heard her sing. R.I.P.' No dates were added.

"I never knew when she was born, I don't think she did. We never celebrated her real birthday, did we?" Sophie had arranged the headstone, she was Saphine's family along with Jacques.

"No we didn't." He smiled. "She would just announce, it's my birthday today. Let's have a party."

"Never the same date twice, and rarely more than three months apart." Sophie had a fond look on her face.

"She must have been at least 120 by that reckoning!" Chuckled Jacques.

"She looked bloody good for her age then." Now they both laughed.

Painfully Jacques leaned knelt down and laid some flowers with all the rest. He sniffed and blinked away the tears, which had appeared. "Thank you for being in my life. You enriched it beyond anything you could imagine. I will never forget you." Now his eyes were tight shut, but tears still streamed down his face.

Sophie held him.

Saphine's death changed them or perhaps they were just ready for a change. A week later they decided to celebrate Saphine's 121st birthday. "So she can be given the key to heaven," Jacques said.

Sophie cooked a meal and set a place for Saphine. She made all her favourite dishes and they drank a bottle of 'her usual,' Chenin Blanc.

There was much laughter as they reminisced about her. Jacques described the night she seduced him, to which Sophie said, "That's not how she described it!"

"So how did she describe it then?"

Sophie repeated almost word for word Saphine's description of her first night with Jacques. At the time it had aroused her, as she had dreamt of such a night with him herself. She had relived the description a number of times in her head when she was alone in bed.

"Did I really? No, it wasn't like that. She got it wrong," he said in defence of his actions.

"No she didn't, that's what you did to me as well."

"Really?" Jacques said, feigning mock surprise.

"But you were better than she said, darling."

Now indignation. "She said I was no good?" It demanded the correct reply.

"No, darling. You are much better than any girl could possibly imagine in her wildest dreams."

"That's okay then." Jacques had a sudden thought. "Did you ever…"

"Nothing to do with you, now finish your dessert. It's time I started your physiotherapy programme! Gently at first, of course." She stroked his leg beneath the table.

Over the next few weeks they talked about the future. Jacques started the conversations. "We're not achieving anything are we? My intelligence gathering and insight into Charlie's mind, and your words have not stopped this war. Sorry, that's not fair, your words do make a difference. The tide is turning in America, your articles and other journalists' work, add weight to the lobbyists and American people who are tired of their sons coming home in body bags. It is me, I don't make a difference."

"Yes you do. You have no idea how many lives you have saved."

"Maybe, but someone else can do that. I'm not a unique talent that can change the course of a war. Your words can at least change attitudes."

"What are you saying, Jacques?"

"Perhaps that I want to stop fighting. I'm not sure. I've been involved in wars since I was sixteen, if you count Dunkirk. Now I'm forty-four, and this is not even my war. I'm a mercenary who has gone out to find conflict."

"No you are not. You work for your country, and the people who govern it deem your presence here to be in its interest. You are not a mercenary and I don't want to hear you say that." She sounded quite cross.

"You're very attractive when you are angry," he said.

278

Sophie just shook her head.

"Let's get married," he said suddenly.

"What?" Sophie's mouth was ajar.

"Let's get married. You and me, to each other." He was grinning now.

"Have you just come up with that idea on the spur of the moment, dear?"

He did not have a clue if she was angry. She had never called him dear. "I suppose so."

"Then I suggest you think about it for a while and if you still think it's a good idea, ask me properly, dear."

Okay, so she was cross and she had successfully made him feel like a five-year-old, or worse still a geriatric five-year-old.

It was an end to the conversation, but not to the idea. As all good five-year-olds he did as he was told, and thought about it.

Three weeks later while Sophie was writing an article and faxing her latest offering from the office in town, he prepared dinner for them both. Not a feast, but the best he could manage. He bought over 200 candles and distributed them throughout the apartment, then lit them. He relieved the local florist of all he had to offer and arranged them everywhere. All apart from the rose petals, these he stripped from the flowers and scattered across the floor. He put on her favourite music and waited for her return.

At 6:30, in she walked. At 6:31, she said yes. At 6:32, she was crying. At 6:33, they were kissing. At 6:35, they were making love.

They got married one week later. In her handbag Sophie had a photograph of Saphine, which she got out so she could witness their marriage.

The only thing that Sophie did not know was that Jacques had telephoned Honeysuckle a few days before the simple ceremony to tell her what they were doing. He wasn't sure why he called, he just knew he had to. They talked for a long time and he realised that Honeysuckle was genuinely happy for them and was sorry she could not be there. She promised that she would throw them a party when they returned. He never mentioned that he'd been shot and had come close to death.

The other call that they both made was to his Mother. He could hear her tears of joy down the phone, and promised her that they would celebrate their wedding with them all soon. Neither did they tell Elizabeth he'd been shot.

Two weeks later he was deemed fit to travel, so they returned to the Isle of Wight and their belated wedding breakfast at Farringford.

They spent a week planning it with Honeysuckle and Elizabeth. If the truth were known it was not really Sophie's thing, but she did it for Elizabeth, she deserved to celebrate her son's marriage and she had been such a good friend. Honeysuckle's enthusiasm got her through it and some of it rubbed off, she found herself actually looking forward to it, especially when Yvette said she could attend and wouldn't miss it for the world.

Yvette arrived the day before and asked to stay with Elizabeth. She wanted to meet the woman who had produced such a remarkable son and to Sophie said, "I'll see bloody Honeysuckle tomorrow anyway." Sophie just giggled.

The day was lovely, Honeysuckle had surpassed herself. The meal was magnificent and the evening's entertainment wonderful. She used every trick she had learned to make sure it was a day they would remember, and a day she would never forget.

Seeing Jacques so happy was one of the most important things in the world to her. She had hated herself for all the years of unhappiness she had given him, although she would not have changed her decisions. This was just one small way she could help to make up for it.

There was something else. It was their day too, hers and Jacques's. It was only in her mind and something she never shared with anyone, but in a little girl way it was the day she had dreamed of as a child. It was always supposed to be their day, but at least she was there.

One thing she did, as part of the celebration and instead of wedding vows, was to persuade both Sophie and Jacques to read a piece of poetry. It was easy to persuade them to read the verse she had chosen when she was just thirteen, when it was to be her who was marrying Jacques.

When they read the lines, she alone was crying, but no one saw her tears.

Her reunion with Yvette was interesting. They had once been adversaries and if Honeysuckle was honest, at one time in her life she hated Yvette more than anyone she had ever known before, or since. Despite what she had done for her, some of that animosity still existed.

Jacques took Yvette over to introduce her to Honeysuckle, who at the time was talking to Sophie and his Mother. "Honeysuckle, here is Yvette."

Yvette said, "Hello, Honeysuckle, it is nice to see you again."

Honeysuckle replied, "So you can speak then."

Sophie spat her drink back into her glass, in complete shock. Elizabeth stood, mouth agog and Jacques stared at Honeysuckle waiting for Yvette's reaction.

Slowly Yvette smiled, then exploded with laughter and hugged Honeysuckle. "Bloody Honeysuckle! It is good to see you. What an adversary you were, and still are."

Honeysuckle was smiling now, and hugged her back.

"What was all that about?" Jacques asked, completely at a loss.

It was Yvette who answered, still giggling. "That is what Honeysuckle said to me after she had spent five hours lecturing me for being so feeble, and I finally spoke." She smiled again at her saviour. "I only said something to shut you up."

"I hated you," said Honeysuckle.

"I know, and I hated you." Both faces told a different story now.

"That was then, now I hear you have two beautiful little girls. I want to hear all about them."

Yet again Sophie marvelled at Honeysuckle, her best friend and the woman who she was in no doubt still loved her husband, Jacques, probably more than life itself.

Jacques sat and watched the three of them from afar. It was the only time all three of them would be together at the same time. Three woman he had loved and still did, but all in different ways. Only one was missing, and her photograph watched them all, smiling, from the mantelpiece.

"Don't ever get married, Buster. Lot of fuss, just live with them." The man put another log on the fire, which was struggling to stay alight.

"Come on, trouble. Let's put something on those beans in your tummy to calm then down."

The man stood up and made his way to the kitchen with Buster in pursuit, his old bones creaking but the mention of beans driving him on.

Twenty-Four

The snow was deeper than Jacques thought it would be. At least four inches had settled overnight, but now it had stopped and the forecaster promised rain by the evening.

"It will probably be tropical by tomorrow, Buster. The British weather, eh! At least you knew what to expect in Vietnam."

Buster was lying in his basket hoping they would not have to go out in the snow and all the way up to the Warren. He'd been out earlier to dispose of the beans and did not like the white stuff he'd found on the lawn.

"The fireside for us again I'm afraid, old boy."

Music to Buster's ears, he settled back into the warm blanket.

"Life was not so exciting after that, Buster. Better, but not as exciting. Which was good, I was not getting any younger and had no desire to be shot again."

He knelt down to clean out the hearth, wincing as he did

so. "Mind you, this was easier in those days."

Nothing that sounded like ham or lunch yet, so Buster pretended to be asleep.

"Mind you, we didn't have a fire in London or Paris." He eased himself up again with a newspaper full of ashes and walked to the back door to deposit them in the bin.

He assumed the position he'd struggled up from earlier and set the fire. "Might as well light it as well, old boy." He struck a match and lit the firelighter he'd set beneath the logs. "There, it will soon be toasty."

"Here you are, boy, something to keep you going." As if by magic he produced a chew from his back pocket and led Buster to the fireside with it as if it were attached to his nose.

A good chew and a warm fire, that is what Buster liked now.

Jacques was sitting in their apartment in Paris, two streets back from the Champs Elysees, where they spent most weekends. During the week he commuted to London where they had another apartment in Kensington, and whenever she could Sophie would go with him.

She was still writing, but articles that did not require her to be on the front line in a war zone. She also did some work for television, the news section of R.T.F. She liked the work and the camera liked her, even though she was nearly sixty. The French still appreciated an attractive older woman.

Jacques still worked for MI6, but in an office with a rather nice view of the Thames. He was given the chance to return to Vietnam after his convalescence, and thought long and hard about it.

He had several more discussions with Sophie about their future, and all they could emphatically agree on was that they both wanted one. She did not want him to be shot again and obviously neither did he. So he had been working in an office for the last fifteen years.

He hated the job, but it paid well and he had become a powerful man in the world of espionage. There were new threats and there had been new wars, and he had played his part. But it was the weekends that he lived for, and his time with Sophie.

They had never had children. They had married too late, but it didn't matter, they had each other and sufficient going on in their lives so they were never bored. They also had the Isle of Wight.

They had bought a cottage by the Warren that they managed to visit quite regularly, and would sometimes even go individually to see Honeysuckle and Elizabeth.

Simon had taught Jacques to play golf, badly, and Sophie would talk to Honeysuckle for hours on end.

They were both beginning to think about retirement and maybe spending a lot more time on the island. Sophie was going to write a novel and Jacques was not going to play golf! He would buy a small yacht and sail.

After they were married things subtly changed with Honeysuckle. She never asked for a kiss or flirted with him again, except as a joke in front of others.

After a few years during one of their visits he and Honeysuckle had become so at ease in each other's presence that he decided to ask her why.

"I miss it you know."

"What?"

"Your flirting, and the look you used to give me. The one that gave me an instant erection."

She giggled. "You mean this one." She looked at him the way she used to, the way that took his breath away.

Even now he could hardly speak, she was still an incredible looking woman who seemed not to age, but he managed to say, "Yes, that one."

She laughed, noticing and enjoying the effect it still had on him. "That's why I don't do it."

"What do you mean?"

She was more serious now. "I want to, I've always wanted to, Jacques, and even though I'm nearly fifty I still want to take you to my bed. Unfortunately I know you would come, no matter how much you love Sophie. And I know how in love with her you are. Being fifty has made it easier for us, Jacques. We can have everything, Sophie, Lissette and Simon, and still hold on to what we have always had."

She was right, of course. He smiled, a sad smile. "I still miss it."

"So do I. You have no idea how much, but I love you now as much as I always have. The form of my longing has just changed. Just to be near you, is enough."

Jacques was quiet, assessing what she had said.

"If we kiss now, you will hate yourself. You did not have then what you have now. Knowing is enough."

She was right, she was always right. "At least we have had the conversation and you are right, knowing is enough."

Honeysuckle smiled. "We have always known, but it is good to remind ourselves. We used to do it with a kiss, now we will just talk about it, my darling sweet Jacques." Tenderly she touched his cheek.

"Why ask for the moon, when we have the stars."

She smiled at his reference to the line from the film, Now Voyager. During the War she had watched the film with Simon and had thought of nothing but Jacques throughout. She had cried at that line. "Yes, that's right, Jacques. That's exactly right. We have the stars."

A few years later he did retire. They sold the London apartment but kept the one in Paris, which they visited regularly, splitting their time fifty/fifty between the island and Paris.

Lissette grew to be quite a beauty whilst Honeysuckle

286

matured like a fine wine, each year added to her allure. Some grey hairs appeared but they just added to her aura. With each new grey hair she seemed to grow wiser, and her capacity to love seemed boundless.

'Beauty and the Beast,' Simon had always called them. Never really knowing a good riposte, Jacques had always allowed it to be the last word, but he watched Honeysuckle grow older and all he could see was her becoming more beautiful with every year that passed. Whenever he left her he felt sad, whenever he went back he felt uplifted just to be in her presence.

Jacques loved Paris too. After all he was half-French and much to everyone's amusement he increasingly took on some of his Father's mannerisms and foibles. He even briefly grew a moustache before Sophie almost took the razor blade to his throat. To Jacques, Paris was culture and excitement. The Isle of Wight was Honeysuckle, and Sophie was both places.

Sophie knew this and did not mind, she was confident that she had enough of him never to have to worry. She also knew Honeysuckle loved him. She had told her that the first day they ever met and she had told her every time they visited, just in case she had forgotten. But Honeysuckle was the most decent person she had ever met, and in that she included Jacques. She knew Honeysuckle would never do anything to hurt her relationship with her husband. On the other hand, Jacques was a man; the best she had ever known, but none the less, just a man!

Lissette got married and had her own children, two lovely little girls. Honeysuckle found new people to love and nurture, two more reasons to be happy. She took to the role of Grandma with the same enthusiasm she had conquered everything she had ever done. Her grandchildren were besotted by her and hung on her every word, to Jacques they appeared to be constantly by her side. The Beast held no fears for them and as they grew up he became known as Beautygramps. Just being near them all was

287

an uplifting experience.

Jacques became their favourite uncle and Aunt Sophie was a Princess. She was the quintessential personification of Parisian chic with an accent bestowed on her in Heaven, who captivated the little ones whenever she visited them from the magical place called Paris.

They were wonderful years filled with great happiness as they all watched the girls grow up. Until one fateful day, the day everything changed.

Jacques woke up and put his arm around Sophie. She was cold. An aneurism had taken her in the night and Jacques had not even woken up. He had not been there for her.

They told him that there was nothing he could have done. It was over in an instant and she would have felt no pain, but he was distraught. He did not have time to tell her he loved her one last time. He had no time to prepare for her passing.

Once again it was Honeysuckle who instinctively knew what to do and how to help him, it was her strength that got him through the next two years. Like a younger sister once again, she was there for him whenever he needed her. It was her shoulder he cried on, her heart kept his beating and her compassion helped heal him. It was simply her love that made Sophie's passing bearable.

He sold the apartment in Paris and moved to the island to be near Honeysuckle. The day after he moved in she appeared at the door with Buster, one of her adored black Labradors. Buster stayed, with instructions to look after the man and love him when she could not be there with him.

Jacques had never had a dog, but within a week he realised that Buster had understood his instructions completely and for two years they were inseparable.

The man was crying. Buster did not like crying so he tried to lick the tears away. It worked, the man laughed and tried to move his head out of the way of the lapping tongue, but gave up and just hugged the dog he loved instead.

"I suppose it must be time for lunch, you silly mutt."

Twenty-Five

Jacques sat on the bench. The sun was about to set over the Needles. It was cold, very cold, forecast to drop to minus ten degrees during the night.

There was an empty space where Buster should have been. He stroked the cold wood and thought of their lunches together.

He had been waiting for Buster. They had both been diagnosed with cancer the same week and Buster had died five days ago. Jacques had buried him in the garden, helped by Honeysuckle, with a box of biscuits and a ham sandwich. They had cried together and had tea whilst talking about and remembering dear Buster. During the past two years hardly a day had past when Buster and Jacques had not been to see Honeysuckle or she had come to the cottage, but he had become Jacques's dog and would not leave his side. "It's because you give him sandwiches," Honeysuckle had said, "and let him sleep in your bed."

It had taken nearly a week to put his affairs in order and he had written one last letter to Honeysuckle. He had waited at the post-box for the postman who he knew well, to make his afternoon collection and handed it to him personally and said that it was very important that Honeysuckle should receive it first thing the next morning. The postman promised that he would hand it to her himself.

He had never told Honeysuckle about his cancer, there was no point. It was never his intention to need care or nursing, but the real reason was that it would have cast a dark shadow over their remaining precious time together. He wanted her to remember those days with affection not sadness.

His life had been so full and vibrant that he had no intention of suffering a slow, painful and ignominious death and already the malignant tumours were starting to sap his strength.

Everything was in place, and now he wanted one last look at the view he'd loved all his life from the place that had been the centre of so many of his happiest and saddest moments. He looked up and imagined the Spitfire and saw the pilot waving to him before he did his victory roll. He could see the boy with a little girl by his side, and then that same girl, now fully grown, kissing him on this very spot, And Buster, dear Buster who, along with Honeysuckle had made the past years bearable.

He turned and traced the letters on the bench S O P H I E. "Well it's nearly time, Sophie, my darling Sophie. Time to come and see you and Buster, he likes sandwiches a lot. Don't let him get hungry." He laughed to himself.

He slipped the pills into his mouth and washed them down with a little hot soup he'd brought. There were no blankets to keep him warm, and when they found his body he would be with them both.

The next day Honeysuckle collected the mail from the postman who had brought it into reception, the usual array of bills and circulars. "This one is for you, Honeysuckle. Jacques

291

gave it to me last evening" She took the letter, puzzled as to why he should have sent it.

It was his handwriting, the handwriting that she had read in so many of his letters over the years, all of which she still kept. She stroked the address he had penned on the envelope and was suddenly anxious. Something was wrong, why would he be writing to her?

She ripped at the envelope in a panic sensing some awful news lay inside.

She read the opening lines and put her hand to her mouth to stifle the scream that did not come. Her legs buckled and she grabbed the desk to steady herself.

"Are you okay, Honeysuckle?" The receptionist asked.

She did not answer but managed to walk, shaking as she did so, to her private lounge to read the whole letter. There she locked the door and settled into the chair by the fire.

Trying to find the courage to read, she hesitatingly began;

My darling Honeysuckle,

When you read this letter I will be gone. I have had cancer these past six months and it is incurable. I have chosen what many may call the coward's way out, and they may be right. But you know me better than any living person and you know that I am not a coward, it is simply the way I have chosen to die.

I know you are crying now and who knows, perhaps I can see you. Try not to cry, my darling, I am not crying because I do not believe this is the end of what we have.

I have loved you all my life, and you have loved me. In this life we have known great happiness together and I will wait for you in the next. No, this is not the end, just the next stage of a journey I believe is just beginning.

I believe we can love many people, as you have done all your life, in that I have tried to emulate you the best way that I could.

It has not been easy. We have sacrificed a portion of our love to accommodate others that we have grown to love. I could not have done that without your guidance, and I would probably have abandoned all the others that I have loved if you had asked it of me, but you did not.

Your love and sacrifice is the most wonderful thing that I have ever witnessed, and you are the noblest person that anyone could ever know. I have been blessed that you chose to love me.

Thank you for giving me Sophie. Yes, she was your gift to me in this life, a gift you need not have given and I believe she will play a part in our future. But even in death I believe my future is with you, Sophie knows this.

Thank you also for Buster, dear Buster. You instinctively knew that I would need him, and in him I found another soul mate. I know you chose him carefully and gave me someone you loved deeply. I am with him now and he says, hello.

I am waiting for you, my darling, but don't hurry, there will be time enough for us. Give yourself to your family for as long as you can. There is so much you can teach them.

These are not the final words you will hear from me, every conversation we have ever had will ring in your ears as they did in mine when I was alive. You constantly spoke to me with your wisdom and your heart.

I do not want to stop writing, but there is no need to carry on. I am with you, in everything around you, in everything you touch, everything you see will remind you of me until we are together again.

I love you more than a thousand letters can say.

Your Jacques x

PS. Sorry there is just one kiss, but that is all I ever got. Oh, but what a kiss!

Honeysuckle was smiling and crying. Even in death Jacques was

293

protecting her, as he had protected all those he loved in life.

* * * * *

It was spring and Honeysuckle had made her daily journey over to the Warren with Molly, Buster's sister. She had taken a detour to see if the tulips Jacques had planted in memory of Sophie were still thriving after the harsh winter. They were.

She sat on the bench and her fingers traced the J of his name on the plaque she had added for him.

She took the ham sandwich she had prepared for Molly from its bag and handed it to her. Molly took it from her with relish, albeit with a great deal more decorum than Buster would have done.

She feasted her eyes on the view that had brought Jacques so much pleasure and sighed.

Within minutes she was a small girl again, tucked beneath his arm with her own arms wrapped around him, watching the Spitfire that roared overhead.

The End

Postscript

Should you visit the Isle of Wight, walk on
Headon Warren. Continue to the top and past the barrows.
Any of the paths will lead you to a bench.
There are no names on this bench, but it inspired this book.
Sit down and take in the view.
Imagine and remember.

Nigel Jones (Author)